TRUST NO ONE

CALEB CROWE

INKUBATOR
BOOKS

Published by Inkubator Books
www.inkubatorbooks.com

Copyright © 2025 by Caleb Crowe

ISBN (eBook): 978-1-83756-646-4
ISBN (Paperback): 978-1-83756-647-1
ISBN (Hardback): 978-1-83756-648-8

Caleb Crowe has asserted his right to be identified as the author of this work.

TRUST NO ONE is a work of fiction. People, places, events, and situations are the product of the author's imagination. Any resemblance to actual persons, living or dead is entirely coincidental.

PROLOGUE

I don't even feel my hands make contact. One second he's in front of me, still trying to charm his way out of it – smiling like I'm being silly – and the next my palms are on his chest. Pushing. Not gently. Not playfully. Just *enough*.

One push. That's all it takes. I don't mean to do it. That's the worst part.

He stumbles backwards against the window and slips, reaching for something to hold onto, fingers grabbing at nothing. There's a stupid, suspended moment where I think he'll catch himself. Where I think maybe he'll bounce back, throw some awful line at me, and carry on as if nothing has happened.

But he doesn't. He goes out. Arms flailing. Face twisted.

Gone.

It doesn't feel real.

Not until the sound. The sound he makes when he hits the ground below. It isn't a scream. Not even a thud. It's a crack. A *snap*. Like something essential has broken. A dull, final kind of sound.

Then nothing.

Just… silence. Just this awful, crooked stillness that turns my stomach inside out. I stand frozen, my heart hammering, my hand still hovering half-raised like I can undo it.

And I don't know what happens next.

I go to look. Everything says help him. But he's beyond help. Arms wrong. Neck unnaturally bent. Blood seeping out through the cracks. Instead, I just stand there. Shaking.

I didn't mean to do it. But who's going to believe that?

So I do the only thing I can do.

I run.

PART ONE

CHAPTER 1
GRACE

I don't realise he's dangerous until he climbs on the chair.

"As you can see, it's full of original features and brimming with character."

No response. Just silence, while the man in front of me frowns up into the corner of the room like he's waiting for it to collapse. Now's when I'm supposed to build a rapport. But this isn't going so well.

That's fine. I can handle awkward viewings. I've sold houses to couples mid-divorce and once to a man who kept a ferret in his glovebox. I glance at my clipboard to remind myself of the name.

"Did you say you're from Scarborough, Justin?" I ask brightly, like we're old friends. I hear my voice ricochet off the walls in the sparsely furnished flat.

"Leeds," he grunts.

That's it.

So much for friendly small talk. But I don't let it ruffle me. I remind myself everyone gets one truly awful day a month to behave like an arsehole. Today must be his.

Justin takes his suit jacket off. That's when he drags a chair across the room and stands on it like he owns the place. He takes a biro out of his pocket and begins to poke at the cornicing. A shower of fine dust drifts into the shaft of sunlight beaming through the curtainless window.

"By 'original features' I assume you mean the dry rot," he says, humourless.

Oh. He's one of *those*. Bitter middle-aged men who mistake being sarcastic for having a personality. He's got the energy of someone who's been waiting his whole life to ruin my morning. The trick is not to rise to the bait. Whenever someone's rude, I narrate them in my head like a David Attenborough documentary: *Here we see the lesser-spotted grumpy man, puffing out his chest to impress potential mates.*

I'm alone in a flat with a stranger, and he's on a chair with a biro in his hand. That's the moment it hits me: this is more than just a bad viewing.

"A little TLC goes a long way in these characterful proper-ties," I sing-song in my best 'just smile and sell' voice. That's my trick. Let them be rude. I stay radiant. "There's exciting potential to enhance the property, which is reflected in the incredibly reasonable price." Dangle the bait. Keep smiling.

He says nothing, just keeps poking his pen deeper into the moulding. I should tell him to get down, but I don't want to make the mood worse. I'll wait and see if he does any real damage. I can see the revolting crack of his arse appearing above the back of his trousers. He's standing on tiptoes to reach up. His shoes are horrible brown brogues, scuffed and unpolished, and they don't go with his cheap, grey, shapeless suit. I manage to keep smiling by imagining him falling off and breaking his fat, hairy neck.

Eventually he finishes worming about and climbs down.

"I thought there was supposed to be a sea view," he says aggressively, squinting disdainfully at the window.

"There are stunning sea glimpses from the bedroom."

"Glimpses!" he scoffs. "I suppose you have to stand on a sodding chair to see those as well…"

Oh, come on, mate. Buy a step ladder and dream big. I bite back what I'd love to say and toss him another platitude from the script. "We're just a stone's throw from the seafront, yet tucked away in a quiet but convenient location."

He moves across the room towards me, suddenly closer than feels normal. His eyes are flat and mean. My chest tightens.

He scowls at me. "Do you really believe any of that cliché bullshit you're spouting?"

Hang on. This doesn't feel right. I've had awkward viewings before, but I've never had one like this. Like he's not here to look at the flat – he's here to look at me. This isn't just a grumpy customer. This feels like something else. Something deliberate.

I realise I'm scared.

It's eleven in the morning. This flat is unoccupied. The other people from the building will be out at work. I'm alone. I'm horribly aware of how vulnerable I am. I clutch my keys hard in my pocket, my little insurance policy, like I'm on a walk home at night and wondering if someone behind is following me.

My mind races. Who knows I'm here with him? He'll have given a name to the office for the appointment. But that doesn't help if he attacks me now. And he could have given a false name anyway. He could be anyone. If I scream, will anyone hear me? Or might screaming provoke him to do something to shut me up?

I try to act like there's nothing wrong. "It's ideally situated, offering the perfect peaceful coastal lifestyle," I say weakly. But my throat is dry. I can hear my voice waver with fear.

He sighs.

"No," he says, shaking his head. "No, no, no, this won't do at all."

He walks towards me, and I step back. But my bag's behind me and I catch my heel on the strap. Suddenly, I'm pitching backwards over it, windmilling my arms. I start to fall as he lunges towards me. I instinctively put my hands up to block him.

My hand hits his face with a muffled crunch. We both freeze.

It's only when he yells out and leaps back, covering his eye, that I remember I'm holding my keys. I watch in horror as he takes his hand away from his face and pokes at his cheekbone, where I can see a small nick. A bead of blood begins to ooze out and trickle down his face. He dabs at it with his hand, then stares at his bloody fingers.

"What the hell are you doing?"

He gawks at me. He looks more surprised than angry. But I know I've provoked him. Once he gets over the shock of it, he could do anything. I'm in trouble.

"I was trying to stop you falling over, you dozy cow!"

He steps back, picks up his jacket and clutches it to his side with his elbow. His bloody hand sticks out like someone directing traffic, trying not to get blood on the material. He starts rifling awkwardly through the pockets with his clean hand.

"You could have had my sodding eye out. Have you got a tissue or something?"

"What?"

"A tissue!" He's annoyed and impatient. "Look, Grace, isn't it? I'm Justin Trott. I'm the new Regional Manager. Have you got a tissue before I get blood all over this suit?"

Shit. My new boss.

I scrabble about in my bag and find a small pack of paper

hankies. I hand one over and watch as he dabs away at his cheekbone where I've stabbed him with the key, peering at the blood on the tissue with an affronted expression, as if it's deliberately offended him. He rips a bit of the tissue off, licks it and sticks it on the cut.

"I've been setting up these viewings with all the staff, playing the difficult customer, getting a feel for the team in action. I can tell you, you're the first person who's physically attacked me."

"Sorry."

Justin Trott. Or Justin Twatt, as Kyle called him back in the office. Now I've met him myself, that seems about right.

He grabs the chair he was standing on, swings it round and sits on it with the back in front of him. He looks like a geography teacher trying to act cool in front of a class of teenage girls.

"Listen, Grace. You're clearly out of your depth with tricky customers. You've got to show them who's boss. You were like a bloody damp flannel at the start, then you all but blinded me. If I was a real customer, we could have a sodding lawsuit on our hands."

The thing about nearly blinding your new boss is that it really sets the tone.

"Sorry," I say again. I try not to stare at the bit of tissue stuck to his face which makes him look ridiculous.

"And listen to you. You've apologised twice. You need a bit of backbone. Houses don't sell themselves. You've got to take charge. You need a killer instinct."

He reaches into his jacket again and pulls out a business card.

"Look," he sighs, like he's had enough of the conversation, "the firm's signed up for an employee coaching programme. One of Mr Lyle's ideas. Touchy-feely bollocks if you ask me, but we've paid for it, so there it is. And if anyone needs some help, it's you. Set up an appointment."

Shit. My first meeting, and he already has a crappy impression of me. He passes me the business card.

Executive Coaching. Oliver Smallwood.

God help me.

CHAPTER 2
OLIVER

Oliver locks, unlocks, locks, unlocks and locks his office door, then makes his way along the narrow, windowless corridor, down the threadbare stairs, through the shop and out onto the street. He pulls his coat around him against the cold and trudges along the residential street, the parked cars glistening under the streetlights from a shower of rain earlier.

No one is around. It's only 5.31 p.m., but it's already dark. He feels the night stretch out in front of him like a marathon he hasn't trained for, dire and exhausting.

He comes to the end of the road and turns onto Northway. It's busier here, cars cutting back and forth, carrying commuters home to their husbands and wives, their children. He waits for a gap in the traffic and scuttles across the road, past a couple of teenage girls eating chips outside Cod Almighty, then turns up a side street and into the ALDI car park. He needs something for dinner, and milk for the morning.

Oliver takes a basket by the doorway and passes the fruit and veg. He thinks about getting some apples, but the idea of chewing his way through an apple feels like hard work, more worthy than pleasurable. He heads for the cereal aisle at the back of the shop. He deliberately avoids the wine section. Drinking at home is a slippery slope he doesn't want to slide down. A few other shoppers are dotted about the place, but Oliver doesn't look at them. He doesn't want to know whether he recognises them or not. He avoids eye contact. He notices the Fruit & Fibre is on offer and puts a box in his basket, assuming it is a healthy choice. Maybe a bowl of something with raisins is one of his five a day?

He scans the refrigerated section of ready meals and opts for a lasagne from the Finest Table range. The portion for one looks pitifully small, so he gets the meal for two. He knows he's developing a bit of a belly and tells himself he doesn't need to eat it all. The Lean & Lovely ready meals are just below, but the other one is in the basket now anyway. He remembers the half bag of frozen peas in the freezer at home and feels better about his life choices.

Toilet roll. Bleach. A litre of semi-skimmed milk. Oliver queues at the self-checkout machine behind a man buying a box of chocolates and a bunch of artificially bright carnations. He sneers inwardly at what he assumes must be some last-minute afterthought birthday or anniversary present, and wonders what the recipient will feel about these tragic offer-ings from a budget supermarket. What do they say about the value of the relationship? Then he unloads the contents of his own basket and considers what they say about him. He scans and loads them quickly into a carrier bag, embarrassed by his lonely hoard for one.

He scans his card to pay and looks up briefly at the secu-rity guard by the door, hoping he has heard the beep of the machine. The guard is looking the other way. Oliver says yes to the offer of a receipt, in case he is challenged in the doorway trying to leave. But when he exits, the guard pays him no attention.

He cuts back and up another side road, heading towards Westborough. He needs to get cash from the bank to pay the window cleaner he still hasn't got round to cancelling. This used to be the thriving heart of the town when he was a boy, but Scarborough has changed in the years he's been away. It just about scrapes a living in summer, but now, in the tourist off-season, it just looks bleak and depressing. It's late January, but the unlit Christmas decorations are still up along the pedestrianised street, the outlines of snowmen and reindeer suspended above him like festive corpses on a gallows. Maybe the man whose job it was to take them down moved away and no one else could be arsed. Scarborough itself has given up.

He should never have come back here, to his shitty little home town. But what choice did he have? He couldn't stay in Leeds, not once Alison left him, not after–

He tries not to think about it.

There's a queue at the cashpoint. The man in front of him is in a thin suit and no coat, and shuffles from one foot to the other to keep warm. The woman at the front turns to her friend and says something Oliver can't quite make out. It might have been "Sticky". The friend turns her head slightly, and he wonders whether she has glanced at him. He knows he tends to think people are looking at him when they aren't. But that doesn't mean she *isn't* looking.

Oliver decides to leave the cash and walks further down the hill towards the sea, then cuts left through the old town, heading for home.

He tried to stay in Leeds for a while after. There was only a small mention in the newspapers about the inquest, and he hoped it might all blow over. But of course, all his friends and family saw it. People pretended to be kind, but he could imagine what they were thinking; he could feel the blame. It seemed like a good plan to come back here for a while. To disappear. But he can see now what a foolish idea that was. This tiny, petty town where nothing ever happens and everyone knows everything about everyone. *Disappear?* He'd laugh if it wasn't so awful.

He unlocks, locks, unlocks, locks and unlocks the front door and goes inside. The hallway is dark. Dark carpet, dark green walls, the dark brown wood of the panelling by the stairs. He goes through and into the small kitchen, unpacks his bag of shopping to the cupboards and the fridge and sits in a straight wooden chair at the table. 5.58 p.m. He thinks about his evening, the lasagne he will take brief comfort from, and then the expanse of night that follows. He wonders how long he can put off the pleasure of the food before he gives in and starts preparing it. He decides to occupy himself with a cup of tea and puts the kettle on to boil.

Inevitably, the report of the inquest made its way onto the Facebook group for his old school. Things died down after a while. But you can never escape it completely.

He takes a cup from the sideboard and drops in a teabag from the old Yorkshire Gold tin on the worktop. He sits and listens to the clicks and ticks of the kettle as the plastic warms and expands, heating the water. He waits for it to come to the boil.

It's always there, either in the looks of other people or in your head. The intrusive thoughts.

CHAPTER 3
GRACE

I don't want to be here, but I'll get through it. Christ, I once sat through *Cats: The Movie* without gnawing my own arm off, so I can survive this.

I've got zero interest in getting coached. But then this isn't coaching, not really. This Oliver bloke is Justin's spy. It's Justin's way of checking whether I'm any good at what I do. I'm not worried though. One hour of fake listening, tick the box, keep the job. Easy. It's just another hoop to jump through. I've jumped through worse.

I remind myself why I'm here: pay the rent, save every penny, get myself back to uni, and rebuild my life, properly this time. One awkward coaching session isn't going to break me.

The place doesn't exactly scream professionalism. It's not even a proper office – more a converted terraced house. I thought I'd come to the wrong place at first. Downstairs is a chiropodist, with a huge cartoon foot painted on the glass, and piles of ugly looking shoes in the window. But the woman inside pointed me to a door at the back, with a tiny sign and stairs that go up to the first floor, where I am now.

I try one door, but it's a depressing little toilet. So I knock on the other door.

"Ah, you must be Grace."

A drab, brown-haired man with beige skin and bags under his eyes swings the door open and smiles at me encouragingly.

"That's right."

He holds the door open and steps to one side, beckoning me in.

The office feels more like a cupboard that someone's tried to pass off as a room, an awkward, leftover space with no function – what we laughingly call on a spec *a generous single* or *ideal for home working*. But fine. He wants to play coach in a cupboard? I can play along.

The carpet matches his face, beige and worn down, and it's frayed where the door scrapes across it. The two chairs don't match. One's faux leather and the other's fabric, but he's tried to disguise the mismatch with identical cushions. The chairs look comfy enough, but they're too big for the room and make the whole place cramped and claustrophobic. The window blind's slightly wonky. Nothing major. Just enough to be irritating.

"So, Grace, welcome. Please, take a seat."

The leather chair looks a bit more like something a psychiatrist would have, so I go for the other one. There's a print of a misty forest on the wall facing me, the sort of thing you get from Dunelm when you're trying to look calm and mindful. On the wall opposite the window, there's a framed motivational quote in swirly writing – *Be the change you wish to see in the world.*

"Have you come far today, or from work? Lancaster & Lyle's just the other side of town, isn't it?"

"Yes. Just off the Esplanade."

He's trying to warm me up with small talk. I give him the

full professional smile, making sure I look relaxed, and definitely not like someone who's worried about their job. I lean back in my chair like I haven't got a care in the world and have another casual look round the office. There's a shelf overloaded with a Buddha head, a dreamcatcher and a stack of pebbles. There's a bookshelf with lots of coaching and self-help books and a Himalayan salt lamp. It's the well-being equivalent of a tired pick-up line, hollow and predictable. I half expect him to turn on the whale music.

"That's good. Relax. Make yourself at home. It's important you feel this is a comfortable, safe space. Is it warm enough for you?"

"Yes, it's fine."

"The diffuser doesn't smell too strong, does it?" he asks with a laugh. "I only bought it this morning, and I'm not sure what I'm doing with it. I think I might have put too much essential oil in. I hope you like scents of the forest!"

"No. It's lovely." Not *enough* essential oil if you ask me. The room smells faintly of tea bags and antiseptic, and whatever disgusting foot-rot drifts up through the floorboards from the chiropodist below.

He seems more nervous than I am, which almost makes me feel sorry for him. Almost. I'm not here to make friends. I'm here to keep this job, keep Justin Twatt off my back, and keep my plan ticking forward. Smile, nod, leave.

I wonder how many people have sat in this chair and said things they probably shouldn't have. I can already feel myself resenting the blandness of it – how it pretends to be neutral, when it's anything but. I won't be drawn in and give anything away. I mustn't drop my guard.

"So, Grace, today isn't a coaching session as such. It's for us to get to know each other, explore what you want to get from our time together and lay down some ground rules which we both feel are important. A sort of contract, if you like."

He looks at me intently as he talks. He smiles. He leans in towards me. I know all about this stuff, the art of building a rapport with clients. We did a one-day course on it. I won't let him fool me and suck me in. He's got a vague sense of authority, though he's only a few years older than me, about forty at a guess. I try to hold eye contact so I'll seem confident. Now I'm properly looking at him, something about him seems familiar. Maybe I've seen him around town.

"That sounds good." Maybe I'm not saying enough. Maybe I seem too guarded. "That sounds like a good way to start," I add.

"So, Grace," he says, still smiling, "let's maybe kick off by asking what you understand by the term *coaching*."

"Well," I say, "it's about helping people develop, isn't it? Professionally and personally. I suppose it's a structured way of making progress – identifying strengths, working on blind spots, that sort of thing."

He nods and smiles. Good. I rehearsed that last night. I know all too well what *this* coaching is. They pretend it's about 'professional development', but really it's work's way of fishing for my weak spots, of getting me to tell them what I'm no good at so they can kick me out without it looking like unfair dismissal.

That won't work with me. I'm on to them. I'm going to come across as the best, most confident estate agent Lancaster & Lyle has ever had.

"Yes," he says, "that's pretty much it." He sits back in his chair then and just looks at me with a vague smile on his lips. We sit in the silence. I know it's a technique, but it's pretty powerful.

Then he leans forward again and looks deep into my eyes, like someone might look at you on a first date.

"I guess what I'd add," he says in a soft voice, "is that coaching isn't advice. It's not therapy. It's not mentorship. It's a conversation that's all about you – your patterns, your possibilities. I'm fully here, fully present, every session – but I don't have an agenda. I don't need you to please me, impress me, or even like me." He smiles. "That's the freedom of this space. Think of me like a mirror. I won't judge what I see, but I will show it to you – clearly. Sometimes for the first time. My job isn't to save you. My job is to walk beside you until you're ready to save yourself."

To my surprise, I feel myself getting pulled in. It sounds great. I've started my career late and I've spent ages without any kind of proper support. To have someone like that in my corner, watching my back and getting me up to speed, would be amazing.

He frowns. "I should let you know that it can be uncomfortable. It's confronting. It's challenging. Sometimes people are stuck, and they need a nudge to free them up. Can I ask how you feel about challenge?"

I know what he doesn't. I've spent years fending for myself and learning how to keep my cards so close to my chest they're basically fused to my ribs. Coaching challenge? Please. I'm here to keep them happy, not spill my secrets. Let him think he's got the upper hand if it keeps my payslip landing each month. It's going to take more than crystals and a macrame dreamcatcher for me to drop my guard.

"Sounds great," I say with a smile. "Bring it on."

"Good," he says, sounding genuinely excited.

Then his face changes. His voice too.

"What we do here, if we do it properly, is unlock something. Not surface-level stuff. Not tips and tricks. I mean the *real* work. The deep patterns. The hidden beliefs you don't even know are running the show." He sounds like a priest giving a sermon. "Coaching, when it works, is transformational. Not in some fluffy, motivational way. I mean *genuinely life-changing*. You shift how you think, how you feel, and how you act. You step into something bigger than who you've been told you are. That's what you're here for. If you're ready."

He leans forward. I feel myself mirror him without meaning to. Shit. Not this.

He's good. He's persuasive. He almost has me.

That's when it clicks. This isn't a coaching room. It's a boxing ring. A battleground.

Fine. Let's dance. He might think he's about to unlock my hidden traumas, rewire my soul and explain why I'm not good enough to do my job, but I've got bills to pay and bigger plans than him. He can throw his punches. I'll just keep bobbing, weaving, and smiling.

CHAPTER 4
OLIVER

Julia turns the bolt and hears the soft click of the lock.

She braces herself, half-anticipating the chaos of the world outside to come bursting through the door. She stands stone-still for a moment, listening. But nothing follows. No raised voices. No footsteps.

Silence.

The locked door. So pointless. He could smash it down in an instant if he wanted.

She slackens a little, steps further inside and turns on the taps with slow, deliberate care. The water gurgles into the bath, muffling the room in bubbling white noise. The air is thick with the scent of bath oils, lavender and chamomile, soft and lulling.

She moves to the sink, placing both hands on the cool porcelain, and leans in toward the mirror. Her reflection stares back, expressionless. The swelling is already obvious. Her right eye, nearly shut, is smudged the deep purple and sickly yellow of a fresh bruise. Her lip is cracked, the skin raw. She barely recognises herself. The steam from the running water swirls up in lazy spirals, creeping across the mirror, distorting her face even more. She watches impassively until the glass clouds over completely, vanishing her away.

The bath is full now. She steps in, the heat enveloping her. She leans back, the water lapping at her collarbone, her breath slowing. She looks down at her gnarled, ugly hands, her pasty body, her legs sprouting hair where she has ceased to care about her appearance.

She thinks of Oliver, his kind voice, and what he told her: She needs to make a change.

She reaches behind and finds the silver handle of the razor she employs sporadically to shave her armpits and legs. She can't remember the last time she used it. She opens the razor to check if the blade has gone dull or rusted. Then she brings the blade down and makes two long, deep gashes in her wrists. She relaxes her arms by her sides and watches dispassionately as the water turns red.

OLIVER LURCHES UPRIGHT, gasping into the darkness. His chest heaves. He grips the sheets – they are clinging to him, soaked through. His skin is slick with sweat, as if he has just got out of a bath himself. His hands shake as he reaches for his phone.

4.00 a.m.

Just a dream. It was just a dream. It isn't real.

Except it *is* real.

Julia is dead. Dead as sure as if he killed her himself.

CHAPTER 5
GRACE

I'm sure it's in here somewhere.

I shove the breakfast bowls to one side, almost drenching myself in cold milky bran flakes, and begin to take out items from the old shoe box. A dried-up gel pen. A broken butterfly clip from Claire's Accessories. A page ripped from *Mizz* magazine with a quiz I've filled in titled *"Are You Too Nice?"* A scrap of wrapping paper with a tag attached.

"What's that?" Adam asks, through a mouthful of granola.

"From Bridget, for my thirteenth birthday." I read the tag.

Happy Birthday, Sprog. From your incredible sister, Bridget.

"She gave me a bottle of Vera Wang Princess. I drowned myself in it like I was trying to fumigate the house. I used the whole lot in a fortnight."

I chuckle at the memory and keep rooting through the box. A straw from a Slush Puppy Paul Wainwright gave me when we went to see *She's the Man* at the York Odeon. A frayed friendship bracelet, from Jennie or Stacey or Zoe. Those agonizingly intense friendships you think will last forever, until they don't.

"Ah, here it is," I say, pulling out a dog-eared, rolled-up photo with stains on the back. The tube has been squashed, and I try to flatten it as I unscroll, using the milk carton to hold one end down while I press away the creases with the heel of my hand. I scan the long line of faces, hunting for myself and my friends.

"Which one's you?" asks Adam, leaning over a little and wincing slightly as he cranes his neck.

"Here," I say, pointing out the serious girl staring back at me with her poker-straight hair and tiny front plaits.

"Ah, look at you. Little emo queen in training," he says with a grin, then shovels another spoonful of granola into his mouth.

I move up the lines to the older kids further back, until I find Bridget, three years above, testing all the rules with her backcombed Amy Winehouse rat's nest, heavy smudged eyeliner and super-skinny tie. This will be just before she messed up most of her GCSEs and left school to fold up jumpers in New Look. I keep looking along the row.

"I knew it."

There he is. Oliver Whatshisname, thinner, but with the same eyes, the same mouth. Unmistakably him.

"I *knew* I recognised him," I say to Adam, pleased with myself for solving it after puzzling overnight. "What did they call him? Sticky or Stick or something, though he doesn't look all that thin. Or maybe it was Twiggy because of his name, Oliver Smallwood?"

"Kids can be *so* creative..." Adam says sarcastically. He peers at the photo and makes a kind of 'huh' noise. But he went to a different school in Malton, and I can tell he's not really interested in all this old Scarborough gossip. I am, though.

"It's all coming back now. People used to make fun of him all the time, even kids in my year, even though he was three years older. He was the idiot who got suspended for nicking the head's wallet. What kind of genius does that in broad daylight? Of course he got caught. All that was before I got there. But everyone knew. Kids gave him hell. Ha! Well, I won't let on I remember him next session, but I'm certainly not taking career advice from the school joke."

"Yeah. And check you've still got your purse on the way out."

I feel better about things now I've put the pieces together. Knowing something about Oliver feels like it gives me a kind of power. And I need every bit of power I can get. Because if I lose this job, there's no chance of saving for uni. And knowing Justin's chosen someone so hopeless to do his dirty work gives me one up on him as well.

"They'll have to do better than that if they want to get rid of me."

"Too right," says Adam. "Congratulations, Inspector Clouseau. You're smarter than the lot of them put together." He begins to get up from his chair with a pained grunt.

"Stay there. I've got it," I say, jumping up to grab his empty bowl and cup from in front of him. "You sit there, have a bit of a rest and a read."

"My hero," he says, grinning. "Rescued from the tyranny of crockery once again."

I take the dirty plates to the sink, then look back at Adam at the table. He leans back in his chair, flipping through his magazine. His dark hair's curling at the ends, where it needs a cut, and there's stubble along his jaw. Even in that stupid neck brace, he still manages to look gorgeous. He's lovely and supportive with my work stuff. He was livid when I told him about that weird incident with Justin pretending to be a buyer. *Monumental arsehole* were his exact words.

A pang of guilt hits me. We'd only been going out for about a month when he got hurt. He was repairing a window in this place when a bit of the frame came away and he tumbled off his ladder. He fell ten feet or so, and a hedge half-broke his fall, but he hurt his back and neck and hasn't been able to work since. That was six months ago. He moved in here for a while so I could look after him, and we both thought it would clear up faster than it has. It's been hard. He wants to work, but there's only so much he can do. That bloody neck brace. He's pretty immobile. Even pushing the hoover round is a strain. And we're both reliant on my money. That's why this stuff at work is so important. I daren't think what will happen if I lose my job.

Bang!

As if on cue, the window blows open with a tremendous racket as the frame thumps against the wall. I nearly have a heart attack. An icy blast of wind blows through the kitchen, riffling through the pages of Adam's magazine and sending the paper items from my memory box skittering across the table and onto the floor. I charge across the room and push the window shut. It's a wonder the glass didn't shatter.

"I must fix that latch," says Adam.

Just add it to the long list of jobs that need doing in this place. Dad got too sick to take them on, and I was too busy looking after him and Mum to do anything about them myself. The place got as old and run-down as my parents. Now they've died and I haven't got the money to get someone in to sort it all out. I know Adam wants to, but there's no way I'm letting him take the risk. What if he ends up even worse?

I kneel on the floor and load the things back into the shoe box – Post-It notes and flavoured ChapStick and old bus tickets. The school photo is still on the table.

"Don't start World War Three," Adam says.

"What do you mean?"

"I'm on your side, you know I am. But don't start a war with this Oliver bloke. At least, not in those pyjamas."

I laugh, despite myself. "Fine. No war in pyjamas."

"That's my girl." He leans back, wincing a little, but his eyes stay on me, soft and proud. "If you think he's reporting it all back to Justin Twatt, just… keep your head down, yeah? Play it smart. You're smarter than any of them."

"Of course I will. Thanks." I know what he's thinking. Same as me. What happens if I get the sack? Suck it up. Don't rock the boat.

I look at Oliver Smallwood's face again, Twiggy or Sticky or whatever they called him. Justin's little spy. He's the guy they've picked to ruin my life. He thinks he's going to sit in that chair and use his pathetic games and exercises to find out all about me.

But I know all about him.

The thief. The idiot.

I roll the photograph up and put the lid back on the box.

If it's World War Three he wants, bring it on. Because this isn't just about my job. This is about my whole future.

And I'll be damned if some smug little thief in a fake coaching room is going to take that away from me.

CHAPTER 6
OLIVER

Oliver stands at the top of the stairs and watches the slow ascent of Maureen's stair-lift.

"I'm sorry, Oliver. This adds a whole new meaning to the word 'patient.'"

He has known Maureen for years. She taught the module on Working Ethically and Professionally for his diploma in therapeutic counselling, then supervised him during his practical training, and she oversaw his Master's in Trauma-Informed Practice. She has a powerful air of calm he admires. This is the first time, though, that he has ever thought of himself as her *patient*.

He always enjoys the peace of the train journey to her home in York, where she has her office. Her house is beautiful, light and airy, calm like its owner. Its rooms and hallways are spacious, and never appear to restrict her movements in her wheelchair. He no longer sees the wheelchair at all. Only this stair-lift impedes her and reminds Oliver that she's hampered by her injury. There are some traumas you adjust to but can never entirely overcome.

The stair-lift reaches the landing and judders to an

unhealthy stop. Oliver frowns as he watches Maureen slide from the seat into her waiting wheelchair.

"Should you get that looked at?"

"Probably. Sometimes it stops halfway up the stairs like it's having a strop."

"Like a teenager in machine form?"

"Exactly. I half-expect it to slam a door at the top." Maureen gives a wry smile and leads the way to her office.

He's familiar with the dark oak panelling, the serious leather chairs, the long, low table with its simple, abstract sculpture. It oozes calm and authority – the complete opposite of his pokey room above the chiropodist. Though Maureen has never seen his office, he's struck by his feeling of embarrassment.

Maureen eases herself into one of the chairs. She could just stay in the wheelchair, Oliver reflects, as he sits opposite her. But perhaps that would make her too vulnerable, when she wants to seem like someone in charge. Not in charge, but dependable. He registers what he's doing, and tries to stop himself from doing this internal analysing. It's not his turn, for once. It's her turn to consider him.

"So, how is coaching?"

"It's okay."

"Okay?" She lets the question hang. They've started.

"It's early days. It feels different. I'm used to seeing clients with real problems, not just work stuff."

"Isn't work a real problem?"

Oliver is reminded of how good she is at this.

"Okay, I get the irony. Here I am, trivialising other people's work problems, while you're counselling me on mine."

"You were a therapist for a long time, Oliver. You've stopped for a while. How does it feel to have set up your new coaching business?"

"I'm glad to be seeing clients again," he says, not sounding particularly glad. Maureen nods slightly but stays silent, inviting Oliver to continue.

"Maybe I'm being unfair," he adds. "I'm sure the issues people come to me with matter to them. I just don't know how much I can care whether Peter ate Jackie's sandwich from the staff fridge, or whether Grace earned enough commission selling houses to go clubbing this weekend."

Silence. Her slight smile. Her sharp, unblinking eyes.

"I know that sounds cruel or uncaring, and of course I'm not like that when I'm coaching clients. But these issues feel so trivial in comparison to the issues I used to deal with in therapy. The people seem trivial compared to the ones with more vital needs."

"Do you have someone in mind?"

She knows he does. "Julia."

Maureen looks up and to the left, gathering a thought.

"I notice you used the phrase *more vital needs*."

"Yes. Urgent. Necessary."

"It's an interesting word, *vital*. It also means alive."

Oliver pictures Julia. Her delicate, thin frame. Pale skin, with faint hints of yellow and purple bruising at the neck and wrists. Her cocooned way of sitting, arms crossed around her in a kind of self-comfort. Her sad, grey eyes. Hands fluttering at her mouth or hair when the questions got too hard. Bruised. Battered. But alive.

"That's the kind of work I still want to be doing. Work that really matters." Oliver replays the banality of his week's sessions over in his head. He half laughs, bitter. "This woman, Grace, from the estate agency. Lancaster & Lyle hired me to do career development with her. But what's the point? She says nothing, drifts off whenever we touch something real. No desire to explore values, beliefs, anything. She's blank. A void. I should be working with people who need me, not these distracting irritations, like a gnat you flap away at but can't escape."

He stops. He imagines what Maureen's heard in his voice. Contempt. Disgust. How can he help when he has contempt for his clients? For himself? He knows he's wrong. But for now, Grace represents everything he despises.

"I know you don't want to hear this, Oliver, but you're not ready. Coaching is a good step. But you're not ready for psychotherapy clients yet."

He's angry. Why is she stopping him from doing the work he has a calling for? He couldn't save Julia, but he can save others. He could be working with people who really need him. *Need* him. He curses himself for choosing Maureen to counsel him. He should have known she'd be too cautious. Maybe that's what she's doing when she hides the wheel-chair. Trying to hide the bit of herself that had an accident, that's scared of risk. But he sees it.

"The work we do requires us to hold our clients with unconditional positive regard. Compassionate detachment. You know this. But right now I think you're struggling to do that."

"I don't blame myself for Julia."

"No?"

"I don't."

"Is it possible you are too involved, Oliver? Too bruised?"

He thinks of the clock, reading ten past noon. The session she had booked but didn't attend. The brute of a boyfriend he couldn't get her to blame or to leave. The razor. The bath turning red.

"I don't," he protests again, his voice wavering, too high-pitched, revealing the lie, convincing neither himself nor Maureen.

"You're in pain, Oliver. I understand it. But our clients have agency. Their choices are their choices. Sometimes they aren't ready or able to take the help we offer. We can offer everything and still lose them. And that's their choice."

Oliver nods, letting her words sink in. "I couldn't save her."

"It's hard for us to accept that they have no hope and can't see a way forward, but that is their truth, not our failure."

Maureen thinks he can't understand how Julia could take her own life. But he understands only too well. Playing his sessions with her over in his head. What else could he have said or done? Blaming himself. Crying on the bathroom floor. Staring into the mirror at his guilty face, a mound of tablets piled in his hand, swallowing, then hunched, vomiting into the toilet. He knows only too well the temptation of leaving these feelings behind, the lure of feeling nothing.

He'll never tell Maureen that. *She's* the one who wouldn't understand.

Oliver blames himself as much as he blames the bully. He was supposed to save her, and he didn't. And now she's dead.

Maureen leans forward, lays a hand on his arm.

"Sometimes we have to hit our lowest point before we can get better. Julia hit hers and couldn't find a way back. But you will, Oliver. I know you will."

He nods and forces a smile.

How can she be sure of that, when he knows for certain that he won't?

CHAPTER 7
GRACE

I balance my cappuccino and Danish on my desk, shove Kyle's abandoned paperwork to the side, and take a deep, smug breath. Warm pastry, proper coffee, and a morning with no client calls until ten. Bliss.

The office still smells faintly of Kyle's stale chicken tikka, but nothing's ruining my mood today. I've got caffeine, sugar, and two idiots I'm going to outperform by lunch. It's called focus.

They're both camped out by the interactive display, talking too loudly and jabbing at the touchscreen like they're closing a million-pound deal. Kyle's fiddling with the laser pointer like it's a toy, clicking it at random spots around the office just to show off. He keeps shining it on my desk like I'm a bloody cat, then pretending it was an accident, but I can hear them laughing behind their hands like naughty schoolboys.

The cinnamon icing sticks to my fingers as I break off a corner. Perfect. Let Kyle and Mohammed prat about with the touchscreen like two toddlers in a soft-play. I'm the one who actually keeps this place running. If it wasn't for me, the two of them would still be googling how to spell 'mortgage'.

Christ knows what the woman by the listings board thinks, what with the curry smell and these two acting like a couple of halfwits on *The Apprentice*. Kyle bounces over to her, buttoning up the jacket of his cheap shiny suit.

"That's a lovely house," he says, clocking the one she's looking at, the three-bed on Orchard Road that's been on the market for a couple of months. "Only just come on, and it's a good price for that area, though I'm sure they'd be open to an offer."

"Thanks," says the woman, "but I'm looking for something with a bigger garden. I think I have what I need." She takes the specs on a couple of houses out of the trays and exits sharpish. I'm not surprised. It's amazing we sell anything in the middle of this chimp's tea party. Kyle sidles back over to Mohammed.

"I wonder if *she'd* be open to an offer," he says, with a revolting laugh. "If she's into gardening, I could plant a few seeds for her."

Mohammed snorts. Kyle grins like he's said something award-winning.

"Classy," I say, without looking up.

Kyle swings round like he's just noticed I'm here. "Oh, morning, Grace. You alright? Bit quiet over there."

"Fine," I say. I don't want to get into it. I go back to what I'm doing, typing up the details for a new listing Kyle viewed yesterday. He always lands these on me. *It's better if you do it, Gracie – you've got that nice way with words. Makes it sound fancy. I'm more of a talker than a typer.* I refused once, and when I saw the rubbish he'd come out with, full of spelling mistakes and grammatical errors, I had to redo it all anyway.

Right. Listing typed up, coffee still hot, Danish half demolished. I'm winning at life this morning. I check my phone under the desk. It's Adam, promising a foot rub tonight if I get home before eight. Motivation comes in many forms.

A smart couple come in. He's got a lovely coat on that shouts money, and she's got a Hermès handbag that costs about ten times what I earn in a week. Mohammed and Kyle spot them, and Kyle flies across the office like a man possessed. We work on commission, so any time someone comes in who looks like they've got two pennies to rub together, those two practically foam at the mouth. Meanwhile, Muggins here is left holding the fort and doesn't get a look-in. Doesn't matter. I'm playing a longer game than they'll ever understand.

Kyle starts greasing them up and goes into serious schmooze-mode, while I get back to typing another listing. I need the photos Kyle took yesterday so I open Outlook.

Ping.

New email from Justin.

Subject: Final Warning – Performance Review

For a second, the words don't register. Then my stomach cartwheels like I've missed a step going downstairs.

"Fuck."

It's out before I can stop myself. I look up and see the smart couple peering over at me. Kyle looks at me like I've just kicked over his sandcastle. I can't believe I'm working with him and *I'm* the one who looks bad.

I click open Justin's email. It's short. Bullet points. Brutal.

Your sales performance has not met expectations.

This is your final warning.

You have four weeks to improve or face further action.

No preamble. No meeting. Just – this.

I reread it twice, three times, searching for the bit where it's a mistake. But it's not.

The couple have left, and Kyle creeps closer, doing a hammy job of pretending to tidy leaflets.

"Oof," he says, peering over. "Someone's in the naughty corner."

I snap my laptop shut.

"Private email," I say sharply.

He raises both hands, grinning like the joke's always on someone else. "Alright, alright. No need to bite. You just looked a bit upset and I was worried about you."

As if. Bloody nosy, more like.

He shrugs. "Well, if it's about sales, maybe it's a sign. Time to hustle, Gracie. Work the charm. Show some leg."

I blink at him.

He winks. "Metaphorically."

Mohammed's staring over from his desk like he's watching a sitcom.

"It's *Grace*," I say, "not Gracie."

"I'm just being friendly," Kyle says in a voice that says *he's* the one who's offended. He ambles back to his desk, grinning at Mohammed.

I carry on typing up the listing. But I can't concentrate, and all I can think about is the email. The injustice of it. I feel angry tears welling up, and I don't want them seeing me upset, so I go into the kitchen and get myself a glass of water. Then I bring it back to my desk and just stare at the screen.

About half an hour later, Mohammed wanders past my workstation.

"Kyle's a dick, but he's not wrong. If you want commission, you've got to jump in a bit more. No one's gonna hand you viewings."

No, they just elbow you out of the way and grab them all for themselves.

"You two book yourselves in for everything that moves," I snap, my voice shaking with anger. "You hog every decent lead and toss me the hopeless cases, then stand there like you're bloody Mother Teresa doing me a favour."

Mohammed looks confused. Kyle looks up from his desk, all mock innocence. "It's not our fault if we're proactive. Can't help it if we're good at our jobs."

I stare at him. I'm thirty-three, and because I took years out to care for my mum, I've been here four years, stuck at junior level – while these two clowns are ten years younger and leapfrog over me.

The computer pings again. This time it's an invite. Sales strategy meeting. HQ. Thursday. I'm not on the list.

Of course I'm not.

Kyle claps his hands. "Right, Mo. You ready for the 11 a.m.? Viewings don't wait."

Mohammed grabs his coat. He glances my way with a kind of pitying look.

Then they're out the door like a pair of eager puppies, jostling over who gets to drive. I'm left in the silence, the fake plant in the corner rustling in the breeze from the fan heater. My coffee's gone cold.

I open the email back up. Final warning. No sugar-coating. No second chances. Like a bolt out of nowhere.

And then it hits me.

Oliver.

I've only had one session with him, but I knew something felt off. Too many questions about the team, about Justin. He said it was all part of 'context gathering'. Said he wanted to help. But now I'm absolutely certain Justin didn't hire him to help at all.

I can picture him now, in Justin's office, giving his snide feedback. *She's struggling. Defensive. Not a cultural fit.* I bet he's very careful with his phrasing. Maybe my file already has a plan in it and Oliver's just ticking the final boxes.

But if they want me gone, they're gonna have to do better than this. I won't make it easy.

Let's see how they handle *me* when I stop playing nice.

CHAPTER 8
OLIVER

Perched on a low stool at a small, round, wooden table, Oliver forms grubby worms of paper as he rubs his finger against a damp beer mat. He sips a pint, his second, an amber ale with some name he didn't catch when he pointed randomly at the pump. He didn't care. This place was never about the beer.

The Anchor. The pub hasn't changed. It still has that stale, hoppy smell and damp carpet, with a worn track from the door to the bar. An old fishing net and a pair of broken lobster baskets hang from the low ceiling above him, and the walls are lined with yellowed pictures of sailors in their thick jumpers and heavy waders, faces creased like the photographs themselves. Probably all dead now, or faded away with the vanishing local fishing trade.

The TV flickers in the corner, showing some snooker match or other with the sound off and no one watching. A hunched man at the bar coughs into his hand to call the barmaid away from her texting and orders another whisky. Two women speak in hushed tones over glasses of wine.

Someone jabs at a quiz machine, which bleeps and jangles with unnecessary enthusiasm.

Oliver picks at a crisp from the packet he has torn open in front of him. He used to think of this as an old man's pub. The kind of place you could disappear into and not be disturbed, safe from the familiar faces from school. Now he looks around and realises this *is* an old man's pub. And somehow, quietly, he's become one of them. He's not even forty, but that's how he feels. Old. Weary. Ground down.

He's disturbed by a laugh from a table at the other end of the room. A group of men, a couple of them in football colours of some team or other. He envies them their common interest, their allegiance to a tribe that binds them together. His only memories of football are the miserable rainy afternoons on the school field, the sting of leather kicked hard against his bare legs, the bruises on his shins, the humiliations of his embarrassed father watching on from the touchline, then not watching at all. The changing room.

He used to go to the pub, in Leeds, with Alison. It was a ritual – pub first, then some new pop-up place she'd found, with exciting seasonal menus and exposed brick. Or, sometimes, a drink after, nursing red wine and swapping stories about their day. Her laugh brightening the quiet corner they'd tumbled into. Her smile.

Now here he is, drinking alone, putting off going home to a house whose silence suffocates him when he's there. The emptiness curls around the door frames. Better to be sitting here facing an empty chair.

He's scanning the huddles of other drinkers when he spots him.

Ash.

Sitting at a table by the window, beer in hand, talking too loudly to his companions, like he owns the place. He's broader now, hair shaved down close where he's started balding at the front. But it's him alright. The grin. That braying laugh.

Oliver freezes. His eyes dart across the table, searching for something to do. He picks up his pint glass, nearly full, and sips slowly, hoping – stupidly – to disappear. The beer tastes bitter and thin. He glances across towards the door and wonders how long it would take to walk from this table and out to the street in a casual way, without being noticed.

"Sticky!"

Too late.

The voice booms across the large room. Oliver imagines every head in the pub turning, locking eyes on him like someone who has just been caught shoplifting. He feels a hot flare of shame crawl up his neck as if he is sinking in scalding water.

Ash is already on his feet, swaggering over. "Bloody hell. You're back, then? Leeds didn't quite pan out?"

Oliver half-looks up, making eye contact without confronting, trying to keep his face neutral. "Just visiting."

Ash claps him too hard on the shoulder.

"Course you are. Back for a bit of peace and quiet, yeah? Shame what happened, the stuff with that woman topping herself on your watch. We read all about it on Facebook. But you were always a clever one. You're bound to bounce back."

Ash leans over and takes one of Oliver's crisps. He crunches away on it, smiling, giving no suggestion he's about to go away. The words are friendly. The tone isn't. Oliver has done enough courses on silent body language to understand what lurks in the shadows between the words. It's the same tone Ash used when he'd call him 'pal' before tripping him in the canteen. The same glint in his eye that said *I'm just messing* – but he wasn't.

And worse.

Oliver sits frozen, like a mouse being played with by a cat.

He notices his finger on the beer mat, the ribbons of paper piling nervously on the table. His heart beats too fast.

He tries not to think about school. The thick dread that used to pool in his stomach every Sunday night. The cold sweat on the walk to the gates. The cracked tarmac. The bike sheds, their paint peeling like old scabs. That sagging school sign, rust biting into its corners. Always grey skies overhead, threatening, like the weather itself was antagonistic.

Ash wasn't the worst of them. Not at first.

No – Ash had been *kind*.

They weren't friends, not really. But Ash used to walk out with him occasionally after class, or let him sit and watch in peace when they were kicking a ball about in the school yard. Say things like, *You're all right, you know. The rest of them are just dickheads.* And Oliver believed him. Because when you're thirteen, and lonely, even the tiniest kindness feels like salvation.

So when Ash slid in next to him in the library one day and whispered, *"Reckon you could help me with something?"* Oliver felt like he'd been singled out for special treatment. He felt chosen.

Just watching the door while he grabbed a confiscated Game Boy, Ash had said. Oliver stood guard outside the school office, eager and grateful. Afterwards, Ash hadn't spoken to him for the rest of the day, but all through lessons that afternoon, through maths and English and science, Oliver could feel the energy crackle in the classroom, the bond between them.

The next day, at morning assembly, the head announced to the entire school that his wallet was gone, "stolen by some sticky-fingered thief." £120 in cash. And a signed photo of him presenting a comically oversized charity cheque to the local MP had been smashed, the prized memento torn on the office floor in a mess of broken glass.

The CCTV showed one boy entering with his jumper pulled over his head, impossible to recognise. But the pupil in the corridor was unmistakable. Oliver. Standing like a sentry outside the office door.

He was suspended for a fortnight.

His parents didn't speak to him for three days, attending the school to repay the stolen sum from their own money. He could hear their raised voices downstairs once he'd been sent to bed, dinnerless and in disgrace. His mum cried in the kitchen when she thought he couldn't hear.

Oliver never told.

Ash didn't even deny it with his mates. Just shrugged and grinned, half-bragging about it without saying anything, basking in a kind of glory, while Oliver was shunned, shamed and humiliated. They started calling him Sticky. Sticky Fingers. Sticky the Sap. His time at school from that day on was more miserable than before. He tried to shrink, to disappear. But everyone joined in. His classmates. Then the whole year. Then the whole school.

The cruellest thing of all was that Ash, whom he had once thought of as a kind of shelter in the storm, became his greatest tormentor. It was blindingly clear to Oliver what he hadn't seen before: that Ash, and people like Ash, are evil. They never get caught, and they don't need to run, because they don't care. They smile. They charm. They thrive.

Ash went on to work in sales somewhere. Big house now, probably. Probably a company car. A wife who laughs at his stories because she can't see how loathsome he is. Loathsome herself. With loathsome kids, no doubt.

Ash grins, all teeth. "We should have a proper catch-up. Get a drink sometime, yeah? For old time's sake."

Oliver attempts a smile. "Yeah." He forces down his nearly full pint in one, praying the nausea he feels won't bring it surging up again, crowning his humiliation. He grabs his jacket and pulls it on. "I've got to be somewhere. I forgot. I'm late."

Oliver lurches towards the door, dizzy with emotion, holding his breath, desperate to get out but not wanting to look like he's running away. Like a rabid dog, he can't let Ash smell the fear.

"See you around, Sticky!"

Ash's voice calls to him jovially as he reaches the door, resists the urge to turn the handle five times, and bursts out gasping into the bracing cold night air.

CHAPTER 9
GRACE

I can feel the stress knotting in my shoulders like someone lacing me up, tighter and tighter. I catch myself, hunched over, elbows locked, and force myself to sit back for a moment, shake my arms out. This crappy wooden dining chair isn't helping, hard as nails and as old as the Magna Carta. Classic Dad. I imagine him admiring it as he bought the set, built for function, not comfort. One more item on the ever-expanding list of things to be upgraded when life gets less... life-y.

When I got home earlier, Adam said I was so wound up he could rub my feet for a week and still not sort out my tension. He ran me a bath instead, loaded it with bubbles and even lit me a couple of scented candles. The room smelt lovely, all rose and sandalwood. I listened to the sound of the water gurgling into the bath as I got undressed. I saw my reflection, strained and tense. It was almost a relief when the mirror clouded up and I didn't have to look at myself anymore. I turned off the taps, slipped into the bath and lay back in the warm water. Adam even brought me a glass of wine.

But no matter how hard I tried to relax, that bloody email kept playing in my head like a crappy song on repeat.

You have four weeks to improve or face further action.

I launched myself out of the bath, dripping and furious, and dried myself roughly with a towel like I was scrubbing Justin off my skin.

And so now I'm at the kitchen table. It's dark out, but I haven't bothered with the main light. Just the under-unit ones. The blue glow from my laptop spreads across the pad of notes I've been scribbling on for an hour – scratchy handwriting, underlined dates, half-legible ramblings I'm trying to pull together as some kind of defence. Exhibit A: I work harder than any of those clowns. Exhibit B: I don't deserve to be shafted. Exhibit C: I'm not the problem here – I'm the bloody solution they're too blinkered to see.

I shiver slightly where the breeze hits my neck from the window Adam couldn't finish repairing. After my bath, he asked me if I wanted anything, but I told him I need to be alone with this for a bit. Now the noise of the TV rattles on from the living room next door while he watches some comedy panel show or other. Every now and then I hear him roar with laughter. We don't go out much, not since the accident, so telly has become our main entertainment. Adam laughs again, and I try to tune it out.

The fan in my laptop hums and clicks. I've still got Justin's email open in another tab, like some kind of masochist. *Your sales performance has not met expectations.* I know it off by heart. Every passive-aggressive keystroke. I scroll down, stare at the sentence like I'm trying to morph it into something else. Spoiler: It doesn't.

I flick back through my diary. Viewings I booked. Specs I wrote. Clients I chased. Properties I pushed. All of it logged, tracked, and utterly ignored. I want to believe it adds up to something; that I can make a case for myself.

Instead, all I can hear is Justin in that terrible first meeting, with his smug little moustache and the square of tissue stuck to his cheek like a warning label. *"You were like a bloody damp flannel at the start... You need a killer instinct."*

Yes, well, not all of us sell houses like we're flogging used cars for commission. Justin only seems to value the kill of the sale, but there wouldn't *be* any sales without me doing all this legwork in the background. And anyway, I don't treat this job like the others, as if it's some kind of religion. I'm saving for uni. That's it. But *that's* why I have to fight this and stick up for myself. If I lose this job, I lose everything. So I'm not just fighting for sales now. I'm fighting to save my job. I'm fighting for my future.

I know exactly what tomorrow's coaching session really is. A trap, gift-wrapped in fake concern and tied up with a corporate bullshit ribbon. Oliver will sit there in his sad little chair with his sad little therapist-y voice, staring into me with his phoney kind eyes. And all the while, he'll be looking for signs of weakness he can report back to Justin Twatt.

I can't give him an inch. That's why I've written it all out. What I've done. What I've learned. What I'll do better. Passionate, not pissed off. Determined, not difficult.

And under no circumstances – no matter what – no tears.

The music goes quiet and the TV clicks off. Adam wanders in, shirtless, still in his neck brace, a bit frayed now from overuse. He watches me from the doorway, waiting patiently while I jot down a few more notes.

"Fancy a cuppa?" he says once I've finished.

"Oh God, yes, please. I've been sat working on this for hours."

He goes over and flicks the kettle on. "Have you got much more to do?"

"I've got the coaching thing tomorrow," I say, keeping my voice light. "Trying to get my head straight."

Adam pulls a face. "What, the wallet thief turned psychiatrist? That's one hell of a career pivot."

"He's not a psychiatrist. It's not therapy. It's supposed to be career development."

He scoffs. "Funny way of developing someone, threatening to sack them."

He tosses a couple of teabags into mugs and pours on the hot water. He peers into the teabag box.

"Did you put a shopping order in?"

"Not yet. I've worked all day, cooked, cleaned, and now I'm trying to not get fired. I'm afraid teabags didn't make the shortlist."

He kisses the top of my head, the way he always does when I'm on edge.

"It's okay, luv. I was just going to say I'll sort it. And don't let them get to you, sweetheart. You're a superstar."

And now I feel like a cow. Because he can see the pressure I'm under. We met when he was doing lots of handyman work. He'd painted the outside of my hairdresser Emma's house, and she gave me his name. He did some work on the roof and the guttering. We hit it off and went on a couple of dates. I thought he was sexy and funny, and it all happened pretty fast.

Then he had the accident. It's not like he *wants* to be on the sidelines, not doing his bit. The brace, the pain – it's all real.

"I'm sorry," I say, squeezing his hand.

"Don't worry, luv. What you're doing, it's important. I'm heading up, give you some space," he says, taking his mug. "Don't be too long, sweetheart. You need sleep."

"Don't worry, I won't."

He goes out and I hear him huffing his way painfully up the stairs.

Sleep. Right. I'll pencil it in between saving my job and

working out how the hell we live within our means. I keep meaning to sit down and go through it all. Half the stuff we're pouring money out on I don't even recognise.

But sleeping and budgeting will have to wait. Tomorrow comes first.

I grab a biscuit for energy, sit back down, have a sip of tea and open a blank document. I've got all the notes. Now I need to pull it together into a kind of script. The one where I don't flinch, don't fumble, don't fall apart.

Oliver said something last time that's been bothering me: *"My job isn't to save you. My job is to walk beside you."* I wonder if he says that to everyone, or if he meant it just for me. Either way, he's wrong. I don't need him. By tomorrow afternoon I'll be ready to save myself.

Upstairs, I hear Adam shifting around, the creak of the mattress, the faint hum of his phone. He'll be asleep soon. And I'll still be here, chasing my tail. I'll pull an all-nighter if I have to.

Tomorrow, I'll sit in that weird little office above the chiropodist, with its shabby walls and fake plant in the corner, and I'll tell him exactly who I am.

I'm Grace Harper. And I am not going down without a fight.

I'm not ready. Not yet. But I will be.

Because if they think they're taking away my future – my job, my plan, my life – they've got another thing coming.

CHAPTER 10
OLIVER

He's been in The Station Tap for almost two hours.

The surprise encounter with Ash unsettled him. Bad enough he's had to navigate the challenges of the last few months, his split with Alison, sorting all his parents' things. Julia. He could do without his childhood trauma getting loaded on top.

For once, the pub isn't just a place to take refuge – he feels he needs a drink to steady his nerves. He's now on his second pint here, alone at a table that's far enough from the window not to be seen from the street, but close enough to the door that he can make a quick getaway if need be.

This place is new. It seems too trendy for this sad town locked in a time-warp, all chalkboard menus and exposed pipework, mismatched stools and filament bulbs that cast the room in a hipster glow. When he lived in Leeds, there were hundreds of places like this. Here in Scarborough, it feels gauche and contemptible.

He nurses a pint of IPA with an absurd name like it's been made up for a dare. It's thick and too sweet, clearly very strong. Not to his taste at all. He drinks it anyway.

The bar is a low hum of sound – clinking glasses and background indie music. There's a table of four women near the window, laughing loudly about someone's hen do, from what he can gather. Two men in fleeces are dissecting a cricket match. He's the only one sitting alone. He's relieved not to recognise anyone in here. He flicks through the news on his phone, opens his messenger app now and again, scrolls through messages from clients, pretending he's chatting with friends.

He thinks about Julia. What might she be doing right now if she were alive? He pictures her sitting at the table, knees tucked up under her, glass in hand, head tilted back in laughter. He can't remember if she ever really laughed. He doesn't think so. Is this the kind of place Julia would have liked? Or would she have hated it as much as him, the self-consciously quirky objects loaded onto the shelves? The overdone reclaimed wood. Might they have shared a laugh about it, bursting out onto the street in a fit of giggles?

He glances out of the window and watches a crowd of people emerging from the theatre opposite, light and jolly after the show. He wonders what it would be like to go to the theatre on his own. Perhaps he might feel like he was amongst people, for once. The danger though is that he might feel even more alone.

He finishes his drink, the third of the evening, maybe fourth. He's not counting. He's not drunk, but there's a woolliness behind his eyes, a dull fuzz around his thoughts. The kind he hopes will anaesthetise his restless brain and make memories slow down.

He should have eaten. He pictures the contents of his fridge at home – a paltry assortment of ready meals for one. A kind of heavy dread comes over him, like a wet overcoat, as he imagines himself eating them. Putting the oven on. Sitting in silence at the kitchen table, waiting for it to heat up. He can't bear the thought.

By the time he leaves the bar, the evening's fully sunk into night, and most places are thinning out. The cold bites at the back of his neck the moment he steps outside. He zips up his jacket and heads up through town. Scarborough in winter feels like a place someone's forgotten to put away.

He orders fish and chips without thinking. Just muscle memory. The neon cod behind the counter flickers like it's winking. The packet warms his chilly hands as he marches along the pavement, steam rising up from the greasy paper. He wants somewhere quiet to eat them, and walks down the hill to the front, past the harsh fluorescents of the arcades and up towards the lifeboat station. He sits on the low wall that faces the sea and unwraps his supper. He picks away at the limp chips and oily batter with his tiny wooden fork. The tide's out. The beach glistens black under the moonlight. The sea itself is a long smear of darkness.

He imagines Julia here. Sitting beside him, coat buttoned up against the sea breeze. Counting the waves as they drag themselves back and forth over the stones. Trying to sneak one of his chips and pretending she hadn't.

He's barely eaten a third when he's had enough. He dumps the rest in an overflowing bin. Wipes his hands on a tissue. Though it's late, it still feels too soon for home.

The Olympia's still lit. He hasn't been bowling since he was a kid. He remembers going once, maybe twice, and hating it. He finds himself pushing the door, and is surprised to find it's open. Inside, everything is brighter than it needs to be. The familiar smell hits him at once, a rush of stale popcorn and bubblegum, catapulting him back twenty years.

He books two games at the counter. He doesn't know why. One wouldn't be enough, and more would be sad. He asks for a lane at the end, away from the birthday group of teens squealing over nachos. He changes into the shoes. They're still warm from the last person. It makes his stomach lurch.

He takes off his jacket and studies the electronic scoring system that wasn't here when he was a kid. He notices a group of teenagers posing for the screen, tongues out and peace signs. He decides against a photo. He leaves his player name blank.

Player 1. Player 2.

He picks a ball that feels the right weight and holds his fingers in front of the air-jet. He plays both sides. Once he starts, he remembers why he hated it so much. He's not good. The ball thuds and veers. Sometimes he hits a few pins. Once he gets a spare. Never a strike. He has no idea why some balls stay on track and others skitter off into the gutter.

He imagines Julia in the booth beside him. Messing it up, laughing at herself. Her cheeks pink from exertion. The way her laugh might have sounded if she'd had reason to enjoy herself.

He finishes both games. 72. Then 85. He is both winner and loser. He doesn't care. The whole thing lasts barely twenty minutes.

Back outside, the cold hits harder. He walks home the long way and tells himself it's to stretch his legs, clear his head. But really, it's just delay. Delay the door. Delay the smell of old curtains and radiator dust and everything that reminds him of what has brought him back, now, to this place.

He unlocks and locks five times, in a familiar pattern.

He walks through the hallway in darkness with his coat still on. The light in the kitchen is stuttering. He's meant for days to replace the bulb. He fills the limescaled kettle and makes tea on autopilot, no sound except the kettle boiling and the tick of the ancient clock. But he's too full of beer to want it, and leaves it untouched on the counter, where it will stay until morning.

He climbs the stairs and reaches the landing. The bedroom smells faintly of furniture polish and cold sheets. He undresses, folds everything neatly, and places it on the chair. The mahogany wardrobe looms at the foot of the bed like a monument, funereal.

He brushes his teeth. He sits on the spongy mattress, then lies down. The other side is empty. He closes his eyes and tries to think of nothing.

Instead, he pictures Julia. How she might have lived. Sitting in a room somewhere, reading. The soft light behind her. The sound of the radiator ticking. Going to bed, content. Hair spread out on the pillow. The rhythmic rise and fall of sleep.

He tries not to think of her, but he can't stop it. He knows he'll fall asleep eventually, but even then, he won't escape. He closes his eyes. He waits for her to come to him in dreams, like always.

CHAPTER 11
GRACE

"I've been thinking about Justin's email," I say brightly. "And I realise now it's a good thing. A challenge. Honestly, I see it as an opportunity to bring out my best self. I've already started tracking my performance metrics and identifying proactive ways to add value to the team."

I pause, satisfied. If there were gold stars for corporate jargon, I'd be bloody covered in them.

Oliver shuts his eyes.

He's sitting opposite me, head slightly tilted. His pen's still in his hand, but resting on the pad like it gave up halfway through a thought. I wait until the silence has gone on long enough to be awkward.

I narrow my eyes.

Is he asleep?

I thought I got a whiff of booze when he invited me in. Has he been on a bender?

I shift slightly in my chair and sniff. Nothing. No reaction. Just that same furrowed brow, like he's deep in contemplation, or dreaming about a tricky Sudoku.

This is meant to be me saving my job. I'm supposed to be

revealing my professional potential. Instead, I'm sitting here wondering if a man in a saggy cardigan is about to drool down himself.

I clear my throat, just loud enough.

He straightens, blinks slowly. "Sorry," he says, smiling faintly. "Thinking."

Right.

I'm not sure what's worse – if he *was* asleep, or if that's his actual reaction to what I just said.

Oliver nods, noncommittal. "And what's motivating this change?"

I can't afford to let him derail me. I spent hours scripting this last night like I was already in the unfair dismissal tribunal. I know exactly what I want him to think: confident, committed, a team player. Someone worth keeping. Someone who'll see all this as character-building. I mentally scroll through what I worked on, trying to pull something from the script.

"I want to be better," I say smoothly. "I want to succeed. Get my finances stable, save up, go back to uni…" – I catch myself – "…*eventually*. But right now, I'm really committed to this job. I want to prove I'm worth it."

"Why now?"

I smile. "I suppose… it's just clicked. The urgency. Justin's inspired me."

He tilts his head. "But what about before? Why didn't it click sooner?"

I flinch. Just slightly.

My brain races with all the reasons I've been underperforming at work. Because I was holding everything together at home. Because I spent years spoon-feeding my father mashed potato and coaxing my mother into taking her pills. Adam's accident. Because it's all been about everyone else except me. Because it's taken all my energy just to survive.

Thinking about it all like this suddenly feels overwhelming. Rage fizzes up behind my ribs. It's pathetic, really, the fact I've bent myself backwards for everyone, and here I am in front of cardigan man, explaining why I'm not trying hard enough. I almost laugh at how ridiculous it is.

I push it down and press my lips into a smile. "Life's complicated."

He nods slowly, like I've said something deep and profound.

There's a beat of silence, and I feel the thread of my carefully prepared story slipping between my fingers. I can't seem to get it back. He doesn't appear as impressed by my determination as I'd hoped he would. I can feel him pulling at the loose threads, unravelling everything I'd stitched together so carefully. And worst of all, I can't stop it.

"I think..." I begin, then stop. I can hear a wobble in my voice. I don't want to sound emotional. Emotional equals weakness in Justin's book. That's exactly the sort of thing a sexist arsehole like him is dying to hang on me.

So I shut up.

Oliver watches me a second longer, then gently sets his notebook aside.

"Let's try something else," he says. "Sometimes if things feel a bit stuck, it's helpful to step back and look at the whole picture."

He gets up, crosses to the small desk by the window, and returns with a piece of A4 and a biro.

"If it's okay with you, we could try a quick exercise," he says. "I call it Support Mapping. Essentially, it helps us understand the networks we can rely on around us."

He starts to sketch a circle on the paper and draws two lines across it, like slicing a cake.

"Think of your life in four quadrants: work, family, friends, and relationships." He writes the words by the side of each slice. "Then you ascribe a value to each. In the middle of the circle, that's zero – no support. The outer ring is ten – solid, reliable, exactly what you need. Rate each of those elements where they honestly sit."

I stare at the circle he's drawn. "What if you don't have some of those?"

He smiles gently. "That's part of the exercise."

So I take the pen.

Friends. I snort. "I'm so committed to work I don't have time for friends," I say, hoping it sounds good. I leave that section blank.

Oliver doesn't comment. Just nods, waiting.

Family. That's Bridget. And the ghosts of my parents, living in the furniture and the wallpaper I haven't got round to changing. I scribble *Bridget* and hesitate. One sister. That's it. How to rate her? Some days it's a ten. Some days a two. Today I settle on a compromise six.

Relationships. I write *Adam*, underline it twice. Honestly, he's the best thing in my life. He's great. It's not easy with his injury, but he tries so hard to look after me in little ways. Baths, candles, daft jokes. He makes a killer cup of tea. I put him at an eight. Because for all his issues, he's mine, and that's enough.

Work. That's easy. I scrawl *Justin, Kyle, Mohammed* in tiny, irritable script and place it somewhere around the 7-mark. Really it's a 3 at best, but I want Oliver to think it's better. Good, but with room for improvement.

I sit back. The page looks ridiculous.

Oliver peers at it. "Great," he says, with what I take to be professional enthusiasm. "What do you notice?"

I laugh despite myself. "Well, if it was an actual wheel, I'd be careening across the road straight into oncoming traffic."

He smiles. "Sure, it's a bit wonky," he says, "but that gives us something to work on."

I just stare at it, knowing I've rated work and family much higher than they are. It hits me like a revelation.

"I don't have much of a support structure," I say, before I can stop myself. The words sound clinical, like I'm describing a fault in a tent pole.

"Well," he says, smiling, "Work looks positive. And your relationship. And you've got me."

I stare at him. He's joking, I think, but I don't know what to do with it.

I think about Bridget. I can't remember the last time she called and checked in to see how I am, unless you count that time she wanted to borrow my stepladder. I pick up the pen angrily and change the rating.

"Actually, that's more like a four. At best."

Oliver leans back. "Tell me about Bridget."

"At school, I was the one who got the good grades. I was the one who was going to do well, go to uni, all that stuff. Bridget was chaos – bunking off, chasing lads, always needing rescuing. Mum and Dad were forever running after her. And I... I just got left to it."

Oliver says nothing. Just listens.

"When they got ill, she was useless. Too busy with Dave. I came home to help out for a bit. Then moved back full-time. I gave up uni. I fed them, changed them, managed the hospice visits. And then... then they died. Bridget got to carry on like nothing happened. Boyfriend, nice car, holidays, decent job. And I ended up back in this shitty little town, living in the house I grew up in, sleeping in their old room. Ten years behind everyone else."

I stop my rant. I notice Oliver's leaning forward now, staring at me. I don't think I've ever been listened to or watched so intently.

"How do you find it? Living in your parents' house?"

My smile tightens. "Oh, it's a laugh a minute. Feels like

I've time-travelled back to being seventeen, except now I pay council tax."

"I'm asking. How do you cope with it?"

I pause, staring at the floor. "When I left for uni, it felt like everything was about to begin – like I was on the cusp of something. But once I came home, it all froze. Same bedroom, same kettle, same bloody curtains. The house became the whole world, and everything outside it just... faded. Like it was never real."

Oliver nods slowly. "Like you never went away at all."

"Exactly," I say, and it escapes sharper than I mean it to.

He pauses and looks away, almost like he's drifted onto another thought. "Like life hasn't moved on. Just stuck. There's no way out," he says quietly.

My eyes snap to his. "What's that supposed to mean?"

He holds my gaze now and looks almost guilty. "It's not a criticism."

No. It's worse. It's true.

He nods, then shifts slightly. "What's work like, day to day?"

"Overwhelming." Something in me jolts. I let out a breath. "Hostile."

"Hostile?"

"Kyle and Mohammed treat the office like a school locker room. They grab all the viewings, hog the leads, give me no chance to earn commission or get noticed doing anything useful. But when anything goes wrong, suddenly it's all my fault, like I'm designated scapegoat of the month."

Oliver says nothing.

"It's like I don't matter. Like I'm just background noise. And Justin–"

I stop. Swallow.

"Justin?"

"Justin makes me feel like I'm one stupid mistake away

from being kicked out. Like he's just waiting for an excuse. One day I'm too soft, the next I'm too aggressive, or not assertive enough, or too assertive. Honestly, if I breathed wrong, he'd probably write it up as a performance concern."

Oliver watches me steadily.

"Some days I feel invisible. Other days, I feel like I'm under a microscope, being poked around by people who've lost the instructions. Either way, it's like they're pulling me apart just to see what breaks first."

He nods. "That sounds exhausting."

"It is."

I didn't plan to say anything. I don't plan to let it spill out like this. But the words rush up, hot and sour, like something I've been holding in too long.

Then tears come suddenly. Hot and stupid. I swipe at them with the heel of my hand.

"I'm sorry," I mutter. "I didn't mean to–"

"You don't have to apologise," Oliver says, voice quiet. "Not here."

I sniff. "Well, don't tell Justin. He'll have me down as unstable."

He smiles faintly. "None of this goes to Justin. This is a safe, confidential space."

I nod, even though I don't fully believe him.

Oliver leans back. "That's a lot to carry."

"No shit."

"And now you're in a job where you're not being recognised, and your boss is undermining you."

"Exactly," I say. "It's all too much. Some days I think about just… giving up."

There's a silence.

Then he asks in the gentlest of voices, "What does giving up look like?"

I think about giving up on trying to better myself, of going up to Justin, telling him where to stick his shitty little job. I could go and work on the checkout or something. The money wouldn't be much worse.

But I don't trust Oliver enough to say all that. I don't look at him. I've said too much already.

I don't answer.

He watches me a moment longer, then softly closes his notebook.

"We've done enough for today," he says.

I nod.

This wasn't how it was meant to go. I walked in here in control. And somehow, without me even noticing, he's turned the whole session inside out.

This hasn't gone to plan.

Not at all.

CHAPTER 12
OLIVER

Maureen's in her usual chair by the window, framed by the soft grey light that drifts in through the blinds. Her wheelchair is tucked behind, discreetly out of sight. It's cold outside, and rain taps at the window, like nervous fingers drumming on a table. But the radiator clunks in the corner, coughing heat into the quiet room.

Oliver is mid-flow, speaking faster than he realises, his hands animated in front of him.

"…it's not what I thought, you know? Coaching. If I'm honest, I dismissed it as shallow, transactional, therapy-lite for the self-absorbed. But it's not. There's depth to it. It's real work."

Maureen nods, her expression encouraging. He's been talking for nearly fifteen minutes, and she hasn't interrupted once. He takes that as a good sign.

"You can actually help people. I'm *helping* people."

Finally, she speaks.

"It's good to see you so energised." She tilts her head. "You sound… lighter."

"I *feel* lighter." He almost leaps out of his chair as he says it.

Her smile is small but warm. "That's good to hear, Oliver. I'm glad."

"I forgot what that felt like. The sense of purpose. A shape to the day."

"And you're finding that rewarding?"

"Revelatory."

Is he ranting? He becomes aware of how he's been talking. How she sees him. He leans back slightly.

She smiles. "Tell me more about that. About why it feels important to be helping others."

"It's… good to be back, in some capacity. Doing something meaningful. Like I've got purpose again."

Maureen waits.

"And helping… I think – because I know what it's like *not* to be helped when it matters."

"Go on."

Oliver shifts in the chair. He's been seeing Maureen for years, off and on. Now she's asked him to come to her twice a week. She knows more about him than almost anyone. Still, there's a small, hard knot lodged behind his ribs whenever she invites him to look inward.

"For so long, I didn't believe in myself. When I was young, school was…" He drifts off, not wanting to complete the thought. "And when I was a teenager… just hell. I was quiet. Easy to mock. Whether I was always that, or I became that because of how people were with me, I don't know. Maybe it doesn't matter. That's what I was, anyway. All the way into university."

He stares at the sculpture on the table between them. The smooth, curved stone, quiet and calming.

"And then I met Alison. Alison saw past all that. She

made me feel… like I mattered. Alison believed in me. Like I could be something."

Maureen looks at him. "And *are* you something?"

"I was. But when things got bad… during the inquest stuff, Alison couldn't handle it. She left."

He pauses and watches a trickle of rain zigzag its way down the window.

"My dad thought anxiety was weakness. Something to be ironed out." His fingers rub against the arm of the chair. "I don't blame her." Rub, rub. One, two, three, four, five. "Well. Not entirely."

Maureen's voice is gentle. "And anyone else you think of when you think about helping?"

Oliver doesn't look at her when he says it. "Julia."

She doesn't speak for a long moment. She only nods. Outside, a siren wails somewhere, up by the Minster. Some crime or tragedy slowly unfolding.

Oliver looks at the floor. "I became a therapist for people like her. People who needed saving. And when I couldn't save her…" He exhales. "That broke something. It's why this coaching thing is so powerful. I'm not saying I'm fixing people, but there's something redemptive about it."

"You're allowed to take meaning from the work," she says. "It's okay to feel good about giving something back. We all draw nourishment from purpose, connection, contribution. And you do seem… brighter, lately. More present. I'm really pleased."

Her approval matters to him more than he expected.

"I had a breakthrough with one of the clients," he says. "I misjudged her at first. She's hard to read. A bit brittle and defensive. But I see it more clearly now. What's going on."

"Oh?"

"Grace. She has this boss, Justin. He's not abusive in a

textbook sense, but oppressive. Belittling. Undermining her constantly. And she just absorbs it all, like it's her fault. I think she's internalised it. Her sense of self-worth is... paper-thin."

Maureen shifts slightly. "And how did you come to that understanding?"

Oliver reaches into his bag, pulls out a notebook, and flicks through pages. "She talks about feeling invisible. Like her energy's all gone. Like she's stuck in this old family house that's filled with the ghosts of the past, and she's just surviving."

He turns the page. "Listen to this. She said, '*It's taken all my energy just to survive.*' And another time, '*There's no way out.*'"

Maureen looks at him quizzically. "And...?"

"And it hit me. I've heard this before."

He reaches for another notebook, battered and dented at the corners, where it has been passed around lawyers, shoved into deep storage and pulled out again.

"Now listen to Julia. When she was talking about Darren, the abusive, controlling boyfriend... '*He makes me feel invisible. It's like I don't matter. Sometimes I just want it all to stop.*'"

Maureen leans forward slightly. He knows she's trying to look blank, but she looks puzzled.

"You see?" He waves the notebook at her. "It's the same pattern."

Silence. Oliver stares at Maureen. He can't work out why she isn't as energised as he is, seeing the obvious connection. Maureen makes a note but doesn't speak. He has to help her understand.

"They both feel powerless. Trapped. Hopeless. That's not just coincidence, Maureen. It's a pattern."

Maureen folds her hands in her lap. She is quiet for a long time.

"It's compelling," she says eventually. "But I want to offer another possibility."

He shifts.

"It's not uncommon," she says carefully, "for therapists or coaches to see patterns in clients. Especially when those clients stir up old wounds. But that doesn't mean the two people are the same."

"I'm not saying they are," he says. "But the themes, Maureen. The language. The emotional patterns. They're too close to ignore."

"Or perhaps close enough to project onto?"

His jaw tightens.

She notes his defensive body language and softens her tone. "I'm not accusing you of anything. But I'd like you to think about the language you're using. You said 'breakthrough.' You said 'revelatory.' You're using words therapists often use to describe their own shifts. Not their client's."

He closes the notebook. "You're making it sound like I'm imagining things. That I'm reading too much into it."

"I'm asking you to consider the possibility that you're not objective. That this work might be activating unresolved feelings."

"I know what transference looks like," he says, almost sulkily. "I know the dangers."

"And yet here we are. You've brought your old notes. You're mining Grace's language for similarities. You're positioning yourself as her lifeline. That concerns me."

He frowns. "That's not entirely fair. I'm just... invested. She matters."

"You said something earlier. That Grace said she thinks about giving up."

He nods. "Yes."

"Do you feel responsible for her?"

"She needs support."

"From you?"

He says nothing.

Maureen leans forward. "You once said, 'I couldn't save Julia.' And now you're talking about Grace in very similar terms. Oliver, is it possible you are trying to save Grace because you couldn't save Julia?"

"I know she's not Julia," he snaps. "But I've been on this road before. I know where it ends. If you go round a bend and crash, isn't it right that the next time you come to that bend you remember it and act differently? And if I can intervene now–"

Maureen closes her notebook gently. "It's not your job to rescue anyone."

"She said she has dark thoughts."

"Then the responsible thing is to signpost, not to insert yourself as the solution."

"She trusts me."

"Does she know you're thinking of her like this?"

He doesn't answer.

They sit in silence.

Eventually, Maureen says, "I think it would be helpful for you to take some space from Grace. Reflect on your role. Your boundaries."

He smiles, but it doesn't reach his eyes. "Of course. You're right." He knows Maureen too well. He knows this game. He knows what she needs to hear. "Of course. I'll think carefully about what you've said."

"Our time is up for today, I'm afraid. But Oliver, I'd like you to come and see me again, later this week."

"Yes. Yes, that would be helpful. Thanks."

Maureen watches him as he packs away the notebooks.

They leave the office in silence. She presses the button on the stairlift, and it hums to life with its usual judder, crawling down the stairs like it resents the effort. Oliver goes ahead, then stands in the hallway and watches her descend, slow as ever, down to the ground floor.

"Later this week, then," he says, and puts his hand on the door to open it.

Her voice stops him.

"I want you to sit with this," she says. "You've come a long way, Oliver. But that doesn't mean you're finished healing. Grace is not Julia. Her problems may echo, but they're not the same. And you're not the same, either."

Oliver nods. "Absolutely. I hear you."

Maureen watches him leave.

Outside, the street glistens and the sky is low and grey. A van is parked on the street outside, with *GlideRight Mobility* painted on the side. Two men get out as he leaves the house, but don't make eye contact. They'll be here to repair the stair-lift. It's typical of Maureen to get them to wait discreetly, to be sure he leaves and they don't interrupt his session. Such is the regard she has for his welfare.

Oliver walks away from the house without looking back, his coat clutched tight around him against the thin rain. He strides off, back towards the train station.

However much Maureen may be concerned for him, he won't let her doubts cloud what he knows in his bones. This isn't about Julia. This is different. Julia came to him too late. Grace has come just in time. Grace needs him. She's flailing in the dark, and he can help her. If he saves her, he saves himself.

She's his second chance. His redemption.

And this time, he won't fail.

CHAPTER 13
GRACE

I let myself in and toss my keys into the dish by the door, where they clatter louder than I mean them to. My shoes come off with two sharp kicks. One lands neatly. The other rebounds off the skirting board like a pistol shot.

The TV mumbles away in the living room – some low, droning true crime thing with a synth-heavy score and breathless narration, the light flickering through the crack in the doorway. I guess Adam hasn't heard me come in. That's okay though. I really don't feel up to talking.

My head is aching. It's not a pain exactly – more like my brain is humming too loudly inside my skull.

I drift through to the kitchen. I can't work out if I'm hungry or not, and open the fridge, hoping for inspiration. There isn't any. Half a bottle of milk, a couple of eggs, and a block of cheddar too sweaty to be appetising.

Work was a shitshow today. I couldn't concentrate, not really. I was typing up the listing for a two-bed on Victoria Avenue and had to rewrite it three times because I called it a 'spacious mid-terrace' when it's barely wide enough to swing a cat. I missed a call from a buyer, and Kyle sniped, "Blink and you miss it, eh? Like your career trajectory." He's such an arsehole. I shouldn't let him get to me, but he does. I got my revenge by taking half a Chinese takeaway he had in the fridge and hiding it in the bin under some kitchen roll. But even listening to him whine about that through lunch didn't cheer me up.

In the afternoon, Justin made an appearance, filling the office with horrible aftershave and passive aggression. He did this thing where he hovered over my desk just long enough to make it awkward, then asked, "You feeling more focused now, Grace? Ready to chase down those leads?" All with that fake smile of his. He pretends he's encouraging, but really it's him saying, *I'm watching you.*

I wanted to say, "Do you sit on the end of *Kyle's* desk, look down his top and ask if *he's* feeling focused?" But I just nodded and smiled until he buggered off.

It's that session with Oliver that's thrown me off balance in a way I didn't anticipate. I keep replaying it in my head. All day it's been like he was there in the office with me. I keep hearing his voice, low and steady, like a metronome ticking over and over through my thoughts.

I drop my bag by the kitchen table and slump into the chair like my bones have given up. My laptop's still there from this morning, the lid half-open, watching me unravel. I flip it shut and rest my forehead on my arms.

I really didn't want to cry yesterday. How bloody embarrassing. I had a plan. I wrote it out. Rehearsed it like a script in the mirror. Insight. Awareness. Just enough vulnerability to seem human, not enough to seem chaotic.

And then Oliver asked that stupid question – *Where do you feel supported in your life?* – and the whole thing came tumbling down. He didn't even push. Just sat there, nodding slowly like one of those bloody toy dogs people have in cars. And like a baby, I let it all come flooding out. About Bridget.

About my parents. About how I'm on the verge of giving up and just quitting.

Now I've said it all out loud, I can't cram it back in the box.

And I don't know if he's reported it all to Justin. Of course, he *says* it's confidential. But he also says he's here to help, and that sounds suspiciously like HR bullshit. For all I know, he's already fired off an email suggesting I get the sack.

"Hey," Adam calls from the living room.

I push myself up from the table and shuffle in. He's curled up on the sofa, blanket around his legs, a half-drunk mug of tea perched on the armrest.

He looks up from the telly. "You okay?"

"Fine."

"Well, *that* sounds convincing." He pauses the programme – a woman in a cardigan stares blankly at a police officer mid-sentence, her mouth gaping open in what looks like a frozen scream.

He pats the seat next to him and gives me that half-smile that always makes my chest loosen, just a little. I sit down, breathing in the smell of his shampoo.

"How was it? You know, the coaching thing? Did you go?"

"Yeah. Yesterday."

"Yesterday? Shit, sorry. And?"

I shrug. "It was fine. Just… weird. He asked me to map everyone in my life. Like a literal map. Circles and numbers. It made me realise just how empty it all looks on paper."

Adam frowns. He wraps his arm around my shoulder, and I lean into him, warm and solid, almost feeling like I could cry again.

"You've got loads of people. Me, your sister–"

"Bridget doesn't count. She's barely spoken to me in years. Only shows up now and then because she feels guilty."

"Still. You're not alone." He reaches over and pats my knee, wincing slightly as he stretches. I know it's meant to be supportive. But it lands like a thud in the middle of the room. *You're not alone* – not a comfort, more a reminder. That I *should* feel better. That I *shouldn't* be struggling. Which I am.

I lean forward, elbows on my knees. "He said I sounded stuck. That there's no way out."

Adam raises an eyebrow. "He sounds like a prick. He doesn't even know you."

I heave a sigh. "I'm sorry, but I've got to do some more work. You keep watching your thing."

"Are you sure? Can I get you anything? Beans a la Toast? Speciality of ze house…"

He makes stupid noises in his cod French accent and twists the ends of an imaginary moustache.

"No, you're okay, thanks, Garçon. You carry on." I glance at frozen-scream woman. "Comedy, is it? It looks hilarious."

"It is. Only three deaths in the first fifteen minutes. No wonder she's in hysterics."

He takes the TV off pause. The light from the screen paints his face a bluish grey.

Back in the kitchen, I open the laptop and create a new document. I name it *Oliver Prep*. This time, I'll stick to the script. No tangents. No truth bombs. Just steady, calm, coachable. Future employee of the month.

I start typing, but everything I write down sounds shit and I just delete it. I can't stop thinking about what Oliver said. Or the way he said it. Like he could see something under my skin. Something even I hadn't noticed.

That I'm stuck. That there's no way out.

I've got this grand plan of going back to uni, but will that ever really happen? I can barely keep on top of the finances now, let alone save for that. And if I lose this job, it's going to get a whole lot worse.

I grab the stack of bills on the counter and open my banking app. I scroll down a long list of transactions. £12.99. £28.45. A £73 charge that I don't remember approving. Subscription? Food shop? I've no idea. I need to sit down and go through it all properly. Work out where it's all going. But not tonight. I don't have the brain for it.

I lean back from my laptop and rest my head in my hands. I'm barely hanging on to this job. If I lose it, there's no backup plan. No savings. No fairy godmother.

Maybe he's right. Maybe there *is* no way out.

But why did he say that? Maybe it was a guess. That's what these coaches do, right? Chuck it out there and see what lands. Dig around until something cracks. Find the weak spot.

Only trouble is, he's right.

I stare at the computer screen, the cursor blinking, like it's impatient, waiting for me to say something. But what can I say? How can I go into the next session with Oliver and say something that puts the genie back in the bottle? How can I save a job I increasingly feel I hate?

Then an idea comes to me. A way I can take back control of at least one shitty corner of my life. Not just flirt with it. Actually do it. I type tentatively.

Resignation email.

Just two words, like a threat, daring me to press send.

From the lounge, I hear Adam laugh at something on the telly.

Part of the idea of it fills me with dread. What would I do? How would we cope, Adam and I? Am I just being selfish? And how will I ever get my uni plan back on the rails?

But if they're going to throw me out, maybe the only control I have is to get in there first.

I stare at the screen, letting the idea sink in, wondering what comes next.

CHAPTER 14
OLIVER

Oliver cancels two appointments and clears the rest of his afternoon.

He locks, unlocks, locks, unlocks and locks his office. His fingers tremble slightly with the effort to keep calm. Five is safe. Five is order. He's been feeling better about things since forming his plans about Grace. But this afternoon, knowing what he intends to do, his nerves have got the better of him.

He walks down through the centre of town. It's only mid-afternoon, but the winter sky is slate grey with ugly looking bulbous clouds, and all the shops have their lights on. It's blustery, and shoppers, hunched in tired anoraks and shapeless overcoats, scamper along, tugging at their flapping carrier bags like unruly kites.

Oliver cuts right at Huntriss Row, past McDonald's and Starbucks, and onto Spa Bridge. Today, the sea is dark and choppy. The tide is out, but hardly anyone is on the beach – only a dog walker wrestling a couple of frisky terriers, and a group of surfers, wetsuited jet-black against the freezing water. The bridge is famed for its incredible view, but also its height, a favourite spot for anyone thinking of suicide. He glances at the sign attached to the ornate iron railings.

SAMARITANS. Whatever you're going through, you don't have to face it alone.

Oliver tries to put ideas of suicide out of his mind as he leans into the wind and heads up to the Esplanade.

He's been thinking a lot about all the things Maureen said, her words looping through his head. Her studied concern, that it's not his responsibility to rescue anyone. That he should stay away from Grace.

Maureen is wrong. Completely, clinically, laughably wrong.

Instead, he's been working on the best way to help Grace, thinking about it all night. He could coach her, sure. Run a dozen exercises with her.

Challenging conversations.

Confidence in the workplace.

Asserting value in toxic hierarchies.

But Grace doesn't need another patronising lesson in self-reliance. He knows she's already exhausted from carrying everything herself. And that would be treating *her* as the problem. As if she's failing. As if her lack of confidence is a defect that needs fixing.

It's not.

If someone breaks into your house and steals your belongings, you don't sit down with the victim and coach them on how not to tempt burglars. You go after the bastard who broke in.

And that bastard is Justin.

Oliver steps into the estate agency office of Lancaster & Lyle. He gives his name to a young man in an overly tight suit, whom he assumes to be Kyle. Then he waits.

He looks around the room, past the boards of property details, and sees Grace, typing at a desk at the back, her face tight with focus. He watches her work, unaware that he is here on a mission to rescue her. He smiles at the idea, that he is operating in secret in the backstages of her life, working to make things better. He imagines himself like Clark Kent, unremarkable as far as she is concerned, while in secret, he is Superman.

As he's musing on this, she looks up from her desk and sees him, does a double-take, then looks back down at her computer screen. He feels a wave of disappointment. Maybe he'd have made a more noble superhero if she hadn't seen him here at all.

After a few minutes, he's shown through to a side office.

"Alright. Oliver, is it?"

Justin reaches out and shakes his hand with a tight grip that Oliver takes to be some kind of statement.

It's a small room, and Justin fills it with his bellowing voice and large frame, bulked up, Oliver assumes, by vanity gym sessions in front of a mirror and pints after Sunday League football. There's a wall-mounted TV with *Cash in the Attic* on mute, and a football shirt in a frame, something red and Premier League, with the name *JUSTO* written across the back.

Justin drops back into his chair like he's reclaiming a throne. He crosses his legs at the ankles and laces his fingers behind his head. "So, Oliver. What can I do you for?"

"Firstly, thanks for agreeing to see me at such short notice. As you know, I've been engaged by Lancaster & Lyle to offer coaching support to some of your employees, and I've already had some really promising conversations around potential for growth and reflection. But I thought it might also be of benefit for me and you to have a chat about the outcomes of this programme. See if we can create a benchmark for what success might look like for all concerned."

"Numbers," says Justin.

"Oliver blinks. "How do you mean?"

"The numbers, mate. The bottom line. That's the goal, right? This touchy-feely stuff is all well and good, but unless it translates into extra commission and closed sales, it's a bloody book club with name tags."

Oliver clears his throat. "Of course. But for many employees, performance is linked to feeling heard and supported."

"Uh-huh," Justin says. "But are they selling more?"

Oliver presses on. "If we cultivate the right environment–"

"I create the right environment," Justin interrupts. "Every morning at the sales meeting. I tell them what's expected, and I don't move the goalposts. It's fair and it's firm. You either know how to get your toe on the ball and finish, or you're on the bench."

He gives Oliver a hard look. Oliver can feel himself being sized up. Sized up and dismissed.

"I'm not here to stroke egos, mate. I'm here to hit targets. Always have been. I was the top seller three years running before I went into management, so I know what I'm talking about."

Oliver has met this type many times before. "It's excellent that you set such clear goals, and that you're able to model the behaviour you want to see in your team," he says, trying to take control of the conversation again by blowing a bit of smoke up Justin's arse.

"I could sell ice to Eskimos, me," Justin goes on, clearly warming to his own myth. "Still can. Problem is, half this lot couldn't sell water to a man on fire. Not hungry enough."

Oliver folds his hands. "Sometimes performance issues come from feeling undermined or undervalued. In some cases, encouragement and praise–"

"Come on," scoffs Justin, interrupting. "What is this, *Blue*

Peter? They're in a sales job. If they don't want to feel pressure, they can piss off to a pottery class."

Oliver exhales through his nose. "The thing is, when people perceive that they are feeling threatened–"

"I don't threaten people. I motivate. And with all due respect, I don't need some head-doctor telling me how to do my job."

Oliver goes very still.

There it is.

He stares at Justin. He sees it now, clear as anything. That same cruel glint. The same swaggering, macho, bullying energy he recognises from school. From Ash and the rest of the pupils who made his life hell. The way they'd taunt and humiliate, then claim it was just a joke. A grown-up version of the same bully in a different uniform.

"I think," Oliver says, keeping his voice level, "that with a little reflection, you might see a more productive way of leading–"

"I think," Justin says, mimicking his tone, "that you might want to remember you're on a three-month contract to talk feelings. I run a business."

Silence.

Oliver lowers his eyes. He can feel himself flushing red from the anger and humiliation. The sense of powerlessness. He knows there's no reaching him. No reasoning.

Oliver stands. "Thanks for your time," he says, trying to look professional, but just wanting to get away.

Justin smirks. "Any time, Doc."

Oliver walks out stiffly. In the main office, Grace is feeding a document into the photocopier. He pretends not to see her, escapes through the front door, and doesn't look back.

CHAPTER 15
GRACE

The second I step inside the restaurant, I know I shouldn't have come.

It's packed and loud. The kind of place that screams FUN with an exclamation mark. Exactly what I'm not feeling right now. One long table down the middle is colonised by a big family party – helium balloons tied to the backs of chairs, kids climbing over everything like it's a soft play centre. A teenage girl unwraps something pink and sparkly, and her friends shriek like she's just pulled a live otter out of the paper. It's the sort of noise that could shatter glass.

"We're meeting people," says Adam to the man at reception. "Table for four. Probably under 'Dave Ashton'."

Everyone's raising their voices over the chaos. The birthday table dominates everything. The whole place has a kind of party atmosphere.

Tonight's been in the diary for a while, but I could do without being here, to be honest. I've been feeling increasingly weird about Bridget recently, her unreliability, her lack of contact and support. I haven't said much about my work problems to her, but I don't feel I should need to. Isn't that what sisters are for? For turning up when things are shit? She should know what's going on. I shouldn't have to spell it out. Plus, today's been particularly bloody weird. Justin hovering about, piling on the pressure. Then that sneaky shit Oliver turning up to report in to his boss. Unbelievable. So much for bloody confidentiality. He looked properly embarrassed when he saw me. I was so furious I couldn't look at him. And then he scampered off, guilty, knowing he'd been caught out.

By the time it got to 5 p.m. I was glad to get away. I left Justin to go through all our figures, knowing he'd find my sales haven't improved. As if it's my fault his lousy branch is dying on its arse. He's so desperate to hang his own failings on someone else, my inevitable firing is getting ever closer.

I was so relieved to get home. I kicked my shoes off and started running a bath. Then Adam came in and reminded me we were supposed to be going out to dinner. I'd completely forgotten. I felt angry and sick. But after moaning I never see Bridget, I could hardly cry off.

So here we are.

The waiter leads us to a table tucked just out of splash range from the birthday chaos. Bridget and Dave are already here – waving, smiling, like nothing's wrong. Like we're all just out for a jolly catch-up.

Bridget jumps up and kisses me on the cheek. "You look nice!"

I don't. I threw on the first clean thing I could find that didn't need ironing.

"You too," I say, hollow and automatic, slipping into the seat opposite her.

Dave beams. "Evening, Grace! Hard day at the grindstone? This'll cheer you up." He pours me a glass of something fizzy.

"Something like that," I murmur.

Adam takes the seat beside me. The neck brace is gone. First time in weeks. He catches me looking.

"Loosened it for tonight," he says, grinning. "Didn't want them to think you'd dragged me out for a date night straight from A&E. Though I wouldn't say no to the occasional bed bath."

"Good plan." I smile and squeeze his hand. It's nice to see him happy and out of the house for once. At least he's having a good time.

"This one," Dave says, nodding at Bridget, "she could sell tyres to a bloke with no car. She's got the gift." He keeps leaning in, kissing her cheek, putting his arm round her and squeezing, making a fuss. Bridget slaps him playfully as if it's flirty and adorable. She's giggling and pouring the wine like it's communion and she's the priestess of Prosecco. She keeps throwing me little looks and smiles as if there's nothing wrong between us. Maybe she's even a bit nervous, like she deep down knows she's done something wrong.

I sip my wine and try not to think about it. I look at the menu and try to find something I'm remotely interested in eating. I nibble at a breadstick like a stressed gerbil and force myself to start enjoying things.

But Bridget's still giggling away like a silly schoolgirl under Dave's attention.

I resent her good mood.

It's not just tonight. It's not just this performance. It's the past few months. The way she's been slowly fading from my life, like a radio station drifting out of tune. Unavailable. Unreliable. Always "swamped." Getting Dave to field her calls. It's like she's rewritten history to make *me* the needy one. Like I wasn't the one who held our parents' hands as they died. Like I haven't been holding everything else together since.

I look around the restaurant. I feel on the outside of it all. Distanced. When did I become so embittered and resentful?

I try to reset. *This is good,* I tell myself. A chance to reconnect with Bridget. Tell her about what's been going on. The shitstorm at work. Justin. Oliver. The creeping suspicion that the 'coaching' is a trap. It would be great to talk it through with her. I still haven't told Adam I'm seriously considering quitting.

"How's work?" Bridget asks, almost as if she knows what I'm thinking. But as I'm about to tell her, Dave pipes up.

"Champagne," he says, "to celebrate Bridget's promotion! Head of fleet and lease! That's a fancy title, eh?"

Bridget blushes like she's embarrassed, but she's loving it. She instantly forgets me. I haven't even opened my mouth and she's off again. She flicks her hair behind her ear, then starts pouring wine into everyone's glasses like she's hosting *Come Dine With Me.*

"I'm telling you, give this one a spreadsheet and a deadline and she'll run the bloody country."

They laugh and kiss like they're on their sodding honeymoon.

Promotion? It's like a slap in the face with a wet towel. It's not that I don't want Bridget to be happy. I do. But there's something so grotesquely unfair about how easily things fall into place for her. All those years she floated around like one of these helium balloons, vanishing for days, turning up with new boyfriends, and then suddenly she lands on her feet and gets everything she wants. Meanwhile, I'm still stuck in our parents' house, failing at a shitty job I never wanted, with a boss who thinks being nice is a terminal disease, and a coach who's spying on my every move.

I close my mouth and put my wine glass down a little too hard.

Adam notices. "You okay?" His thumb brushes lightly against mine under the table.

"Fine," I say, forcing a smile.

He leans closer and drops his voice. "If you want, I'll fake a migraine so we can sneak out early. I can clutch my head dramatically and everything, stagger about, knock over a few tables for effect."

I almost smile at that, but shake my head. "No, it's fine. I just need a minute."

I excuse myself to the loo.

I stand in the toilet cubicle, gripping the edge of the sink, staring at my face in the mirror. I look tired. Older than 33. I'm not going to cry. I'm not.

When I get back to the table, even more champagne has arrived, and Dave's sending bottles over to the neighbouring tables like he's some kind of local celebrity. Bridget's chinking her glass with some random woman in the big birthday group. Christ, even a restaurant full of strangers gets more attention from Bridget than I do.

I can't take it anymore.

"Sorry," I say, as brightly as I can manage. "I'm feeling a bit off. I think something from lunch has disagreed with me."

Bridget's brow furrows. "Oh no, you okay?"

I nod. Smile. Lie. "Yeah, just think I need to lie down. You have a good time. Honestly. Congratulations on your promotion."

Adam looks at me, concerned. "Want me to come with you?"

"No. Stay. Enjoy the rest of the night. I'll be fine." To be honest, I just want to be on my own.

Dave stands to let me out. "Hope it's nothing serious, Grace."

"Thanks." I fake another smile.

As I head toward the door, I hear the birthday table

behind me burst into another round of "Happy Birthday" and I want to scream. I push through the door and out into the cold.

I need quiet.

I need to think.

Because right now, I'm not sure what takes more strength – staying and fighting or just walking away.

CHAPTER 16
OLIVER

He strides quickly, back across the bridge, the wind beating his face, sharp and cold. The rain has picked up since earlier, and he's soaked within minutes. Trousers clinging to his legs. Hair dripping into his eyes. He feels sick. Humiliation, shame and fury churn together like the sea. He was stupid to think this would work. It hasn't just gone poorly – it has imploded. All that planning, all that gentle phrasing. Justin didn't just dismiss his ideas – he bludgeoned them and left them shattered on the floor.

So much for being a superhero.

By the time Oliver gets home, he's shaking from cold. His key slips on the lock and clatters to the floor. He picks it up with numb fingers and fumbles again. Then finally, he gets inside.

Lock. Unlock. Lock. Unlock. Lock.

His hand lingers on the key for a moment longer than usual. The house has felt like a prison most nights. But tonight it's a refuge. A place to hide.

He goes upstairs and peels off his waterlogged coat. His shoes squelch with every step. He goes to the bathroom and rubs at his hair with a towel, but the mirror catches him. He stops.

His reflection is pale and hollow-eyed. The bags under his eyes are darker than usual. For a long time, he just looks. Not really at the surface, but deeper.

He thinks of Julia. Locking the door. Placing both hands on the cool porcelain. Her reflection staring back, expressionless.

He grips the edges of the sink. He tried to help her, too. Tried and failed. And now she's gone, because of him. Because he was too slow, too uncertain. And what was it Maureen said? That it wasn't his job to rescue people? That he should leave Grace alone?

He thinks of Grace. Where is she now? Who is looking out for her? He remembers her face in the office, looking up at him from her desk with those pleading eyes. That flicker of something unspoken. If he turns his back on her now, then everything Julia taught him is meaningless.

He failed her.

But he won't make the same mistake twice.

He goes to the kitchen to look at the clock. 5.15 p.m. If he hurries, he can still catch Justin.

Oliver grabs his coat. It's still wet. He yanks open the front door, and the wind hits him like a punch. It grabs hold of the door too, yanking it back on its hinges like it wants to tear it off the frame. He wrestles it closed behind him, then runs.

The car is parked two streets away. His fingers are so numb that he can barely get the key in the lock. When he finally does, the wind catches the door again and nearly rips it from his hand. He climbs inside and slams it shut. He pushes back the hair plastered to his forehead. Wipes the rain off his face like he's just stepped out of a shower. His shirt clings to him like a second skin.

He starts the engine.

The wipers spring into life, flapping against the deluge. The dashboard light glows a soft amber. The car pulls away.

He takes the back route toward the Esplanade, weaving through tight side streets, trying to avoid the worst of the rush-hour traffic. His eyes flick to the clock on the dash. 5.24 p.m.

He practices what he's going to say to Justin, speaking it out loud in the empty car, seeing how the words sound.

"Justin, glad I caught you. We got off on the wrong foot earlier. My fault entirely. Look, I'm not here to criticise. You want results. I understand that. I want that too. But people like Grace, they don't respond to pressure the way others do. If you ease off just a little – just slightly – it might unlock something incredible."

He loses confidence in what he's saying, tries again, different forms of words. Different tones.

"You'll get more from her by backing her than by breaking her. She could become your best agent. Your secret weapon."

He reaches the Esplanade. The buildings are barely visible through the curtain of rain, indistinct and hazy, their windows glowing faintly in the gloom. If there is a moon, the clouds obscure it. To the left, a big black wall of nothing where the black sea simmers beneath the black sky.

He pulls up opposite the office and looks out through his rain-streaked window.

Closed. Of course. He's missed him. Of course he has.

Oliver relaxes his hands on the steering wheel, the knuckles white where he's been gripping so hard. Rain drums on the roof. The wipers thud back and forth. He sits there, breathing hard.

He has let Grace down.

Again.

He breathes slowly and leans forward, trying to quiet the noise in his head. The steering wheel is cold against his brow.

He listens to the purr of the engine, the hypnotic rhythm of the wipers and the rain. He's tired. So tired, perhaps he could just rest here forever.

He has no idea how long he stays like that. Eventually, he sits back. His eyes glance slowly across the road.

Movement.

A light shifts inside the office. A shadow. A figure.

The door opens.

It's Justin. Unmistakable in that swagger. The glint of a ringed hand as he turns the key in the lock.

Oliver's heart stutters.

This is his chance. He can get out, wave him down, suggest they go for a pint and talk it through. Be friendly, persuasive.

Even as he thinks this, his foot presses gently on the accelerator.

Justin is standing under his open umbrella, his face illuminated as he scrolls through something on his phone.

Oliver can explain it all. Grace's value. Her potential. The need for compassion.

The car speeds forward. The tyres thump as they cross the kerb. Onto the pavement. The engine growls. The car jerks forward. Justin looks up, too late.

The impact is sudden and savage. His body hits the bonnet with a deafening thud. His head cracks against the windscreen, sending spiderwebs of glass tracing outward. Then he's gone, flipped, rolling across the car's roof with a thundering noise, like a person falling heavily downstairs, before flying off, silent and out of sight, through the air and onto the verge behind.

The car skids to a stop.

Oliver stares ahead, panting.

The rain sounds louder now. Each droplet like a tiny

drumbeat. The wipers keep moving. Back and forth. Back and forth.

That's not how it works with men like Justin. They don't sit down. They don't talk. They laugh in your face and make you hate yourself for trying.

Oliver gets out slowly and walks round behind the car, into the red glow of the taillights. He paces back along the glistening pavement. At first he can't see anything. He's surprised he has travelled this far. Was he going that fast? Perhaps he's passed him. Then a dull shape. For a second, it looks like a hedge, up on the dark verge. A bin bag waiting to be collected. A pile of coats. Something left behind.

Oliver kneels and touches Justin's shoulder like he's trying to get his attention. He shakes him gently, as if careful not to startle him as he wakes from sleep. It's enough to unbalance him, and Justin rolls down and over on the grass verge. The lacklustre streetlight catches his face, revealing a dark wound on his forehead. His face is slack, his body twisted at an unnatural angle. Blood and rain mix at his temple, streaking down toward his ear. His lifeless eyes stare directly at Oliver.

Oliver stands.

He breathes.

And for the first time in weeks, the voices in his head are quiet.

PART TWO

CHAPTER 17
OLIVER

Oliver drives the car quietly up the narrow back lane behind his house and brings it gently to a stop. The wipers are off because he's anxious about the noise, and in any case, he can barely see anything through the splintered glass of the windscreen. How he made it back in one piece is a miracle.

He sits in the dark interior for a moment. His heart is still thumping, like it hasn't realised the moment has passed.

The lane is deserted. No other cars. No movement.

He hopes he parked without anyone hearing. Though the idea that anyone would find it remarkable to hear a car on a road makes no sense.

But they don't know what he knows.

The wind drives the rain sideways in sheets, stinging his face as he steps out. He glances up at the rows of brick terraces. Most of the bedroom windows are dark. Downstairs, a few TVs flicker, throwing bluish light across the sitting rooms. Everyone's inside. Warm. Oblivious.

He's startled by a brief flash of light, and for a second, he panics that someone is photographing him. But that's immediately followed by a bang and a rumble echoing off the walls of the houses, like the sound Justin's body made as it rumbled across the roof of his car.

Thunder.

He ducks through the gate and into the back garden, careful not to let the latch snap. His sodden coat flaps like seaweed around his legs. He lets himself in the back door. Once. Twice. Three, four, five.

He stands in the gloom, breathing hard. The silence in the house is thick, and he can hear his pulse hammering in his ears. He listens for any sound of the outside world, but there's only the drumming of the rain on the window and the steady ticking of the kitchen clock.

He reaches for the pile of old newspapers by the door and lays himself a path of stepping stones to the sink. He bends and pulls things from the utility cupboard: the mop bucket, washing up liquid, dish sponges.

He races outside again, his bucket full of hot, soapy water from the kitchen sink. The car waits like an injured beast under the sodium glare of the streetlamp.

He starts at the front.

More by touch than by sight, he can tell the bonnet is buckled, the dent like a crater, pooling water. He wipes, rinses, and scrubs. The sponge leaves greasy trails of suds across the metal, yellowy-pink from the hue of the light. The broken headlamp looks like an empty eye socket. He leans in, careful not to cut himself on the sharp edge of the glass, and picks out something caught in the grille. It's stringy.

Fibres of cloth?

Hair?

Whatever it is, it could be incriminating. He carefully puts it in his pocket.

He refills his bucket with fresh water, back and forth, and

carries on. He tells himself this is what anyone would do. Anyone. It's basic damage control. He's fixing things. He's fixing everything.

A story forms in his head as he washes.

A dog. It ran out into the road. I tried to brake but it was too late. It was dark. The rain made it impossible to see. No time to stop. I hit it. It was a big dog. An Alsatian, maybe. Or further out of town. A deer? They have those around here, don't they? Maybe it darted across a country road. Is that believable?

His mind races through versions. His hands work mechanically.

He tries not to think about it, the dead animal, its shattered body, its eyes staring into his.

But then: If it was a dog, where's the collar? Wouldn't you be expected to report it? Aren't they microchipped? Has anyone reported their dog missing? And what kind of dog causes this much damage anyway? And what about the dent pattern? The police can match that to a human form, can't they? Head, shoulder, hip.

No. That won't do.

He'll need a better story.

His legs ache from crouching. His fingers are raw and pink from the heat of the water and the scrubbing. He's rinsing the same panel for the third time, and still he can't stop.

It has to be spotless.

Eventually, after more buckets than he can count, he judges it good enough. He tips the water out, sluicing it into the drain at the side of the road. The bubbles swirl away. In any case, it's still raining heavily and seems set to continue all night.

He trudges back indoors. The door locks again, five times. Always five.

He extends the newspaper path and pulls a bedsheet from the washing basket on the work surface. He spreads the sheet out across the tiles, the same way his mum used to when painting walls. He takes off his clothes right there in the kitchen, standing barefoot on the sheet. His coat is heavy with water. His shirt sticks to his chest; his trousers squelch as he peels them away. His underpants last, soaked and clinging.

Naked. He bunches everything into the sheet, the newspapers too, and ties the corners in a knot. It reminds him of that formless shape on the grass verge. The bundle looks obscene.

He showers with water almost too hot to stand. It stings his frozen skin, reddens his back. He washes twice, three times, hair, face, and body. He scours his nails with the scrubbing brush, then does it again.

As he dries himself, his reflection in the mirror is sallow and warped by steam. A dark blotch is spreading along his cheekbone, purple and grey, and there's a scratch near his temple. He must have clipped the steering wheel as he screeched to a halt. Or maybe bashed the doorframe as he bumped over the curb. He can't remember. It's all a blur.

He wraps himself in his father's old dressing gown, the fabric scratchy, the sleeves too long. The weight of it anchors him, somehow. Like a ritual.

Downstairs, in the living room, he begins to build the fire. He balls up newspaper, lays kindling, and arranges logs in a careful pyramid. He lights it and watches as the fire licks upward.

So far, he hasn't switched the lights on in the house. He moves in shadow. But now the flames begin to warm the room with an orange glow. The first heat makes him realise how cold he's been. He presses his hands close, skin prickling.

One by one, he feeds the clothes in. They hiss with rainwater, and he goes slowly, careful not to drown the fire. The shirt dries, then curls into embers like a dead leaf. The trousers boil and smoulder, seams glowing. His socks crackle like bacon, then begin to burn, black smoke coiling up the chimney.

The coat is hardest. He fetches scissors from the kitchen and cuts it into strips, then feeds them to the fire, pacing them out so as not to smother the flames. He finds the lump of whatever it was clinging to the grille of the car and burns that too.

It takes more than an hour. By the end, his throat stings from the smoke. The fire settles into a dull, persistent glow. The smell is thick and sour, singed wool and melting nylon. He sits down in the armchair and lets himself breathe.

His mind, though, doesn't quiet.

The image comes back, over and over. Justin's eyes, wide. The sound of his body hitting the windscreen. The roll. The thud. The moment his head lolled, blood blooming from the gash in his forehead. Oliver sees it every time he blinks.

He thinks of Julia. Her damaged face in the mirror. The colours of her bruises. The steam blurring her away.

And Grace.

Where is she now? Has she just got home? Does she feel it too – a shift in the world, the erasure of something malevolent? Or is she sitting in her living room, dreading returning to the office on Monday, not knowing she's been saved from her oppressor?

He pictures her when she finds out. Her face, pale under the office lights. Surprise. Relief. Maybe tears. Gratitude, even. One day, she'll understand.

Later, brushing his teeth, he notices the bruising. His reflection catches him off guard. The right side of his jaw is already darkening, a purpling swell under the skin. His cheekbone is tender to the touch. He leans closer to the mirror, watching himself the way someone might watch an animal from behind glass.

Again, another image rises. Not his. *Hers.* Julia.

Leaning into her mirror, placing her palms flat on the porcelain of the sink. That awful purple swelling blooming across one eye. Her face mottled with colours that don't belong. The way she stares at herself, like she's already disappeared. Then the steam rising, clouding her reflection. Erasing it.

His stomach churns.

That's what he's saved Grace from.

It's nearly 1 a.m. when he lies on top of the bed. He stares at the ceiling, limbs twitching with excess adrenaline. He imagines police lights outside the window. He waits for a knock on the door. A forensic team combing the grass for paint chips. CCTV. Witnesses.

He doesn't *know* there aren't any.

He gets up and checks the locks again. One. Two. Three. Four. Five.

In the living room, the fire has burned low. He stirs the ashes with the poker. Everything's gone. There's no evidence. No DNA. No fibres.

No proof.

And yet, a nagging thread of doubt clings to him. A loose stitch. What if he missed something?

Still, beneath the dread, something else stirs.

It's not guilt. Not exactly.

It's relief.

And underneath that – fainter, but undeniable – something like joy.

He made a difference. He took action. All those years of swallowing it down, of fantasising about speaking back, pushing back, fighting back – and tonight, he did it.

He did it for the boy he used to be, who sat alone at lunch and watched others laugh at his expense.

He did it for Julia.

He did it for Grace.

The world has shifted.

And he's the one who moved it.

CHAPTER 18
GRACE

It's all over Facebook.

I saw it last night when I got back early from the restaurant. Messages and posts from people I knew at school. Someone who knows someone who heard something. Then a bit on the *Scarborough Evening News* website. Then *The Yorkshire Post* picked it up. And eventually, a mention of it at the end of the ITV regional news.

I just sat there, staring at the TV, mouth gaping open like an idiot, then spent the rest of the evening scrolling through my phone for updates. *LOCAL ESTATE AGENT KILLED IN SCARBOROUGH HIT-AND-RUN.* This morning, it was on the local breakfast bulletin. They even dug out his company photo – smug grin and fake tan, like he's auditioning for *Love Island.*

It doesn't feel real.

I head in to work. All morning, there's a weird atmosphere. Phones still ring, the kettle still clicks off with a little sigh, and Mohammed's already eaten a packet of Hula Hoops before nine. But nothing's normal. It doesn't feel like grief, and it comes home to me that I'm not the only one who wasn't that fond of Justin. It's more like a kind of morbid fascination. Like when you pass an overturned lorry and everyone slows down to rubberneck.

Should I feel worse? Is it wrong that I don't?

Kyle and Mohammed keep checking their phones. At one point, when I go for a coffee, I hear them muttering by the sink. "Bet he was bladdered," says Kyle, with a kind of half-grin. "Probably trying to hail a taxi and stepped in front of a lorry. Tragic."

No way they're mourning. They're gossiping. Justin's death is a great talking point – more interesting than moaning about microwaving curry in the kitchen or stealing someone's Müller Corner. No one's doing any work today, that's for sure. It's like our teacher called in sick and now it's a free period. So here I am, sitting at my desk with a tepid drink and a stale digestive, pretending I can concentrate on anything but the fact that my line manager is dead.

Around 10 a.m., a police car pulls up on the double yellows outside. We crane our necks to have a look. Two uniformed officers get out and start walking towards the office. We all instinctively get our noses down in some work, like we're an unruly class of naughty school kids and someone just yelled that the teacher is coming.

They talk to Kyle first, and then Mohammed, and when it comes to me, my stomach does a small somersault and lands badly. I haven't done anything wrong, but it still feels like I've been called to the headteacher's office. They usher me into the side room and both pull out notebooks.

When did I last see Justin?

Last night, I say, when I left at about 5 p.m. He was staying late to go over sales figures.

Anything unusual about him? Did he seem upset? Concerned? Different in any way?

I can't say what I'm thinking, which is that he seemed less

of an arsehole than he usually is. So I just say he seemed normal.

Did he mention meeting anyone?

I shake my head.

They scribble their notes in their little notebooks.

"Let us know if you think of anything else," one says.

And that's it.

When I get back to my desk, Kyle smirks. "Did they discover you were driving a blacked-out van last night? Let me know if you need me to cook you up an alibi."

I blink. "Hilarious."

The door opens again, and a tall, grey-haired man in an expensive dark coat walks through.

Kyle immediately straightens his tie. "That's Patrick Lyle," he hisses through clenched teeth at Mohammed like a shit ventriloquist, and the two of them sit up to attention like royalty has just come in. I've only seen him once before, at last year's regional Christmas party. Patrick Lyle of *Lancaster & Lyle*, the big boss.

He shakes hands with the police and murmurs something respectful. Then he turns and scans the office like he's sizing the place up. He's got that look prospective buyers sometimes have in houses, where they're imagining knocking a load of the walls down. My guess is he's come here to pick up where Justin left off. And once he looks in the files and works out what Justin had in store for me, I'll be out on my ear.

He glances at me, offers a polite smile. "Ms Harper? Could I see you in about half an hour?"

Fantastic. Enough time to catastrophise, not enough to flee the country. I nod and try to act normal, like I wasn't just mentally going over that resignation email.

He disappears into the side office with the police, and I open my computer and stare at it, trying to look busy. I'm not even reading. My brain won't come into focus.

I think of Bridget, champagne glass in hand, celebrating her promotion. And here I am, less than twenty-four hours later, about to get the sack. It's so bloody unfair. I debate texting Adam. *Feeling sick. Might leave.* Just walk out, skip the meeting, spare myself the indignity. I could be back home, snuggled up on the sofa together with a cup of tea and *Pointless.* He'd shout answers at the telly, I'd mock the contestants' eyebrows. Bliss. But I can imagine the smug look on Kyle and Mohammed's faces, me running away. Don't *forget to leave your lanyard on the way out.* I refuse to give them the pleasure.

Eventually, the door opens and Patrick appears. "Grace, please."

I have that feeling of dread you get when they call your name at the dentist.

The blinds in the little meeting room are closed. He pulls out a chair for me like he's inviting me to dinner.

"Firstly," he says, "thank you for being here today. I know it's all been… highly unusual."

That's one way of putting it.

"How are you feeling? Are you okay? I know Justin's death must be a shock for everyone."

Once again, I'm reminded that I'm finding the whole thing more novel than upsetting. Also, that I'm much more worried about myself and my job than I am about recently deceased Justin. But I don't say that. Instead, I just say, "I'm fine, thanks."

"Good, good…" says Patrick. He kind of drifts off as he looks at me. Then he puts his elbows on the desk and laces his fingers together, resting his chin on them. "Listen, Grace, I'll be completely frank with you. I've seen Justin's notes. But more importantly, I've read between the lines."

Here it comes.

"We've been keeping a close eye on the Scarborough

branch. Justin's death is sudden, obviously. But our concerns predate this week."

I nod slowly, waiting for the hammer.

"Sales figures aren't where they should be," he continues. "Client feedback has been inconsistent. And frankly, leadership has been... aggressive."

I brace.

He sighs. "Kyle and Mohammed are enthusiastic, I'll give them that. But I'm not looking for someone to high-five their way to a sale. That's not why we founded this firm. I'm looking for a steadying influence. I need an adult in the room."

I don't quite follow what he's saying. Is he having a total clear-out of all of us and replacing the whole team?

"You're not the loudest voice in the room, Grace," he says. "But that doesn't mean you're not valuable. Quite the opposite. You're dependable. And we need that. There's too much noise right now. I want someone calm enough to cut through it. And I commend you for stepping forward for the coaching programme. That speaks volumes."

A cold bolt of confusion runs down my spine. It takes me a second to realise what he's saying. Is this... going well?

He leans forward. "Would you be willing to act up in a team-leader capacity?"

My brain scrambles to keep up. Just yesterday I was almost pressing 'send' on a resignation email. Now I'm being offered promotion.

"I..." I clear my throat. "I'm not sure what to say."

He smiles. "Just say yes. We'll work out the rest later."

He stands. I follow suit. He extends a hand.

"Congratulations, Grace. Let's see what you can do."

I leave the room on legs that feel like they've forgotten how knees work. Kyle raises an eyebrow with a vague smile on his face, assuming I've just been fired. Mohammed glances up from his screen. I offer them nothing. Let them sweat. But inside I'm thinking, *say hello to your new boss, boys. How do you like that?*

Back at my desk, I sit like I'm afraid the chair will collapse. My heart's thudding in my ears. I catch myself smoothing my hair with the back of my hand like some teenage intern.

A promotion. After everything.

I stare at my screen, still trying to get my head around what just happened. I've spent weeks clinging on by my fingernails. Now I'm at the top of the cliff.

What now? What the hell now?

CHAPTER 19
OLIVER

Oliver hasn't slept. His heart is racing so fast he thinks he's in danger of having a heart attack. Once the practical task of cleaning the car and his clothes is over, a new kind of anxiety begins to creep in: the knowledge that he will almost certainly get caught. The idea takes hold like ivy on brickwork and won't let go, spreading its roots into him until he can think of nothing else.

He's been on his phone since the small hours, scouring local news sites, crime forums and Facebook groups for any kind of information. Justin's death is on all of them, but there's precious little detail.

Local estate agent killed in suspected hit-and-run. Police are appealing for witnesses.

That's all they have so far from what he can see. No mention of any suspects, no car description, no incriminating CCTV footage with Oliver's pixelated face unquestionably enlarged.

But who knows if any of that is true? Even if the police have information, they're hardly likely to share it with the news, are they? Warn the perpetrator that they are on to them. They could be on their way right now and he wouldn't know it. Dozens of them, parked around the corner in their vans. The first thing he'd know about it would be them smashing his door down, boots on the stairs, torches in his eyes, someone yelling his name. He's seen enough episodes of *Police Interceptors* to know how that plays out.

The sun is just up, and a thin yellow light forces its way through the patchy clouds. He gets up and creeps out in his dressing gown, into the narrow back lane to inspect the car in daylight. He's cleaned it well enough, and the heavy rain has helped, but the damage is extensive, much more so than he anticipated. The left wing is crumpled like a tin can, and a dent in the bonnet carries the ghostly outline of something that might be a footprint. Or a knee. Or a skull. He traces his finger across the metal, then pulls his hand away in disgust. One headlight is gone completely, and the other is dangling like an eye knocked loose in its socket. The windscreen has a fat spiderweb crack across the passenger side.

He runs through the options in his head. He could take it to a small backstreet place that probably won't ask questions. But won't the police have told all the garages to keep an eye out for this sort of damage? He imagines the mechanic staring at the car, sucking air through his teeth.

Because what does it look like?

It looks exactly like what it is – a car used to run someone down in cold blood.

He goes back inside and gets himself ready, as quickly as possible, like he's off for a normal day out. He puts on his jacket, grabs the keys, then goes and sits behind the wheel. He starts it up tentatively. He can't risk driving far, but he needs to do something.

He creeps a few hundred metres to the end of the lane, then turns onto the side street so the car faces the main road. The road's still quiet. The drab early light falls on the uniform terraces, the houses grey and hunched together like pensioners on a bench. He sits there with the engine ticking over.

An anxious fifteen minutes pass while he furtively checks in his mirrors, praying no one will walk up the lane behind him.

Then he sees her. A woman from two doors up, walking her son to school on the main road. He lets them pass, waits until they've rounded the corner, then takes a deep breath, lightly squeezes his foot on the accelerator and lets the car coast out onto the road.

They're walking ahead. He follows them slowly, making sure he doesn't let them know he's there. Then, when he feels he's close enough, he rams his foot onto the accelerator and yanks the steering wheel hard left.

The engine races and the car jolts as it mounts the pavement, slamming into a large tree. The impact is immediate and brutal. Oliver's body slams forward. His seat belt slices into his shoulder. His temple smacks the doorframe, exploding into burning hot pain. For a moment, he's blind. Then, vision returns, swimming red. He blinks through the blur and sees the woman running back toward him, dragging her son, shouting something.

Oliver gets out slowly, hands raised like he's surrendering. A couple of front doors open, and people stand on their steps, brought out by the noise of the crash. A neighbour in slippers. Another man, pulling on a coat over his pyjamas.

Someone asks Oliver if he needs an ambulance. He's confused, but raises his hand to the pain in his head and feels the warm, sticky blood running down his cheek, dripping onto his jacket. He shakes his head, voice faint. "No, no. I'll be fine. Just the shock."

He tries to play the part of the shaken, embarrassed, self-effacing victim. But it doesn't take much effort. The car is a mess and, from the look on people's faces, he assumes he is too. He asks for witness names "for the insurance," and types names and numbers into his phone with trembling hands. At least he has that now. A story. A tree, witnesses, a very public crash.

People drift away to leave him with his car. The front left wheel is twisted into the arch, leaning at a strange angle, clearly undrivable. The tree has a large gash in the trunk. He's hit it a lot faster than he was expecting. He has no option but to call the AA, who tell him assistance could be up to two hours.

He waits, shivering in the car with the engine off. Every time a person walks past or a car goes down the street, he thinks it could be someone about to report him. At one point, a car slows down and opens its window. The driver leans out towards the tangled wreckage. Oliver thinks they're offering to help.

"You can't park there, mate," shouts the driver with a laugh, and speeds off.

After ninety minutes, the tow truck arrives and hauls the car away, leaving Oliver with the name of a garage scribbled on a card.

Oliver walks the short distance up the road home. Back inside, he locks and unlocks the door five times. He goes to the closed curtains and peeks outside. Things are quiet.

In the bathroom, he examines the damage to his face. There's a gash on his temple, clotted with blood, and a bruise around his eye that is already beginning to close up. He pokes the eyelid tentatively and can feel the puffy swelling.

He opens the cabinet and pulls out a First Aid tin his mother must have left; plasters, iodine, ancient gauze in a yellowed paper wrapper. He cleans the wound and guesses he probably needs stitches, but he can't face going out again.

He imagines Julia, pressing a cotton ball to her bruised face. He dabs and tapes and hopes for the best.

He checks the news again. Nothing new. He watches the same footage again and again – the same photo of Justin, the same photo of the estate agency where he was just yesterday, and the same uneventful shots of the crime scene taped off. Same quote from the police, urging witnesses to come forward. Nonetheless, he can't relax. He keeps expecting a knock at the door. Sirens. Flashing lights.

The silence feels weighted, like it's listening back. He has a sudden thought that his mobile phone signal will place him at the scene of the crime. In a panic, he turns his phone off, but a part of him still hears the faint static. Then he realises it's too late for that, and even if his phone is now giving his location away, it makes no difference, as he's in his own home. He shakes himself. He has to start thinking straight.

At lunchtime he realises he hasn't eaten since yesterday. His stomach growls, but the fridge is empty. He pulls on an anorak and puts the hood up to cover the gauze. He walks to the corner shop and grabs bread, milk, crisps and some pre-packed sandwiches. Then he considers he might need supplies for longer and gets another loaf, eight tins of beans and some frozen pizzas, a box of plasters and dressings, disinfectant and some paracetamol.

The man at the checkout starts to ring up the contents of Oliver's basket. "Big night in, is it?" he asks drily.

Oliver glances at a noticeboard on the wall next to the till. There's a Crimestoppers poster pinned to it. A simple slogan in bold red above a phone number.

Know Something? See Something? Say Something!

Oliver's breath catches. He imagines someone seeing the poster, remembering a nugget of information from the evening, calling the number and cracking the case. As he pays, his elbow 'accidentally' knocks the leaflet to the floor. He crouches, scoops it up and shoves it into his carrier bag.

"At least the rain's eased off," says the checkout guy.

Oliver mumbles something noncommittal and flees.

On his way back from the shop, he spots a man across the street, standing very still beside a lamppost. Oliver wonders if he's watching him, but he can't be sure.

He doesn't leave the house for the next three days. He doesn't open the curtains. He spends the time on high alert. He toasts bread and warms beans, and watches the news. Every footstep outside is a threat. Every parked car a surveillance van. He sleeps in nervous bursts, jumping at creaks and shadows. The house becomes both sanctuary and prison. One night he hears a siren and lies flat, waiting. But no one comes.

On the fourth day, he scrolls to the *Scarborough Evening News* website. The article has dropped down the news order, and the headline still reads *"Police appeal for witnesses in estate agent hit-and-run."* There's a fuller story now. There aren't any suspects. Apparently, the CCTV camera on the Esplanade was struck by lightning during the storm. It was out of action at the time of the incident.

It's a boring story for anyone else reading it, but Oliver sinks into a chair and laughs. He hears the noise coming out of him, a high, brittle sound that startles even him, and realises he's spent the last four days in almost complete silence.

The cut on his head seems to be healing okay, and he only needs a large plaster now, rather than a full bandage. On the morning of the fifth day, he calls the garage. The car is ready. He walks the two miles, heart hammering, wondering if the police will leap out and grab him the moment he takes his keys.

The mechanic hands him the paperwork while he pays.

"Hell of a mess," he says. "You hit a wall or something?"

"Tree," Oliver replies. "Skidded and lost control."

"I'd hate to see the tree. Lucky your engine was okay."

Oliver smiles thinly, signs the papers, and drives home. No one stops him. No one asks questions. He feels oddly calm. The new headlights work. The windscreen's been replaced. The dents hammered out. Even the paintwork's been matched. From the outside, you'd never know.

Later, he opens the curtains and sits by the window, watching a cat tiptoe along the back fence.

It's over.

Or it seems to be.

He lies in bed that night, staring at the ceiling, and feels... what? Relief? Not quite. Not guilt, either. A strange, electric hum under the skin. Not joy. Not peace.

Exhilaration.

He did something. Something bold. Something final.

And Grace – Grace is safe now. She'll never even know.

CHAPTER 20
GRACE

"So, Grace," he says, leaning forward in his chair with that professional half-smile that's supposed to say 'safe space' but always makes me feel like I'm going to be handed bad news about a terminal illness. "How's your week been?"

He already knows, of course. He must do. Justin's death is headline news in Scarborough. The hit-and-run's a murder enquiry now. All the police statements. The CCTV that wasn't working because of the storm. Everyone loves a bit of drama, and this one came with thunder and lightning.

"It's been weird," I say. "I assume you heard about Justin."

A flicker. A blink that's half a second too long.

"Yes," he says. "Terrible."

I can't read him. He was in the office that day, presumably reporting to Justin about me. How well did he know him? Maybe they were friends? Whatever they were, he doesn't react. But what he doesn't know is that I've planned super-carefully for this meeting. Because even with Justin gone, I still don't trust Oliver.

By rights, I shouldn't even be here. With Justin dead, it lets me off the hook. I almost didn't come. But this morning it dawned on me like a frying pan to the back of the head: This coaching programme didn't start with Justin. It's Patrick Lyle's big idea. I can't just drop it. I don't want to give him an excuse to backtrack and take the promotion away – or even sack me, like Justin was planning to.

So here I am, back in this grotty little therapist's cave above the chiropodist, in my usual baggy seat by the window, with a delightful view of the flaking windowsill and seagull shit. And today, I'm on a mission: sound capable, look sane, avoid sobbing like a baby. I have to keep up the act. I've been playing babysitter with office toddlers for months, so I can do this. Smile, nod, and for God's sake don't look like someone who's mentally researching part-time degree options in her lunch break.

"I suppose you've heard the other news, too," I say.

He raises an eyebrow, inviting me to continue.

"I got promoted. Acting manager." I need to keep the shock and awe out of my voice and sound like it's the best thing that's ever happened to me. "Patrick Lyle offered me the job."

Oliver beams. "Congratulations, Grace. That's fantastic. Really fantastic."

There's a warmth in his voice that makes me feel oddly... pleased. He seems almost as happy as Adam was. He sounds genuinely delighted. I wasn't expecting that. I find myself smiling.

"You sound a little surprised he chose you," he says, more a question than a statement. I thought I'd masked it, but apparently not.

"Well, yeah. I guess I am. He said I wasn't the loudest person in the room. I sometimes worry about that. But maybe that's a good thing."

Oliver nods thoughtfully. "Quiet strength can often go unnoticed. But it can be the most powerful kind."

That's good. He sounds like he believes I'm not a complete liability.

"Anyway," I say, not wanting to make too big a thing of it, "the job's temporary. Acting up. But still…" I shrug. "It's nice to be appreciated."

It's true. I don't want to speak ill of the dead, but *up yours, Justin*. Not such a loser now, am I?

Oliver reaches for a notebook. "Would it be helpful to explore what opportunities you see in this role? And any challenges?"

Okay. We're going to do a bit of coaching stuff. I trot out one of my statements prepared for maximum positive impact.

"Maybe the big opportunity… is someone finally recognising I can actually do this. I know the job. I've got the experience, I'm ambitious to do my best and maybe even keep climbing…"

As if. The minute I've got enough money for my uni fees, I'll be out of the door like a shot. Can't let Oliver know that though.

"You just need the confidence," Oliver chimes in.

How has he seen that? I guess there is a little bit of me that wonders whether I'll actually be able to pull it off. It feels okay to admit he's partly right. "Yeah, well, when you get knocked back or overlooked, you can definitely lose confidence."

"And confidence breeds confidence," he says. "So maybe this is your opportunity to go from strength to strength."

He gives me a warm smile, and I must admit it feels like I've got a cheerleader in my corner. I'm even feeling positive about the promotion. Especially as it's come with a pay rise to boost the uni fund. It feels like things are back on track.

"And what about challenges?" he asks.

"Kyle and Mohammed," I say without a pause. "They're already giving me looks like I've pissed on their chips."

Too casual. I sound like I'm bitching. I need to recalibrate. At least I didn't say that I could do Kyle's and Mohammed's jobs with one eye closed and a broken arm. But that's not a great look in female leadership, so I keep that bit in my head.

But Oliver just smiles. "I know what you mean." He pauses. "They're not supportive?"

I raise an eyebrow. "Not really, no."

Support.

I get a sudden flash of that exercise we did last time, and my hopeless support structure. I think about Bridget and why I haven't phoned to tell her my good news. It feels like something's gone badly wrong between us. But I've promised myself I won't cry again in here, so I don't mention her.

"You said that Patrick recognised some of your quieter qualities. Which ones do you think helped you stand out?"

I stop and think properly about myself.

"I know it sounds weird, but I think I'm nice. I guess I don't just talk. I listen. I care about doing the job well. I'm a decent person to be around. I don't shout over people in meetings."

Oliver smiles. "Those aren't just nice traits. They're leadership traits."

And for a moment, I believe him.

Maybe he *is* a good coach. That meltdown last week, the tears, the anger – I hated it. But maybe that's what I needed. Perhaps it shook something loose. I've felt more focused since. More capable. And more on target to achieve what I want.

Oliver starts going off on one. He talks about transition, about impostor syndrome, about grounding techniques. And it's all good stuff. It is. Still, there's something… off. I think he's trying to make himself sound absolutely essential to me, like I have to keep coming to him as a coach. I guess maybe he needs the money.

There's something else too. Every now and then, a word choice lands strange. Like when he says, "Sometimes, in order for someone to grow, the obstacle in their way has to be removed."

I nod, but my stomach does a little flip.

Removed. What a word.

But then I think, maybe what I'm feeling that's off about it all is my own guilt. What's happened is that *Justin* has been removed. That's what Justin was. A blockage. Like a turd in a u-bend. Or a fat-berg in a drain.

What an awful thing to think about someone who's just died. I shouldn't feel glad. But I do. Does that make me a terrible person? But I can't help it. And I definitely can't let Oliver see it on my face.

"I don't want you to think I'm celebrating," I say. "About Justin. I wouldn't have wanted to get a promotion this way."

"Of course."

"I mean, his poor wife..." I trail off. I don't have anything positive to say.

We sit there in silence. Oliver's face is unreadable. Like he's holding something back. I can't work out what he's thinking.

Eventually, the session comes to an end. I feel like I've done okay. Said the right things. Shown enthusiasm. But something's gnawing at the back of my brain, like the thought equivalent of a stone in my shoe that I can't shake loose.

Outside in the street, I check my phone. No messages from Bridget. I cross the road and walk back toward the car park.

I've got the job. And I think, for now, I've kept it.

But for all his supportive words, I feel Oliver watching

me. Staring into me. Waiting for me to do… something. What am I giving away? My lack of ambition? My relief that Justin's dead? My plans to leave? Is he going to say something to Patrick to pull the rug out from under me?

I don't feel triumphant. It all feels… precarious.

I feel like I'm standing on a frozen lake. It looks solid. And all the while, Oliver's out there with a stone in his hand, ready to test the ice.

CHAPTER 21
OLIVER

The door clicked shut a few moments ago, and now her absence settles over the room like a hush in church.

Oliver sits back in his chair, hands folded loosely in his lap, and closes his eyes. He imagines her walking back through the narrow street toward her car, coat collar up against the wind. She looked lighter today. Taller, somehow. The weight lifted. The small smile that slipped out when she talked about work.

And it isn't just the promotion. Something has shifted in her life. The shadow is gone. She's going to be all right now. She's free.

And he did that.

No more intimidating looks from her boss. No more dismissive emails. No more walking into the office every morning, braced for humiliation. She's going to grow and flourish, like a plant given room to breathe once the weeds have been hacked away.

He'd only gone to talk, to reason with the man, to help him see what he was doing wrong. But some people can't be reasoned with – like some of his clients in the past, who could never see the answer when it was staring them right in the face. He wanted to shake them. To slap them into conscious-ness. *Wake up!*

But Justin wouldn't wake up. He refused to. That's what bullies do. They refuse to learn, too pig-headedly certain that they are right. They lack the capacity to change. What Justin needed was a more direct intervention.

He's spent his life helping people. Sitting in rooms like this one, reflecting, questioning, gently nudging. Holding up mirrors. But the world outside the therapy room isn't so tidy. Sometimes a single action does more than a thousand sessions.

Oliver opens his eyes and looks again at the chair Grace was sitting in. The curve of the cushion still holding her shape, the little indent in the arm where her elbow rested, as if the room hasn't quite let her go. It reminds him of the curve Justin's body made in his bonnet, the twisted curve of Justin's body itself as it tumbled down the grass verge.

He pushes the thought aside.

He needs to clear his head. He grabs his keys and steps outside.

He walks down the road, the terraces shoulder to shoulder on either side. He aims for the old town, through alleys and back routes he's known since childhood. The streets are patchy with light, the low sun cutting long shad-ows. His hands are cold, but the cold feels good. Grounding.

He passes charity shops, their windows stuffed with sun-faded books and chipped crockery. A teenager skateboards past, hood up, earphones in, his wheels clattering against the cracked pavement. He climbs the hill toward the castle, walking fast, his heartbeat loud in his ears.

At the top, he pauses to catch his breath, turning toward St Anne's church. Its doors are closed, but the graveyard's always open. He wanders between the stones until he finds the small, weather-worn marker beneath the yew. Anne Brontë. He sits on the bench opposite. An unfamiliar calm settles over him.

Anne Brontë. The forgotten one. The overlooked. The quiet sister in a family of loud voices. She died young, didn't she? Not quite thirty. He remembers that from somewhere. All that potential, snuffed out.

He picks a blade of grass from beside her grave and twirls it between his fingers. Then, without thinking why, he chews it. It tastes of damp and soil and old stone. He swallows, and wonders if Anne's body, rotting underground for the best part of two hundred years, has fed this grass. If some tiny part of her, the cells of her, are now in him.

The idea thrills him. Transference. Transformation.

That's what death does, he realises. That's what Justin's death has done. It has fed Grace. Enriched her so that now she can grow into her full potential. Justin was dead weight. Rot. And now he's compost.

Oliver chuckles at the thought. It bubbles out of him before he can stop it. A passing dog walker gives him a side-long glance, and Oliver lowers his head, stifling his grin but unable to stop it entirely.

He gets up and strides down toward the sea. The path winds down to the harbour, where the tide is out and the wet sand gleams like a mirror. A couple walk hand in hand by the boats, heads close together. The worst of the winter storms sometimes shut this road down. The waves come up and slap the tarmac so hard they peel it up like skin from sunburn, rip the road back into the sea. But today is crisp and bright. A good day.

He thinks about the next session with Grace. About the things she might say. The look she gave him today – vulnerable, but grateful. There's trust in her now. She knows he's different. He sees her in a way no one else does. She's begun to rely on him. And she doesn't even know the extent of what he's done for her.

He rounds the bend and walks into a corner shop near the quay. It's mostly tourists down here in summer – ice creams, crab lines, postcards with rude jokes. But today it's empty.

The man behind the counter barely glances up from his phone, smirking at something he's reading.

Recognition slams into him.

It's one of them. From school. Ash's friend. The one who used to jeer when Oliver walked by, mimicking his voice, shoving him in the corridor. He's forgotten this one's name – Dean maybe, or Liam – but he hasn't forgotten the smirk. He remembers him in horrible detail.

But the man doesn't recognise him at all.

Oliver browses the shelves, the seaside rock and the cheap souvenirs, tat made from shells and driftwood. He glances at the newspapers and magazines, the cigarettes and vapes, the chewing gum. He picks up a Twix and slips it into his pocket. He walks past the till with casual slowness. He doesn't pay. Just wraps his hand around the chocolate in his pocket and walks out.

He doesn't have to play by other people's rules anymore. He's doing the work no one else has the guts to do. Making a difference.

He tears off the corner of the packet as he heads uphill again, the gradient slow and steady. The chocolate and toffee melt deliciously in his mouth.

He feels invincible.

CHAPTER 22
GRACE

My inbox is overflowing again.

I scroll through it with one hand while holding a banana in the other, because I didn't have time for breakfast. I've been in since seven.

It's only been a week since Patrick promoted me, and I'm already fantasising about going back in time and politely declining. I'm drowning in admin. Sales logs, performance updates, response targets, and a new 'customer engagement' spreadsheet. It feels like I've been made Captain of the Titanic just in time to manage the feedback forms.

Yesterday morning, I arrived to an email from Patrick Lyle. Subject line: *Checking In*.

All friendly on the surface – asking how things are going, how I'm settling into the role. But I can't help thinking there's more to it than just polite interest. Is he fishing, beginning to think he's made a terrible mistake?

Then this morning at about 8.30 a.m. another message comes through. Patrick Lyle again.

My stomach dips.

Would I be able to pull together a short strategy paper for

him by the end of the week? Something covering market assessment, potential growth areas, and a three-year income projection. He's reviewing regional operations, and he'd like to include Scarborough.

I stare at the screen and take a long, slow breath. A *short* strategy paper. As if that's not five days of utter panic and bad dreams in Word format. Because obviously, that's what I do now – strategic planning, on top of sales figures, performance management, and running a bloody boys' club.

This is even worse than just doing my old job and keeping my head down. Now I'm single-handedly responsible for the success of the branch. All I wanted was to save enough to go to uni, but now I've got to pretend I'm passionate about forging a career in estate agency.

Kyle and Mohammed come in at about nine. I try to get them focused on sales without setting them off on one of their puerile routines. I'm aiming to keep things light and upbeat, but still seem like the boss. I keep hearing myself use the word 'strategic'. I notice I've said it about three times, then shut up as I'm obviously trying too hard.

"Gracie," Kyle calls across the room half an hour later, leaning back in his chair like he thinks he's in the West Wing. "Printer's jammed again. What's the strategy on that?"

I glance over the top of my monitor. "First off, it's Grace. Second, try not cramming sixteen pages of Rightmove printouts in at once."

He grins, clearly delighted to have got a rise out of me. "Roger that, boss lady."

I used to think if I was in charge, everything would run smoother. Turns out, being the boss means wrestling spreadsheets while Kyle plays Apprentice in the corner and Mohammed disappears for 'offsite client liaison', which I'm pretty certain is code for getting sausage rolls from Greggs.

Plus, now I'm relying on Kyle and Mohammed for the

front-facing stuff. Viewings. Calls. Vendors. Which would be fine if either of them saw me as their actual manager. Kyle, in particular, is starting to wear thin. He calls me "Guv'nor" in that same sarcastic voice every time he walks past my desk. He's also taken to 'helping' by forwarding all his emails to me with the subject line *Thoughts?* as if I'm his sodding PA. Around mid-morning, he CC's me into a chain about a boiler inspection, and when I ask what he wants me to do with it, he says, "Just giving you visibility." He went on some half-day business admin course last year, and now he thinks a certificate in Excel makes him Bill Gates. He keeps it framed on his desk like it's an MBA from Harvard. He's used the phrase "synergise the pipeline" twice today, and it's not even lunch.

I'm starting to worry I've bitten off more than I can chew. Now I've said I'll take on this job, I have to do it properly, even if it is just a means to an end. I still can't afford to get sacked. If anything, there's more pressure on me now than there was with bloody Justin. Is this what Oliver meant by impostor syndrome? Perhaps I should think about getting more help from him? I don't really know what I'm doing, and I suspect everyone can see it.

Then, just after 4 p.m., the police arrive again.

They don't make a fuss, just flash their IDs and ask to speak to me in private. I wonder if they've come to update me on stuff with Justin, now I'm manager. I take them through to the side office.

We sit. One of them, a woman with severe, angular features and hair wrenched up in a tight ponytail, opens a notebook. The other one, a miserable-looking man who hasn't said a word yet, just watches.

"We're re-interviewing some of Justin's colleagues," she says. "Standard follow-up."

I nod. "Sure thing. How can I help?"

"Can I ask where you were the night Mr Trott died?"

My mind blanks for a beat. Then it kicks in.

"I was at dinner with my sister and her boyfriend. And my boyfriend."

"Can we take their names?"

I give them Adam, Bridget and Dave's details, and the name of the restaurant.

She jots them down. "And after that?"

"I went home."

"Alone?"

"Yes. Adam got back later."

"What time?"

"About eleven."

"And what time did you leave?"

"I dunno. Around eight, I think."

"Eight?" She looks at me. "So you *didn't* go to dinner?"

"No, I... er, I did. But I left early."

Her lip curls slightly. "What did you do between leaving the restaurant and Adam getting home?"

"I stayed in. Read some news reports."

"About Mr Trott?"

I nod.

She's watching me too closely. I feel like I've walked into a trap.

"Any reason you left early?"

"I felt ill." I hesitate. Better to tell them the full truth. "It was... a difficult evening. I'd had some news at work. And my sister and I sort of argued."

"What about?"

"I don't know. Family stuff. Just... a silly disagreement."

"And what was your news at work?"

This is awkward. "I was given a formal warning."

"By whom?"

"Well... by Justin."

They exchange a look. Not suspicious exactly, but...

noted. It hadn't occurred to me before that I don't really have an alibi. But I don't. And I left dinner early, in a temper. And I'd had a run-in of sorts with Justin. It doesn't matter how innocent I am. In front of the police, trying to account for every minute, I feel guilty. Like I've already been found out. I hated Justin. He formally warned me. Now he's dead, and I have his job.

The questions keep coming. Did anyone see you come home? No. Did you go back out? No. Did you speak to Mr Trott that evening? No.

It's all reasonable. All calm. But the longer it goes on, the more I feel like I'm being pulled into something. I look like I'm guilty.

Eventually, they thank me and leave. I sit in the side office for a while, trying to gather myself, but I can't. It's like all the air's gone out of me. That felt like a bloody interrogation.

I go back to my desk and start typing numbers into a spreadsheet, but I can't concentrate. I don't want to look up, but I suspect Kyle and Mohammed are sneaking looks my way, trying to work out what that conversation was all about. Why did the police interview me and not them?

At 4:58 p.m. sharp, Kyle packs up with a theatrical yawn.

"Don't stay too late, boss," he says. "Wouldn't want you burning out."

If he were any more smug, he'd need a licence.

Kyle and Mohammed leave. I sit at the desk for a while in the quiet office, doing nothing. I should warn Bridget that the police might call her to check about the restaurant. Anyway, I've been looking for an excuse to get in touch with her, and I won't get one more obvious than this.

I pull out my phone and dial Bridget.

It rings for a while, then Dave answers.

"Grace! Hey. You alright?"

"Hi, yeah. Sorry. Is Bridget around?"

A pause.

"She's... just tied up with something. Can I pass on a message?"

He sounds nice enough. Apologetic. But something in his tone is too smooth.

"Oh. Right. No, it's fine."

"Okay. I'll tell her you called."

"Thanks." I should just leave it there. But instead I blurt, "She just hasn't called me for a while, that's all."

There's a silence.

"Yeah," he says, too quickly. "She's just been swamped."

"Okay. Thanks."

He hesitates. "She's in the bath. She's not great at staying on top of messages. You know what she's like."

I do. It's always like this. Bridget being too busy. Bridget being unavailable. And always Dave, playing the buffer for her.

"No worries," I say, my heart sinking.

"Listen, she'll probably be out in a minute. I'll tell her you called."

"Thanks."

I hang up and wait for half an hour. If she's really in the bath, she must be bloody drowning. I stare at the phone. It doesn't ring.

I can see through the window that it's dark outside now, and the wind's picked up. I press my fingers to my temples, trying to will away the headache that's building behind my eyes. Then I call Adam.

"Hi, luv. You okay? You sound tired."

"Yeah, I'm fine," I lie. "It's been a busy day, that's all."

I don't tell him about the police. I can't face thinking about it.

"I'm really sorry, Adam, but I'm going to hang on here for

a bit longer. Do you mind? Patrick wants me to do some five-year strategic growth plan thingy."

"Oof. Big boss stuff. You can do that in your sleep."

"I probably will be asleep. It's so tedious. I don't even really want this job, but now I've got it, I can see it's going to be pretty demanding."

"You're smashing it, Grace. Honestly. I'm proud of you."

That makes me smile.

"It's fine. I knew you were a high-flier. Do him a *ten*-year strategic growth plan thingy. He'll shit himself."

"Thanks."

"I'll knock you up a carbonara when you get in."

"Aw, thanks, baby. Irresistible."

I hang up.

It's great Adam believes in me. But instead of feeling reassured, I feel pressure. Like if I mess this up, I won't just be disappointing myself – I'll be letting him down, too.

I sit at my desk for another three hours, surrounded by scribbled notes and half-drunk mugs of tea. I'm meant to be sketching out this strategy paper, but I can't write anything. I stare at the blank screen with it all whirling round in my head. Bridget avoiding me. The police questioning me. And a job that's going to get me fired for sure if I don't nail it.

No pressure, then. Just my sister, the police, and my entire future hanging by a thread.

CHAPTER 23
OLIVER

Oliver hurries up the high street, the shopping in his Bag For Life swinging at his side. He isn't comfortable being out without his phone to hand. What if he doesn't hear it ringing because of the passing traffic? What if he doesn't feel it vibrate? He pats his pocket like a compulsive tic, checking it's still there.

Not just any call. A call from *her*.

He crosses the road at a gallop and nearly slips on a slick patch near the gutter.

Grace hasn't called and hasn't replied to his email. But he shouldn't read too much into that. She's busy. She has a new job. People get snowed under. But something in him still fizzes with anticipation. After everything that's happened, everything he's *done*, she's bound to reach out. She's smart.

Their last session went well. More than well – it was a kind of breakthrough. There was a clarity behind her eyes. She is starting to realise that she doesn't have to suffer anymore, that she isn't trapped. And when she spoke about her new role at work, he saw something flicker through her. Vitality. Liberation. A spark.

But he'd also seen the fear. That part of her still waiting for the rug to be pulled out from under her; the part that still needs him. And it's his job – his *privilege* – to guide her through these choppy waters. To make sure she doesn't retreat into that place of self-doubt. That she never ends up like Julia.

As he approaches the corner near his street, something tightens in his chest. There, looming to his right, is the tree. The gouge in the trunk where his car struck it has deepened slightly since he last walked past. Probably weathering, or maybe someone's peeled away some of the loose outer bark. A fine line of rain glistens in the wound, giving it the uncanny look of a stitched-up scar.

The image hijacks him: Justin's face as he lies in the grass, his head twisted at the wrong angle. That deep canyon in his forehead. The water pooling and mingling with blood until it's impossible to tell which is which.

Oliver pulls his scarf tighter. No. Not now. That chapter is closed.

He rounds the corner back onto his street and pauses. One of his neighbours is out trimming the hedge. Oliver wonders if she heard anything. But no – her smile is pleasant, if a little wary. She doesn't know.

Of course she doesn't. No one does.

He walks briskly the rest of the way home, fumbles his key in the lock, and pushes the door open with his shoulder. The dull hush of the hallway folds around him like a thick blanket.

He heads to the kitchen and unpacks the shopping, lining up tins on the counter: soup, baked beans, some Ambrosia rice pudding. It's the kind of food you get when you're planning to bunker in for a while. Basic. Nourishing. Easy. He hasn't been out much of late. But perhaps that will change.

It's only as he's putting the last of the items away that he realises he didn't do the usual lock-unlock-lock-unlock-lock ritual. Didn't even think about it.

He freezes for a beat.

But nothing happens. No surge of anxiety, no rising tide of dread.

A new calm has taken root.

As he puts the milk away, he finds himself smiling. Maybe this is what peace feels like. Justin's absence is like a stone removed from Grace's shoe, and from his own chest. There's no reasoning with people like that. They're blunt instruments, bludgeoning their way through the world. He's seen it again and again. People like Justin are *dangerous*. They harm people. You can't let emotion cloud your judgment in such cases. You have to be clinical and impassive, like destroying a dangerous dog.

Oliver walks into the living room and sits at the small table under the window. He opens his laptop and checks his inbox.

No reply.

He frowns and opens the sent folder. He reads through his sent email from yesterday, carefully, line by line, trying to imagine it from Grace's perspective.

It's warm. Encouraging. Full of practical next steps. He's outlined areas they could work on: Impostor Syndrome, managing upwards, setting emotional boundaries, assertive communication, values clarification. He's even included a note about how changes at work can often reverberate through personal relationships, too.

Was it too vague? Has he not outlined the benefits precisely enough?

Maybe.

He begins drafting a new version, fleshing out a list of possible coaching strands.

Recognising Your Wins – counteracting negative bias and building resilience.

Navigating Ambiguity – making confident decisions when there's no clear path.

Conflict Management – from avoidance to constructive engagement.

Workplace Archetypes – recognising personality types and managing dynamics.

Stress Containers – understanding emotional bandwidth and release strategies.

He doesn't mention Justin by name, but he does refer to 'recent workplace challenges' and how Grace has already shown courage and adaptability in stepping up.

He reads through it one more time. In case he's leaving too much to be inferred between the lines, he adds a final paragraph about consistency in coaching, how more regular sessions could help solidify her progress. He suggests that two sessions a week initially might be of benefit.

He signs off with care. *Always here to support you – Oliver.*

He hits send, then gets up from his desk and attends to some chores around the house. He's let things run to seed a bit of late. He gets the ancient hoover out and gives the place a good run around. He finds some Vim in the cupboard under the sink, and a torn-up sheet made into cloths, and he gives the bathroom a good scrub. He changes the bedding. He works with a sense of purpose, and even though he doesn't much care for the cleaning itself, he likes what it represents. A fresh new start.

He goes back and checks his inbox.

Still no reply to the first message or the new one.

Maybe it didn't land. Spam filters are a minefield these days. He copies the new message into a second email, changes the subject line to *Following up – just in case this didn't reach you yesterday*, and sends it again.

He sits back and scrolls idly through his calendar. Two client appointments tomorrow, neither of which fills him with joy. The first is a dull man in his forties who works in facilities management, whatever that is, and wants help "being taken seriously" at work. The second is a twenty-something HR officer who burst into tears in their last session because she thinks she's too nice to be promoted.

He sends short emails to both, cancelling their appointments, and explaining a scheduling conflict. He uses the word *regretfully*, but feels no regret at all. He needs to make sure he has an open diary for when Grace gets back to him. The idea of being tied up listening to their trivia when Grace might be reaching out is unthinkable.

He goes and makes a cup of tea, though he's not particularly thirsty, then returns to his laptop and refreshes his inbox again.

Nothing.

That's fine. She's probably still swamped adjusting to the new role.

He scrolls absently through the news. There's still a tiny paragraph about Justin's death in the regional sidebar, but it's slid halfway down the page, replaced by a story about an otter rescue and a think-piece on Yorkshire's pothole crisis.

He sips his tea and stares out of the window. Rain drizzles over the glass, making the outside world seem out of focus and unreal. A car rolls past, tyres hissing on the wet road. He killed a man. And nothing happened. The police haven't come. No sirens. No pounding at the door. The world hasn't stopped spinning. He's still here. He's still him. An even better him than he was before.

He refreshes his email one more time.

Still nothing.

That's okay. She's got a lot on her plate. There's no hurry.

The room glows a pale orange from the late afternoon sun

slanting in through the blinds. Everything is going according to plan. He saved her.

He dips his biscuit in his tea and refreshes his email again. He's looking forward to getting her message so they can begin the real work in earnest.

CHAPTER 24
GRACE

I stare at my screen with my mouth hanging open like some idiot zombified by a stage hypnotist.

Fourteen emails from Oliver in three days.

Fourteen.

Every time I try to get on with something important, *ping*, there's another one. Subject lines like *Checking In – Just a Thought!* or *Additional Reflections on Impostor Syndrome*. They're stacking up like junk mail on a doormat. The last one includes a PDF coaching model that reads like an IKEA guide for assembling your own emotional breakdown.

God. He must be really desperate for work.

I can't carry on like this. I push my chair back decisively from the desk and stand up.

"Oop, someone means business," chimes Kyle. "Early lunch, is it, Gracie?"

I think about how good it would feel to throw a hole punch at his head. But instead, I march into the side office and shut the door.

Oliver answers on the first ring, as if he's been hovering over his phone, waiting to pounce.

"Grace!" He's all bright and chatty. "How are you? Thanks for getting back to me–"

"Sorry it's taken me so long to get in touch," I cut in. "I've wanted to call, but it's been crazy busy here."

"I can imagine. The many challenges of a new role. As you'll have seen from my email, I think that might be an area where I can offer some support."

"Things are going fantastically, actually," I say, making my voice as cheerful as possible.

There's an awkward silence. He wasn't expecting that. It's rubbish, obviously, but there's no way I'm telling him I'm drowning in work and wishing I'd never been given this bloody promotion. I certainly don't want to give the impression I need any more coaching. Fourteen emails are fourteen too many, and I want this over as quickly as possible.

"Oh," he says. "That's... wonderful. I'm so pleased. What's been working for you, specifically, do you think?"

Time to blow some smoke up his arse.

"Well, pretty much everything. The coaching really helped. I've definitely turned a corner. I'm loving the new job, to be honest. I'd never have got to that point without you."

"Well–" he tries to interrupt, but I press on.

"It's going so well I think we can probably wrap up now. I don't need the sessions anymore. I'm really grateful. But it's time for me to go it alone."

"Grace," he says, like someone who's about to talk me into a three-year broadband contract, "sometimes continuing support through periods of change–"

"I'm so grateful for everything you've done," I say, with as much finality as possible. "I just wanted to say thank you. For everything."

There's a long pause. Then a clipped, "Right. Well. If you ever want to reconnect, you know where I am." He sounds hurt, like someone being dumped. Which he is.

"Thanks," I say, then hang up before he can say anything else.

That's that.

I breathe out so hard I sound like a punctured lilo. God, that's a relief. No more soul-searching, no more mapping my emotional support systems. No more sitting in that depressing little office. Something about him was too pushy, too invasive. Like the coaching equivalent of a bloke staring at your tits.

Though promotion has been pretty crappy so far, one perk of being in charge is that I can politely tell people to sod off. I can stop with Oliver and not have to justify it to anyone. I was only doing the sessions because Justin made me. And now this last thread linking me to Justin has been cut. And if Patrick asks why I've stopped, I'll make something up, tell him how brilliant the coaching was, and how smart he was to send me on it.

I go back to my desk and wake up my computer, half-expecting another email from Oliver.

But it's worse.

That stupid bloody screensaver again. A pixelated GIF of a kitten giving a thumbs-up, with a flashing speech bubble saying 'BETTER LUCK NEXT PROMOTION' in Comic Sans. Kyle's handiwork, of course, though he denied it when I confronted him. I've been trying to get rid of it for days.

Mohammed's pretending to work, but Kyle doesn't even bother to hide his smirk. "I think you might've been hacked there, Gracie."

I can see the pair of them practically shaking with suppressed laughter. Their version of workplace banter: death by a thousand dad jokes.

I sigh and log off. I don't want it making me look like a ditsy teenager on work experience, not with Patrick Lyle due any minute. Patrick, the actual boss, with actual power and actual opinions about whether or not this entire Scarborough branch is worth saving. He's looking to me to turn things around, and here I am, struggling with a poxy screensaver.

I pull out my folder with the revenue ideas I've been nursing like the Holy Grail. I've combed through ten years of residential sales figures and they're flatter than a pancake on a yoga mat. We're not going to increase profits there. I've considered what happens if we put a big push on rentals, but it's a small market, and if we expand, I'd need a dedicated agent, which would swallow any gains. I've put hours to it, and even I think I'm beginning to sound like a convincing estate agent bore. Next thing, I'll be driving a car with the company name on the door.

As I'm looking over my notes, Patrick arrives and strides across the office towards me, oozing confidence. He's in a nice suit and coat, and there's a kind of dapper sharpness about him. He looks like if you threw him into a hedge, he'd come out with his hair still perfect. In contrast, I've hardly slept for a week and I feel like a wreck. The bags under my eyes have got bags under them, and my skin is a mess. It makes me feel even less prepared.

"Shall we take a stroll?" he says. "Get some air?"

We walk across the bridge towards the harbour. The wind's a bit of a shock to the system, but it blows the cobwebs out of my frontal lobes and sharpens me up a bit. I'll need it.

"I always enjoy a chance to come through to Scarborough," he says, as we make our way round The Grand Hotel.

Really? Why would anyone want to come here? It's that small town thing: outsiders find it quaint and charming; insiders find it suffocating and can't wait to get away. It's a dump really. As if to prove my point, we walk past a seagull disembowelling a chip.

We get a table in a place on the pier with a sea view, all

white tiles and overpriced calamari. I'd kill for a glass of wine, but Patrick orders a mineral water and I feel I have to copy him. He seems perfectly relaxed, but I'm sweating buckets. I wonder if I should take my jacket off. But will sweat patches show through my blouse?

"I'm interested to hear what ideas you've got for me," he says.

This is it. Now or never.

"Commercial," I say. I practised it in front of the bathroom mirror, trying to get a little twinkle. I try to read his face. I was hoping for a Eureka moment, but instead Patrick just curls his nose up a bit. I feel like running across the restaurant, throwing myself out of the window and drowning in the sea. But instead, I keep going.

"The housing market's flat, and rental's a non-starter. I've been looking at the commercial sector," I say. "There are a couple of big warehouse properties just outside town sitting vacant since the pandemic. They're costing the owners a fortune just in upkeep and security. Dead weight."

Patrick raises an eyebrow. "There's a reason they're vacant," he says, unenthusiastically. "No one wants them."

"Not true. Not exactly…"

I try to make it sound teasing and mysterious, to reel him in. And he does lean forward – but not out of interest. He just takes a pack of breadsticks from the jar on the table and starts to unwrap them. If anything, he's bored.

I press on regardless. "I've spoken to one of the owners. They're open to movement. I think we could get sole agency, reposition the pricing, and target a niche buyer. It'd take work, but the payoff could be huge."

I sound like I've swallowed the sales manual. Jesus. I'm fluent in estate agent, God help me. But it seems to be getting through to Patrick. He leans back and threads his fingers together, thinking. "Why is no one else doing it?"

"Look, Patrick, people used to think you bought books from bookshops until Amazon came along. Just because we're the first, it doesn't make it wrong."

Christ. It's just a couple of shitty warehouses, not NASA. I think I've oversold it.

He puts his breadstick down. "And you think you can do this?"

"I think we have to *try.*"

I keep my face still, as neutral as I can, and smile like I've already got the deal in the bag. Or maybe like a gambler holding a shit hand and hoping no one can spot it.

Finally, he says, "Okay, you've got a month. Make something happen."

Great.

That's what I wanted, right? To keep the job. Prove I'm worth it. Get through this, save enough, go back to uni. Only now I've stuck my head above the parapet, and the second I fail, I'll be on the scrapheap.

Later, back home, I'm in the kitchen staring at a half-finished budget spreadsheet and chewing my nails to bits, like that'll help anything. Adam comes in.

"You look tense," he says. "You okay?"

I tell him about Patrick. About the warehouses. About the fact that I've just gone from 'bit tense' to DEFCON 1.

He listens. Nods. Massages my knotted shoulders. Says all the right things.

"You're going to be amazing," he says. "You're the smartest person I know. And I know someone who won twenty pounds on a pub quiz machine, so I know what I'm talking about."

He's smiling, earnest. He *means* it.

I smile back and try not to let Adam see my insides are turning somersaults.

"I'll be right back," I say, forcing brightness into my voice and giving him a kiss. "Just need a wee."

I feel ridiculous. Hiding from my own boyfriend in my own bathroom. He's proud of me. Which should be lovely. It is lovely. So why do I have this terrible feeling everything's going to crumble all around me? Maybe it's because now I've got another person I can't afford to disappoint.

The more faith he has in me, the more it feels like a weight pressing down on me. I've stuck my neck out and made big promises. If I mess up now, it'll be a terrible black mark against me. All the pressure of that expectation, from Patrick, from Adam. I *have* to live up to it now, or I can kiss goodbye to my job, my wages and my chances of getting back to university. I *have* to succeed.

I splash cold water on my face and stare at my reflection.

You're doing great. You're absolutely fine. You're not about to crack.

Then, somewhere from deep inside, I hear Justin's voice, "You've got to take charge. You need a killer instinct."

I shudder and try to shake him off. But the cold water doesn't help much. Nothing does. Because now the pressure isn't coming from outside. It's coming from me.

I didn't want to become this. The boss. The fixer. The woman who saves the Scarborough branch. But I've sold that version of me now – to Patrick, and to Adam. And if I don't deliver, the whole thing collapses like a sandcastle.

CHAPTER 25
OLIVER

He doesn't know what to do with himself.

He feels a void in his life again, now she is no longer there to fill it.

Grace is gone.

Not dead, of course. Not lost in the way Julia is lost. But absent nonetheless. He feels it like a severed limb. The coaching sessions were the highlight of his days. She was once so open and so trusting, but now she seems behind glass, unreachable. He imagines himself like a ship, tossed on the waves of a storm. Grace was the anchor that gave stability and structure to his life. But now that anchor is lost.

He tries not to be bitter. He recalls what she said. She's flourishing. He helped her do that. That's what matters. Of course.

But he's not blind to the irony: the better she does, the more irrelevant he becomes. And though it's only been a few days since she politely thanked him and said she no longer needed coaching, the embers of the fire have gone cold. It already feels like an ending.

Loneliness is not new to Oliver. He remembers it from

school – the feeling of not belonging. He recalls the way the other children would band together on the playground, a blur of laughter and elbows, while he hovered at the edges like an afterthought. When he did get attention, it was hostile. At home, his parents were kind but distant, a pair of shadows moving through the rooms.

He wanders Scarborough, threading his way through the streets he used to pass through as a child, like a ghost retracing the living world. He's been trying to call it 'mindful walking', the sort he used to recommend to clients: take in the world, feel the ground beneath your feet, the air on your skin. But he's just looping back and forth with nowhere to go.

He climbs up through the old town, where the terraces are tighter and the streets feel like they might close in on you. He tries to do the things locals do. He orders a bacon bap from the kiosk by the lifeboat station. He watches the old men play bowls in Peasholm Park. He paces the high street and pretends to browse shop windows. He hasn't the drive or enthusiasm for his other clients, doesn't return their calls, and his appointment diary is empty.

He walks up through the quiet roads behind the Esplanade, dragging his feet along the uneven paving slabs, past shuttered guesthouses with faded floral curtains still drawn in the afternoon and black mould blooming at the edges of windowpanes. He passes the church with its desperate, needy signpost – *You're one in EIGHT BILLION and GOD loves YOU* – and heads down toward the Italian Gardens. The wind off the sea bites through his coat, and the air tastes faintly of salt. He stands at the rail and looks out across the water. It's slate-grey and restless, churning with white tips, stretching to a point lost in mist where the sea meets the sky.

Below him, the gardens stretch out in formal terraces, half-dormant for winter. The place is bleak at this time of year. The flowerbeds are ragged with frost-burnt stems. The lily pond is filmed with debris, beer cans like mini icebergs. Life stripped back to the bone.

He walks the loop slowly, pausing at the benches.

For Rita & William Froggatt – Who enjoyed this place.

To Edith. A Promise Kept! Enjoy The View Forever.

In Loving Memory of Margaret and George Pickering.

"COUNT YOUR BLESSINGS"

The past clawing into the present with skeletal fingers. Each one a reminder that even the loved become the forgotten, eventually. Memories to bring joy, but all the more depressing for that. Grave markers with armrests.

He picks a bench near the top and sits, hugging his coat tighter. He thinks about Alison. The life they'd built together in Leeds. Nights with pasta and fruity red wine, watching quiz shows on the sofa. The way she used to hold a wine glass with both hands, like it might run away. Her laugh. Sunday mornings when they swapped the paper back and forth, each quietly knowing the other was the safest place they'd ever been.

He'd done good work then, too. Therapy that made a difference. He mattered.

Then Julia happened. Then... all of it.

He came skulking back here, like a sick dog crawling behind the furniture. And that's what he was – licking his injuries.

Until Grace.

He hadn't seen her coming. Someone who needed more help than she knew. He saw in her something broken, like Julia had been, but still savable. Still warm.

He'd saved her.

He knows he shouldn't feel bitter. This must be what parents feel when their children grow up and no longer ask for help. You're proud, of course. You want them to thrive. It's a celebration when they fly the nest. But it stings – the way they leave you behind without looking back.

The bench is too cold now. He gets up, hands buried deep in his coat pockets, and drifts in the direction of town. He lets his eyes flick up the road toward the row of buildings where her office sits. He tells himself it's coincidence he's ended here. Just a stroll. No different from a dozen other people doing the same.

But he's already mapped her office hours in his head.

THAT WEEK, he finds himself loitering in the Italian Gardens most lunchtimes. He brings a sandwich in a brown paper bag, or a flask of soup, blowing on his frozen hands, waiting for her to come out. She doesn't. Once, he sees her fleetingly, on the phone as she exits the office, pacing and frowning, before she disappears down the street.

She doesn't notice him. Not once. He tells himself it's because she's busy, not because she's avoiding him.

He starts walking where she walks. Not following her. Just aligning. Merely taking an interest, gently wondering if their paths might cross. One day, she heads down Ramshill Road toward the seafront. She's moving quickly, head down, wrapped in a thick green scarf. He crosses to the other side of the road and trails behind at a safe distance. She pauses near the Rotunda Museum to lace her shoe, then moves on. He follows.

He imagines how it will go, the accidental meeting. "Grace?" he'll say, surprised but warm. She'll look up and smile, pleased to see him. "I've been meaning to get in touch," she'll say. "The support you gave me was amazing." They'll have coffee. Catch up.

But when it finally happens, it's nothing like that.

He's coming up Westborough when he sees her crossing at the lights. He angles toward her, waving gently.

"Grace?"

She stops. Her eyes register him and then immediately scan the street. "Oh," she says. "Hi."

"You look well," he says, breath a little short from the hill. "Busy?"

She smiles tightly. "Always."

There's a pause. He tries again. "I was just thinking, we never really got the chance to reflect on the work we did together. Maybe we could grab a coffee sometime? Or a drink?"

"Oh. I–" she falters. "I don't think that's a good idea."

The smile is still on her face, but it seems plastered on like a mask. She's uncomfortable. He can see that now. She must be under terrible pressure at work to look so tense.

"I just think," she adds, "it might be... complicated. Thank you, though. For everything. I really do appreciate it."

And then she's gone, walking fast, her boots clipping the pavement.

He imagines the workload she must be facing now. In such a hurry. Hardly time for lunch, let alone chitchat or a coffee. He'd love to suggest ways in which she might approach managing the stress to avoid burnout. He stands there for a long time, the wind cutting into him.

Later, at home, he sits in his living room, dinner on the table, shepherd's pie untouched.

He replays the conversation over and over. Her tone. Her body language. That little twitch in her jaw, like she was holding something back.

He can't believe she said no. After everything he's done.

She's confused. That must be it. She's overwhelmed. New job, new pressure. That kind of stress warps how people see things. She doesn't understand. She doesn't *know*. If she knew

– if she understood what he did for her – then she wouldn't walk away so casually.

She'd be grateful.

She *should* be grateful.

He grips the knife and fork until his knuckles go white.

It's not her fault, he tells himself. She's confused. That's what's happening. She just needs more time.

If only she knew.

If only she understood.

She's *wrong* about him.

He's sure he can make her see that.

CHAPTER 26
GRACE

"So I just want you both to keep your ears open," I say.

Kyle's leaning back in his chair, arms folded, legs stretched like he's on a sun lounger in Marbella. Mohammed's got his notepad open, but I can see it's mostly doodles and a crude cartoon of what looks suspiciously like me with devil horns. Wonderful.

"If you come across any leads – people looking for space, light industrial, that kind of thing – any ideas, I'd like to know."

They're staring at me like I've announced we're pivoting out of estate agency and into circus management. Mohammed nods once, slowly. Kyle shifts restlessly in his chair and sighs dramatically, like I've asked him to donate a kidney.

"I mean, obviously, without it taking time away from your core work," I add. "It's just a bit of prospecting, if you've got a quiet half hour between viewings."

Kyle snorts. "A quiet half hour. That's adorable."

"I'm just saying–" I start, but Kyle's on a rant.

"I'd *love* a quiet half hour, Grace. I really would. Maybe I could get my nails done. But when I'm not out on viewings, I'm doing feedback calls. Or trying to hit my sales targets so I can afford electricity this winter. I'm flat-out doing valuations, fielding buyer queries, managing chains–"

"Chains?" I interrupt. "You've got *two* properties under offer."

He blinks. "Which is two more than you."

I don't rise to it. I won't give him the satisfaction. Mohammed watches us go back and forth, his head swivelling like he's watching the tennis.

"Look, I know you're busy–"

"And if I'm doing less proper work just to chase ghosts in disused warehouses, where's my commission going to come from, eh?" he says, all mock-aggrieved. "Do we have a bonus scheme now for flogging asbestos-riddled death traps?"

"It's a team effort," I say, fighting the urge to shout at him. "It's about the bigger picture."

Kyle grins, leans back in his chair and laces his fingers behind his head like he's won. "Sure. Happy to help with your treasure hunt whenever I'm not out earning my actual wage."

Mohammed keeps out of it and pretends to have something fascinating to deal with on his phone.

The meeting wraps up with lots of vague nods and the sense that neither of them is going to lift a finger unless it directly benefits them. They shuffle back to their desks, deliberately slow. I stay at the glass table in the middle of the office with my stomach in knots. So that's where we are. We've stopped pretending. They're not just lazy or unhelpful – they're actively undermining me, willing me to fail. Hoping I'll mess this up so one of them can swoop in and claim the job. They don't care which of them it is. Just so long as it's not me.

I head back to my desk, and when I turn my monitor on,

the bloody cat screensaver is back. Except, instead of having its thumb up, it's now crying. Showers of tears are cascading across the screen, and the speech bubble is flashing 'ALEXA, PLAY "EVERYBODY HURTS" BY R.E.M.'

Kyle coughs loudly behind me. "You okay, Gracie? Computer giving you grief again?"

I'm fizzing with rage.

I try to shake it off and go back to the research like my life depends on it – because it does. If there's an angle to turn what I've promised into something concrete, I have to find it. I pull a big wodge of papers from my bag – *The Guardian, The Observer, The Telegraph* and *The Financial Times* – and start combing through the business sections. *The Financial Times* makes me feel like I'm trying to decode ancient scripture, but I'm getting the hang of it. I've made a list of seven businesses that might – *might* – have an interest in expanding into our neck of the woods. If I can find even one lead, something solid to show Patrick when he checks in again, it might buy me a bit more time.

But it's impossible to concentrate, because Kyle keeps pinging bullshit questions over. What's the Wi-Fi password? Where do we keep spare light bulbs? Have I seen the petty cash for some teabags?

It's all stuff he knows. After the third interruption, I stand up and walk over.

"What's your coffee order?"

His smirk falters. "Wait, you're going?"

"No," I say, producing my credit card. "You are."

He looks from me to the card like I've offered him a shit in a box. I smile sweetly. "Cappuccino for me. Get whatever Mohammed wants, too. And something sweet for the team. Cakes. My treat."

He doesn't move.

"I'll need the receipt," I add.

"Sure," he says. "Happy to be of service." He takes the card and heads out, walking with the sort of flounce kids do when they've just been sent to their rooms. But he's a kid who can't resist the lure of a free doughnut.

I sit back down feeling... not triumphant exactly, but something close. Like I've reminded him who's in charge.

Which lasts about three seconds. As he leaves the office, he stares back at me through the window with a look that lingers just too long. He's not smirking now. He's all pure hatred. It's quite a shock and it sends a shiver right down me.

But I can't let ruffling his feathers get to me. Sometimes, to stay afloat, you've got to paddle harder than anyone else. Even if you're scared the tide's pulling you under.

CHAPTER 27
OLIVER

He knows her schedule. Her patterns. He knows where she gets coffee in the morning. He knows her walk – businesslike, but with a slight hesitation at pedestrian crossings, like she's already halfway inside her next meeting.

He sees her everywhere. A glimpse of her hair in a crowd. A coat that looks like hers in a shop doorway. Yesterday, he followed a woman all the way into WHSmith before realising it wasn't her.

HE DISTRACTS himself with a walk down to the front. He always thinks of the sea as grounding, its timeless enormity making his concerns seem petty and insignificant in comparison. But today, even the sea looks off. It's low tide, the water dragging itself reluctantly away from the harbour wall like it's too much effort.

He goes into the Harbour Bar and orders an ice cream sundae. But it just sits there, taunting him by being the sort of thing someone having fun would eat. He tries a mouthful, but its claggy sweetness isn't to his taste. He's embarrassed by what the girls in their pastel blue and yellow aprons might think if he leaves it uneaten, so he pretends he needs the toilet, then sneaks out through the side door.

Later, at dusk, the craving to see her again becomes unbearable.

He tells himself it's nothing – just a walk, some air, no agenda. But he walks past the estate agent's again. Slower this time. More deliberate.

She's still there. He can see her now, standing by the printer, arms folded. She's in conversation with that lanky moron, Kyle. Oliver watches their interaction like a lip-reader decoding a spy tape. He doesn't like the way Kyle's smirking. Nor does he care for the way Grace shifts her weight from one foot to the other. Defensive.

Though she may not see that she needs it, *he* still sees himself as her coach, her supporter. Her protector.

Maybe she's afraid. Afraid of what it means to get better. Afraid of how much she needs him.

Or maybe – maybe – someone's poisoning her against him. Patrick Lyle, perhaps. He seems the type. Slick. Smiling. A politician in estate agent clothing. Probably wants Grace in his pocket. Doesn't want her thinking for herself.

Oliver checks his watch. He's been here for about two hours now. It's dark and very cold. He can barely feel his feet, but he daren't leave his post. Kyle and the other one, Mohammed, leave together just after 5.00 p.m.

Now Grace is on her own in the office.

At 6:07 p.m. she emerges from the building. She heads east, coat collar turned up against the cold. He waits a beat, then follows from a distance. Not close enough so she'll know he's there, but near enough to ensure she's okay.

She stops outside a corner shop. Goes in. Comes out with a paper bag. Walks another hundred yards to the bus stop and sits. A car slows nearby and he jolts, spinning round. No one's looking at him. Just a taxi, waiting for a fare.

She's checking her phone. He can't read her expression. Then a bus pulls in, and she boards without looking back. He stays rooted to the pavement until the bus pulls away, then he walks home, fast, adrenaline humming in his ears.

That night, he can't settle. He keeps composing email messages in his mind. But he decides not to send them. It's not the right time.

She'll get in touch when she's ready.

She'll come round.

And when she does, he'll be there.

THE NEXT MORNING, Oliver stands at the kitchen window, watching the wind pick at the washing line. A single forgotten peg swings like a metronome. The kettle begins to boil, and steam fogs the edge of the window, a slow blur that spreads until the whole garden looks out of focus.

He checks his phone. There's another voicemail from Maureen, the second he's ignored. She'll be wanting to arrange another session he hasn't the heart for.

He wonders what he would say to himself if he were his therapist.

"Oliver," he says aloud to the empty room, one hand resting on the countertop. "Do you think you might be over-investing in a single outcome?"

His voice, breaking the silence, almost makes him laugh. Stating the obvious. He knows that much. But is it unhealthy? Or just... focus? Surely there's a difference.

"Let's reframe this. Let's look at the behaviour, not just the thought. Is it serving you?"

Is it serving him? No.

But that's not the same as saying it's wrong.

He carries a mug of tea into the hallway and pauses, noticing the paint on the banister, cracked and chipped at the curve of the handrail. How long has it looked like that? Years, probably. Decades. He suddenly becomes aware of the air in here – thick, musty, over-warmed by the gas heater. The smell of old upholstery and mothballs.

He looks around the hallway and sees it properly for the first time in months.

This isn't a house. It's a mausoleum.

He lives in a memory, like a ghost haunting the life he once lived. Every surface holds the echo of someone else – his father's coat still hanging in the hall, mimicking the old man's stooped shoulders; the finial on the newel post where his mother used to pause before puffing her way upstairs.

This can't go on.

He starts with the upstairs wardrobe, dragging out suits his father hadn't worn in the last ten years of his life. Fusty wool and elbow patches, the scent of pipe tobacco. Into bin bags they go. Shirts, socks, drawers of tangled cufflinks and ties intertwined like fighting snakes. His mother's things are harder. He finds her perfume, the bottle still half full. The smell hits him like an ambush. Her dressing table, still laid out with a ring of talcum powder and a cracked hairbrush.

He moves quickly and methodically. Three bags to the charity shop, five to the tip. Old VHS tapes, yellowed books, spines cracked, shedding their pages like autumn leaves. He finds one drawer stuffed with envelopes, letters from people whose names he doesn't recognise. His parents' friends, presumably, long-dead or demented. He throws those out, too.

He sets about his old bedroom. Dog-eared exercise books, an ancient copy of *The Guinness Book of Records*, a badgeless green jumper from the miserable two weeks he was a Cub Scout.

Then, under his old school reports, in a box labelled *Oliver
– Primary to Sixth Form*, he finds a small tube of paper, like an
ancient scroll. He unrolls it.

A photo.

Class of 2003, maybe 2004. The usual tiered rows of sullen
teenage faces, boys in worn, stretched jumpers, girls in scratty
ponytails and cheap hairbands. He doesn't want to look, not
really, but his eyes flicker down the ranks almost invol-
untarily.

There he is. Fourth row, end of the line. He'd be about
fifteen here. Even in the black and white of the printout, his
hollow, vacant expression looks bruised. A skinny, haunted
thing. His blazer hanging off him, his collar chewed with
nerves. The boy everyone laughed at.

He goes along the row, the parade of tormentors. Faces
that make something twist inside him. There's Ash, scruffy
and tie-less, grinning like he owns the place. And others,
names he doesn't know but whose faces are etched into his
brain, who threw pencils at him, tipped his bag out, pissed in
his PE shoes. Oliver can feel his stomach turn. He glances at
rows below him, younger kids who inherited the idea he was
fair game for bullying from the older ones and joined in.

But then he sees her.

Three rows down. Left-hand corner.

She's younger. Must be twelve. Thirteen at most. But
there's no mistaking the round curve of her cheekbones, the
slight tilt of her head.

Grace.

He freezes.

Grace went to his school.

She never said.

She's looked him in the eye, spoken to him like he was
just some stranger hired to coach her – and all the while, she
knew. She knew who he was.

Which means she knew *what* he was. The weakling. The joke.

His stomach drops. He thinks back to her face in their sessions. The way she tilted her head. That slight smile. The glances she sometimes gave him at the end of a sentence.

Were those sympathy? Or pity?

Or were they amusement? Was she laughing at him?

He blinks at the photo, his skin buzzing like it's been plugged into the mains. He tries to find something in her expression, some hint of what she thought of him. But twelve-year-old girls don't put those kinds of thoughts in school photos.

He can't breathe for a second.

She knew. Of course she did. Everyone in that place knew him. And now she's seen him again – broken, still living in his parents' house. Perhaps she thinks he hasn't changed at all.

But surely she can't be like the others. She came to him for help. She let herself cry in front of him. She told him things she hadn't told anyone.

Or was that just another manipulation? He can't be sure anymore.

He has to know. He has to find out if she's made a fool of him all over again. And if she has laughed at him – if she is like the others…

Well–

Then he'll know what he has to do.

CHAPTER 28
GRACE

I stare at next week's calendar. The date's been sitting there, nagging away at me, lurking in my path like a landmine.

Bridget's birthday.

It's been two weeks since that awful dinner I walked out of, and I've not heard a word from her. I've wanted to call, but I left it, acting like some stupid teenage girl after a first date, hoping she'd call first. But she hasn't.

I've told myself a dozen times that it's her problem. That I've reached out enough. But the truth is she's my sister. I know how to tie my shoelaces because she showed me. It's ridiculous, this silent standoff.

So before I can talk myself out of it, I send her a text.

Hey. I'd love to celebrate your birthday – & share my good news. I'll book the 4 of us a table. Nxt Friday okay? My treat x

The little blue ticks appear under the message almost immediately. But that's it. No reply. Nothing. Read. Ignored. Perfect.

I go onto Google Maps and look up spa hotels that aren't too far away. I find a really lovely one up the coast in Ravenscar that has a deal on. It's got a gym as well, and a swimming pool. Even though money is tight with only me working, I book us a weekend package. Overnight stay, two treatments each, champagne afternoon tea. I imagine us wrapped in white robes, and drinking fizz in the hot tub, slagging off old boyfriends. It makes me smile. It's a stupid spend, but I figure it's worth it. I want to fix this. I want us to be okay again. Sisters, not strangers.

I send her the confirmation link with a message.

Booked us a girlie spa weekend for your birthday. Just the 2 of us. Pampering & bubbles. U deserve it. x

Blue ticks again, but no reply.

The following day I head into work. Kyle's done something weird with the printer settings, so every document comes out in an enormous font. Plus, my spellchecker has been set to French. I feel more like a crèche assistant than a manager.

But I'm still here. I haven't been sacked. That's a win.

I try to concentrate on some commercial property leads for a couple of hours, then look at my phone messages again. Still nothing. I hate myself for checking. I feel like a needy teenager. Still, I go ahead and book a restaurant and text Bridget the details.

Eventually, Friday night rolls around. I dig out the dress I wore to Adam's brother's wedding. It smells a bit musty from where it's been hung in the wardrobe so long, but I give it a spray with perfume. I do my hair and make an effort with my makeup. I look at myself in the mirror and feel pleased with how I've scrubbed up.

Adam puts on a smart shirt. A real one. With buttons. He shaves.

"Buy a ticket, why don't you?" he says when he spots me staring at him.

"Happily," I say. "Front row, please. I can't help it. You're gorgeous."

"I'm not the only one," he says, giving me a sultry look. And I do feel nice, getting dressed up. He wanders over to me and we have a little snog.

We get to the restaurant. It's the new Italian one in the old town, cosy, quite posh, but buzzy enough to feel normal. I'm excited to see Bridget, but weirdly nervous.

We get shown to our table and wait.

And wait.

Fifteen minutes past the booking. I'm just checking my phone to see if she's texted that she's on her way, or has got held up, when Dave rings. Not Bridget. Dave. He sounds sheepish.

"Grace, I'm really sorry. We're not going to make it. A thing came up with Bridget's work today. They pulled her in last-minute for a meeting with the regional boss-guy and it's dragged on. He's only in town today and they've insisted they carry on over dinner."

What a load of bullshit.

"Right," I say. "Of course."

Adam's looking at me all puzzled. He can tell from my tone of voice that something's up.

"She's only just messaged me," Dave goes on, "and she just can't get out of it. Anyway, I'm really sorry."

He does sound genuinely sorry. But the apology's from him, not Bridget. She couldn't even be arsed to lie to me in person.

After we hang up, I just stare at the menu.

"Don't tell me; she's not coming?" Adam asks, already reaching for my hand.

"Nope. Too busy apparently, in an 'urgent' meeting. What kind of urgent meeting can she have all night? She works in bloody car rentals!"

Adam leans across the table and puts his hand on mine. "Sorry, luv." He wrinkles his nose in a sympathetic smile.

I'm so pissed off. And I'm hurt. I can feel tears welling up inside me, so I hang onto the anger instead. I'm buggered if I'm going to let myself cry. "Let's just go home," I say.

Adam shakes his head. "No," he says. "No way. We're out. We're dressed. I've had my annual wash and put on clean underpants."

I smile. "Are you sure? How's your neck?"

He rubs his neck a little. "It's fine. Let's stay. We can still celebrate your promotion 'til my head comes off."

I nod, but part of me wants to tell him the truth – that I don't want the bloody promotion. I just want enough money to leave. But that would sound ungrateful. And a bit insane. And anyway, he's right. Sod her.

"Alright then," I say. "Let's order one of everything."

The champagne is eye-wateringly expensive, so we pull back from that and toast to my promotion with prosecco. Adam tells me how proud he is and how amazing I've been. I have pasta and chicken and tiramisu.

But my stomach keeps knotting. My own sister couldn't even text back. The thought nags away at me all weekend.

Back at work on Monday, I try to focus, but my head's all over the place. I find myself rereading the same sentence in an email about ten times, not taking anything in. Kyle asks me if I need any help 'decoding the big words' and I nearly launch a stapler at him.

Eventually, I can't take it anymore. I text Dave and ask if he's got time to meet for a quick chat. He suggests The Sailors Arms at 5.30 p.m.

When I arrive, he's already there, at a corner table, pint in hand.

"Thanks for meeting me," I say.

"Of course." He pushes a seat out for me beside him. "I figured this was coming."

Now I'm here, I don't really know how to start what I

want to say. The best I can manage is "Look, Bridget... Is she okay?"

"She's fine," he says. "Busy and stressed. But fine."

"I just... I don't get it. She's my sister. I've really tried. I've sent texts, booked a whole bloody spa weekend. She didn't even say thank you."

Dave shifts uncomfortably and sips his drink. "She saw them. She just... didn't know what to say."

"That's insane. I texted her three times."

"Grace, look. I probably shouldn't get involved, but..."

I lean in. "But what?"

He sighs. "She feels like... you always got the spotlight. With your parents. At the end, when they were ill... She thinks you monopolised them."

I laugh. "You mean like, with hospital appointments or changing adult nappies?"

But Dave doesn't laugh. He doesn't even blink. That's when it really comes home to me: this isn't a joke.

"I'm not saying it's true," he adds quickly. "But that's how she sees it. Like you made yourself the Good Daughter. That you came home and took over everything. And now you've got the house, and she's... left out."

I stare at the sticky pub table, the overlapping rings of old beer like some kind of baffling Venn diagram. None of it makes sense.

"I didn't swoop in with a halo. I came back because no one else bloody did. She could've been there too, but she wasn't. So I was."

"Feelings aren't always logical."

"Right. Because giving up uni, wiping Dad's chin for two years, and holding Mum's hand while she died – that was just me stealing the spotlight, was it?"

"She sees you in the house she grew up in and it just... gets under her skin."

"Then why doesn't she just *talk* to me?" I say. "Why act like I don't exist?"

He spreads his hands helplessly. "She thinks you turned them against her. That they loved you more because you were there and she wasn't."

My throat tightens. "That's insane."

"But that's how she sees it."

We sit in silence.

Outside in the car park, it's dark and cold, and it's started raining. We stand under the entrance porch, doing up our coats.

"Look, I don't want to get caught in the middle of something between you two," he says.

"I know. I'm sorry I messaged you."

"No, it's okay. There's just nothing I can do about it. Sorry."

He gives me a hug. A kind of awkward shoulder-press.

"I'm sorry," he says. "I really am."

"Thanks, Dave."

I watch him drive away, his taillights shrinking into the dark, and I just stand there. Then I head home alone, hands in pockets, keys cold in my hand, wondering what the hell I did to deserve being shut out by the only person I thought would always be on my side.

CHAPTER 29
OLIVER

He sees them from the far end of the pub car park, half-shielded by a hedge. It's dusk and the light from the porch silhouettes them in a grainy amber, like a bad dream caught on CCTV. Stabs of thin rain cut across the light like knives.

Oliver squints behind the branches. At first, he can't hear what they're saying, only fragments. They're standing close, too close for anything casual. Comfortable and familiar.

Grace leans in and hugs the man. Her breath fogs in the air.

The man's face tips into profile. For a moment, Oliver thinks he's made a mistake. That maybe he's just tired or overwrought, seeing things. But then the man turns, and Oliver sees him properly. Recognition hits him like a sledgehammer to the chest.

Ash.

They release their embrace, and Ash walks towards his car. Oliver hears Grace call after, "Thanks, Dave."

The name might be *Dave* now, but the face is pure Ash. *Dave Ashworth*. Ash. Unmistakably. He'll never forget that face. The grinning puppet-master of his adolescent humiliation. The ringleader of everything. The boy who ruined his life.

A flush rises up Oliver's neck.

And now here it is again. Ash laughing with Grace. Something inside him twists. She's not just meeting him. She *knows* him. She's *close* to him. Like old friends. Like allies.

He stands there puzzling it out, barely aware of the rain and the cold.

Of course. It all fits. She never once mentioned school. Never once asked if they'd met before. She knew. She recognised him the moment they met. Of course she did. It's the very reason she came to him. The bullied kid. The school joke. Sticky Fingers.

He stares at her again, still standing in the light of the pub entrance after Ash has left, watching her companion drive away. Not a flicker of shame or discomfort.

His stomach churns with the familiar hollowness of embarrassment and humiliation. All this time, he thought he was helping her, rescuing her. From Justin. From her job. From herself. All the vulnerability, the emotional honesty... and she played him. Just like Ash did all those years ago. *You're different, Oliver. You're all right.* Before asking him to watch the door. Before setting him up to take the fall.

Grace is no different. Kindness first, just enough to make him feel seen. Then the manipulation. The appeal to his better nature. She must have been watching him get sucked in, week after week, reeling out her rehearsed vulnerabilities. The emotional lure. She cried. She talked about the pressure. The despair. She made herself the victim and him the saviour.

What if she never needed saving?

He thought he'd done it *for her*. But maybe it wasn't his idea at all. Maybe the whole idea was *hers*.

She hadn't asked him to kill Justin. Of course she hadn't. Not explicitly. Not with words. She was far too smart for that.

The way she walked out of that last session, radiant with confidence, with the new job she inherited from the dead man. She'd said it was his coaching that saved her. But what if it was something else entirely?

His mind races. Scene after scene replays itself – but now with a new script, darker and sharper. Grace in her office, letting Oliver glimpse her frustration. Grace in the sessions, timid and damaged. Pulling him in at just the right moment. Like a fisherman giving a cunning tug on the line.

He suddenly sees the whole thing in reverse, like rewinding a film. Grace telling him about the bullying. Grace with the watery eyes. Grace with the sobs she never quite let out. It wasn't trauma. It was bait. A lure.

It was all a performance. She manipulated him; she *forced* him into killing Justin. She wanted the path clear. And now she's got everything she wanted. She's the boss. All poise and authority.

And here she is, celebrating with *Ash*. Hugging *Ash*.

Oliver closes his eyes for a second. The anger rises like acid. His head feels tight, his heart hammering. She's just like the others. He can feel himself being pulled backwards, to the lonely boy with the oversized blazer. Does she still see him as that boy in the back row? The joke? The freak?

He watches her walk away from the pub until she disappears into the shadows. He scrubs at his eyes with the heel of his hand, trying to get his thoughts straight. There's a high whine ringing in his ears, like a kettle screaming. For a moment, the image of Julia flashes up. Julia, who trusted him. Julia, who needed his help. Julia, who hadn't made it. That was different. That was a failure.

This is betrayal.

His mind won't stop. The shape of it all becomes clear. Grace is not some wounded bird. She's a predator. She didn't need his help. She used it. She used *him,* just like all the bullies did before.

It's a revelation. It's like waking from a dream, realising he's been sleepwalking for weeks, maybe longer. He wasn't coaching her. He was being played. Maybe that's why she shut down the coaching so quickly. Going back to Kyle and Mohammed, telling them what a weirdo he is. They're all in the office laughing. He can picture it now, Kyle mimicking his voice, Grace cracking up. And her laughter over drinks with Ash. *God, he actually did it. He actually killed Justin. What a mug.*

She thought she could use him. She thought he was weak.

Rage moves through him like something physical, hot and sharp. Maybe *this* was always what he was meant for. Some people are here to help. Others are here to punish.

His pulse steadies as something calcifies in his chest. She has no idea what she's unleashed.

It's not about saving her now.

Grace doesn't need saving.

She needs *stopping*.

PART THREE

CHAPTER 30
GRACE

The office is full-on playground warfare.

It's not just the pranks. My phone charger's tangled in about a million knots again. The Ethernet cable looks like it's been yanked out and jammed back in. And I keep thinking about those weird transactions on my bank statement last week. Just little things - £4.99 for some random app I don't remember downloading. A Deliveroo order I'm sure I never made. Other stuff. I've checked with my bank and they say they're all legit.

Could Kyle and Mohammed be using my phone? I leave it on my desk all the time. What's to stop them picking it up when I nip into the kitchen or take a call on the landline in the side room? It wouldn't take much. A few taps on Apple Pay and they're buying vape juice and novelty socks in my name. I wouldn't put it past them.

But how would they even know my security questions? There's no way. Still, I don't trust them. I change all my passwords, shove my phone into my drawer and lock it. No more being careless.

They're always watching me too. Trying to sneak a look at

my computer screen. Trying to earwig on my phone calls. They've started doing this thing where they go quiet when I walk past, which would be fine if they didn't start smirking like schoolboys, like I'm some sort of travelling circus act, The Incredible Failing Estate Agent. *Roll up, roll up! Watch her drop the ball! Gasp as she botches another lead! Thrill as she fails to tame two overpaid man-babies!*

They're not the only ones. It's only Wednesday, and Patrick's already had two Zooms with me this week and just emailed to say he'll "pop in" tomorrow. I don't buy it for a second. It won't be a friendly drop-in. It'll be him sniffing around like a fox by the bins outside a chicken shop, looking for weakness. He's absurdly nice about it, of course – cuff-links and charm and that whole "I just want to understand" thing. But I'm not stupid. This is the prelude to a seal cull. I smile on the calls, act upbeat, drop in words like *momentum* and *strategic potential* so I'll sound like I know what I'm doing. But the warehouse plan's stalling, and I feel like a con artist flogging knock-off Rolexes from the back of a van.

It feels like I'm being watched from all angles. When I walk home after work, I keep looking over my shoulder, half-expecting someone to be there. I tell myself it's just the pressure, but still… it's like something's shadowing me. Another week of this and I'll be checking under my bed, like a frightened kid looking for monsters.

At lunch I go out to the Italian Gardens with a takeaway coffee. It's where I usually reset, breathe, and pretend I'm not drowning. But today the calm doesn't land. Something's off. The air's sharp and cold, and the wind keeps dragging eerie seagull cries across. I sit on the damp bench with my cardboard cup and try to shake the feeling, but even the gulls look suspicious. One of them tilts its head like it knows something I don't. I catch myself turning around. There's nothing there, of course. Just the churn of the tide and someone's Labrador snorting at a sandwich wrapper. But I still keep checking. I can't shake the feeling I'm being tracked. Like someone's watching me come apart, one bit at a time.

With Patrick coming tomorrow, I make a decision. Kyle and Mohammed are off residential sales as of now. Full commercial focus. It's a risk, cutting our income stream to prop up a long shot, but the only way to survive this is one massive win with those warehouses. Eggs, meet basket.

I use some of our ad budget for a feature in a trade magazine I've found called *The European Business Register*. It's a gamble, but I've come up blank on UK leads, and I've already exhausted every angle in the local press. We need to pitch to overseas investors. Business types after cheap units near a port. Some tech warehouse, or designer furniture importer, or maybe a craft gin bottling plant or something. I don't bloody know. But the buyers are out there. Somewhere. They have to be.

Problem is, the photos we've got are crap. They make the place look like a condemned power station, not a thrilling multi-use commercial opportunity. We need something that says *industrial renaissance* rather than *apocalyptic rat museum*.

Kyle's our best photographer, unfortunately. He's got that whole faux-artsy vibe and acts like he's Stanley Kubrick – but it's the one area where he actually knows what he's doing.

"I knew it," he says, as I dangle the agency camera in front of him. "You love me really."

"You're marginally better than a potato with a lens. Don't let it go to your head."

We're on the verge of what sounds like office bants, but of course, he has to ruin it.

"Can't though. Sorry. I'm already double-booked – *working*, you know, selling houses, covering for other people's mistakes, carrying this branch on my beautifully sculpted shoulders..."

"You're doing the shoot," I say emphatically. "That's final." I pull him off a viewing and throw him his anorak. "Where did you park the car?"

The car, surprise, surprise, is disgusting. I haven't done a viewing for weeks, so Kyle and Mohammed have taken it over. It's like chimps have got into it at a safari park. Sweet wrappers, crushed cans, a half-eaten sausage roll still in its greasy paper bag. It stinks of Lynx. I grimace and tell him to clean it out later.

"What?" he says. "It's lived-in."

"It's a biohazard."

He sets off like he's on *Top Gear*, braking hard at every roundabout and singing along to something that sounds like a car alarm with lyrics. We head out of town, along the derelict stretch of the old industrial estate. Rows of skeletal buildings with rusted signage and chain-link fencing gone slack. The warehouse we're pitching is the biggest. An enormous concrete shell, with shattered windows like it's had its teeth punched out in a fight.

We pull up in the huge, empty car park. I unlock the gate, and we step inside.

Pale daylight filters in through the gaps, making long, striped lines on the floor. It's vast and eerie, and silent, except for the tick-tick-tick of water dripping from somewhere high up in the rafters. Rain's come in through the broken glass and pooled across the floor in shallow, oily lakes. Moss is colonising the corners and weeds have begun to push through the concrete, forcing their way between the cracks. An old forklift sits rusting in one corner, like a fossilised relic from some ancient civilisation.

Kyle whistles. "Well, this isn't creepy at all."

"Don't be a dick."

"No, seriously," he says, lifting the camera. "I think this is where they shot all those *Saw* films."

I ignore him and walk further in. A broken pipe hangs from the ceiling and I nearly take my eye out with it in the gloom. I slip on something greasy hidden under a puddle and yelp, windmilling to keep balance. I just about catch myself against a rusted support beam. When I look, my hand is grazed. I stare at it as tiny pinpricks of blood come to the surface.

Kyle doesn't move to help.

"Careful," he says. "You could have a nasty accident in here."

He says it with a half-smile, but there's something in the way his eyes linger that makes my spine tighten. I remember that stare he gave me in the office a few weeks ago, full of hate. He looks like he wouldn't lose sleep if I fell and broke my neck.

There's no one around. No witnesses. No security. If something happened, it would be hours before anyone found me. My palm burns. It's ridiculous – I know that – but something cold creeps into my chest. I think of Justin. How he was killed. The hit-and-run. No suspects.

For a split second, I wonder. Could Kyle have...?

No. That's mad.

Isn't it?

I glance at him. He's watching me.

"I'm fine," I say quickly, wrapping a tissue around my hand.

We walk back toward the centre of the room. I scribble notes in a pad, while I keep him in my peripheral vision. My heart's beating too fast. The stupid thing is, I *don't* believe Kyle killed Justin. Probably. Almost certainly. But when someone keeps trying to undermine you, you overthink everything.

He goes behind me to take some photos from the far end.

There's a sudden noise, and I spin round in fear. But it's just a pigeon taking off from a beam above.

I can't keep walking on eggshells.

"I know you think this is a waste of time," I say. My voice comes out higher than I expected, and I sound nervous. "But if we don't make this sale, there won't *be* a branch. You won't be able to mutter about me behind my back unless you're doing it while we're both down the Job Centre."

He lowers the camera.

"Do I get a badge if I behave?" he says.

"You get a hefty commission if it works. And a bonus. And if it doesn't, we're all unemployed."

We hold eye contact for a beat. I half-expect him to laugh or brush it off. But he doesn't.

Then he steps towards me. Something's shifted. I feel myself lean back a fraction, scared of what he'll do next.

"Fine. I'll put a portfolio together tonight."

I'm stunned. "You will?"

He shrugs. "Might as well. Beats flogging another three-bed semi with damp problems."

I nod, trying to hide my relief. "Thanks."

Kyle goes back to snapping pictures and I trail behind him, arms crossed, trying to stop shaking. This isn't how promotion is supposed to feel. This isn't promotion. This isn't progress. It's a trap. The sooner I earn enough money to get to university the better. I turn my face toward the cracked skylight and let the cold light hit my skin. Just a warehouse, I tell myself. Just a job.

We head back in near silence, the car's heater wheezing. I drive this time while Kyle's quiet and focused for once, fiddling with camera settings. Even so, I don't trust it. I don't trust him. But maybe I don't need to. Maybe I just need to make this sale, for now. We'll see what comes after.

Back at the office, I let Kyle and Mohammed go home

early. I start drafting the copy for the warehouse listing. My fingers feel stiff on the keyboard. Normally I'd enjoy having the place to myself, music on, shoes off… but I still feel weirdly anxious. I glance toward the window, half-expecting to see someone out there, lurking in the gloom, watching.

Of course, there's no one there. Just a seagull perched on the railing, staring in.

But the feeling won't go away. That sense of being watched. I feel a chill, so I rub my arms and try to laugh at myself. Ridiculous. Probably just stress.

I've made it this far. I can keep going.

But I still can't shake it.

Like something's coming, and I'm the only one who hasn't seen it yet.

CHAPTER 31
OLIVER

He would be lying if he said he hasn't considered it.

Killing Grace.

The thought comes unbidden the night he sees her with Ash, or Dave, or whatever he's calling himself these days. He's barely slept since. The idea blooms in his mind like mould – dark and damp, quietly expanding. Like someone else has planted it in his skull. For a while, he can't stop turning it over, jotting things down on the back of a Tesco receipt in the car.

Follow to pub – wine glass (sedative?).

Push – bridge – note (suicide?).

Break-in – blood? Struggle? DNA evidence??

Electrical fault (fire?).

It seduces him, the idea that he could dispose of Grace as completely as he did Justin, wipe a bad person off the face of the Earth. He settles into the thought as he looks at her face in the school photograph, slowly tearing it into strips. Then again. And again. Flushing the pieces down the toilet two at a time. He enjoys imagining the scene of their final meeting as he walks around town, the things he'll say before he snuffs her out. He finds himself in LIDL, of all places, rehearsing the conversation he'll have with her while he stares at the discount bin of pre-packed sandwiches.

"She'll thank me," he says out loud. Or maybe he just thinks he's said it. A woman with a half-full trolley stares at him. But perhaps she is just trying to get past. He mumbles something about fat content, pretending to be reading a label.

Back home, he sets his mug of tea down on the worktop and exhales slowly through his nose. There's nothing wrong with making a list, he tells himself. That's fine. Controlled. Clinical. Just some initial brainstorming. Options are not actions.

Anyway, he understands where that came from. He's only human after all. Our feelings are our feelings. We must be kind to ourselves. Forgive ourselves. He remembers when Julia died, the cycle of pain and guilt, self-loathing and anger, a mass of uncontrolled emotions that ate him up and almost destroyed him. But that was just reflex. Primitive stuff. Amygdala nonsense.

He's past that now. That's not who he is anymore.

"I'm past that now." He says it aloud as he stares into his mug of tea like it might reveal something to him.

The important thing, Oliver reminds himself, is not to act impulsively.

That's what he would tell a client in this situation; someone hurt, angry, and desperate for meaning. "Don't react," he says decisively to the empty room. "Impulse is the enemy of clarity."

He lets this settle into his chest like the weight of a calm, well-anchored breath. He's proud of himself for resisting the early instincts: rage, retaliation, reckless thoughts. Those would have been the old responses, from a time when he lacked structure. When pain dictated his choices.

No. He's better now. Entirely rebalanced.

He stands in the kitchen, grounding himself – heel to toe, heel to toe – looking out at the square of neglected grey garden and the sloping wooden fence. The sky is grey too, like unmarked slate.

No, he's not going to let his emotions decide for him, like last time. That was Julia-era Oliver. He's grounded now. He's processed the trauma. He's rebuilt. No one can take that away from him. Certainly not Grace.

What he needs is a detached sense of perspective.

He makes more tea and carries it into the living room, then takes a notebook from the pile beside the armchair and uncaps his pen. Outside, a car passes, headlights sweeping across the drawn curtains like a searchlight. Let them look. He's not doing anything wrong.

What is the presenting issue?

He writes it neatly at the top of the page and underlines it twice.

Grace.

He lets the name sit there like a diagnosis.

What does she represent?

The betrayal of trust.

The manipulation of therapeutic boundaries.

The deception of someone who presented as vulnerable but was in fact coercive.

He writes each one as a bullet point, the dots like small wounds.

But Grace is his client.

She is still in need.

The problem is, she doesn't know it. She thinks she's finished. That she's 'better'. That she can terminate the coaching arrangement because she's got a shiny job title and no one breathing down her neck. But that's the danger zone. That's when relapse occurs. False confidence. Premature autonomy. Classic self-saboteur behaviour.

He rubs the side of his nose with his thumb. As Maureen always says, *progress isn't linear*. And she's right. There are setbacks. But you recognise them. You respond with compassion, not reaction.

He opens a clean page in the notebook and begins writing.

Treatment Plan: Grace Harper

1. Destabilise.

2. Isolate.

3. Reveal.

4. Rebuild.

It's elegant, really. A clean arc. He pauses to admire his clarity. It's astonishing how organised the mind becomes once you remove the emotional fog. No more swirling, ambiguous feelings. Just direction and purpose. Maureen will be proud of him. She always says his strength is in systems. In seeing structure where others see chaos. *"You find clarity in confusion,"* she told him once.

He's not the one in chaos. Grace is. She's the one spiralling – failing at work, lashing out at the people trying to help her, hiding behind fake smiles and pretend strength.

That's it. That's the truth.

Grace doesn't need removing. She needs rescuing. She needs her mirror shattered, so she can finally look into her real face. What she has now, all of that is just armour. And he can break it. Only then will the work *really* begin.

He can almost feel the moment arriving. It makes him giddy. Not manic. Not manic. Courage is not the absence of fear. It's acting in spite of it.

Perhaps he'll go for a walk near the seafront to steady himself.

He wanders into the hallway, stops in front of the mirror by the coat hooks. He checks his posture. His eyes. Still clear. Still steady. That's good.

He speaks to himself in the mirror. "You're not doing this *to* her. You're doing it *for* her."

He closes his eyes and pictures Grace. Grateful and changed. Crying, perhaps. With joy.

"You saw me when no one else did."

Yes, she'll say that. Eventually.

He thinks about Maureen. Her kind, lined face. Her calming voice cutting through the surface to the heart of things: "*Sometimes we have to hit our lowest point before we can get better.*"

She's right. Sometimes healing begins with a nudge. A knock. A fall.

He'll help Grace fall.

And then he'll catch her.

CHAPTER 32
GRACE

I can feel the tension chewing through my insides like battery acid. Patrick Lyle is due at the office for a catch-up in less than an hour, and I've got precisely nothing.

Across the room, Kyle's perched on the corner of Mohammed's desk like a smug little gnome, showing him the warehouse photos.

"It's all about the focal length. I went long lens so I could soften the grime, blur the sharpness of the broken tiles. You shoot wide and suddenly it's all cracked asbestos and dead pigeons."

Mohammed nods, like he's getting a masterclass from Steven Spielberg. I want to scream.

"I should have taken a few snaps of what it really looks like. We could have sold the place to someone who has a fetish for condemned slaughterhouses."

I grudgingly have to admit his photos are pretty good. At least they make the place look less like the location in a Netflix crime drama. But the advert went in *European Business Register* three days ago, and since then we've had the grand total of zero calls. We even paid the web guy to give the listing top billing on our homepage. But literally no one has emailed. Not even a phone call from someone wanting to turn it into a skate park or an illegal rave venue. Not a peep.

Kyle, of course, is loving it. He keeps making these *I'm not saying I told you so* faces, which he clearly is. He stretches theatrically and heads to the coffee machine.

"So, Gracie," he says, "what's your Plan B when this whole ship goes tits up? Don't say waitressing. Think of those poor customers."

"Don't worry," I reply. "I'll just follow you into stand-up comedy. You're hilarious."

He smirks. "Aw, thanks. That really means a lot coming from someone as funny as you."

I go into the toilet and splash water on my face. I need five minutes on my own. It feels like everyone's crowding round, watching me, waiting for me to fail. Not just Kyle and Mohammed. It's Patrick Lyle. It's even Adam, asking *"how are things going"* every night, being wonderful and supportive but somehow ramping up the pressure. It's the ghost of Justin, sneering in the corner like some corporate poltergeist.

I stare at my reflection and see the stress lines. My skin's dry. My eyes are baggy. Not exactly the image of confidence for a branch manager about to pitch to the boss.

I know Kyle's game. He wants me flustered. He wants me to unravel before Patrick even walks through the door. And the most frustrating thing is, it's working. The pressure's been mounting for days, and I can feel it rising up my spine. But if the branch closes altogether, then at least we'd *all* be out on our arses – Kyle too. I try to see that as some sort of consolation.

I rehearse what I'll say to Patrick. But every version ends with polite sympathy and a cardboard box under my arm. I imagine going home and telling Adam. Imagine telling the bank. Imagine going on Universal Credit with nothing but own-brand baked beans and soup for dinner. And even worse, I imagine my plans of going to uni and getting my life back on track all going up in smoke.

I can't hide in the loo forever. It's pathetic. I head back to my desk and refresh Outlook. Still no enquiries. I sit for a minute, pretending to look calm and busy, wondering how long I should leave it before refreshing again. My fingers hover over my keyboard, when the phone rings.

Unknown number. Great. Scam likely. Probably someone trying to sell me cryptocurrency or a kidney.

"Lancaster & Lyle," I say, in my best 'I'm totally competent' voice.

"Hello. Is that Lancaster & Lyle, Scarborough Branch?"

I try to place his accent. It's not British, that's for sure.

"It is, yes. How can I help you?"

"Good morning. May I speak to Grace Harper?"

I blink. "Speaking."

"This is Martijn de Vries, from Eindhoven. I saw your advert in *EBR Monthly*. About the warehouse space."

I nearly fall off my chair.

"I was hoping you could give me some more details. Confirm dimensions. And tell me more about site access and freight shipping options."

"Of course!"

I scramble to open the listing while he tells me about his firm. He's the CEO of a Dutch e-bike company. They're expanding and looking for UK locations for an electric bike manufacturing arm. "The UK market is growing quickly," he says, with his smooth Dutch vowels, "and post-Brexit logistics are... how shall we say, not ideal. But if we can assemble locally, that makes it better for us."

I frantically scribble notes. I hit all my talking points. Ports. Logistics. Space. Good-value land. You'd think I was pitching for the Olympics.

Martijn seems genuinely engaged. "That sounds promising. I'd like you to send me everything you have – floor plans, access routes and photos."

"Yes, I'll send them straight away." I try not to sound like a giddy teenager who's just been asked on a date.

He gives me the company website and his work email. Then he pauses. "Actually, I am travelling a great deal this week, so perhaps it is best that you have my mobile. And my direct email also is easier than going through the office."

He gives it to me. I repeat it back, just to be sure. I can barely hold the pen.

"Very well," he says. "I'll look out for your email."

The call ends. I stare at the phone, stunned.

"Kyle!" I shout. "Mohammed! Get over here."

They come over, wary.

Then I launch from my chair. "We've got one!" I yell into the office. Kyle and Mohammed blink at me like startled meerkats. "Martijn de Vries," I say. "Dutch e-bike company."

Kyle raises one eyebrow. "That's… incredible. I assumed EBR's circulation was you and a bot in Lithuania."

I ignore him. I'm already at my screen, typing like a lunatic. Mohammed's peering over my shoulder as we gather around my computer and pull up his company's website. *Blue Pedal.* It's glossy, professional, terrifyingly slick. Big fonts, smooth animations, aspirational photos of impossibly fit blond people zipping past traffic jams on gleaming, perfect bikes. According to their press kit, they're the fourth-largest electric cycle brand in Europe. There's a photograph of Martijn in all his saintly glory. My saviour.

Kyle makes a pained noise like he's been punched.

"Told you the light was great in those shots," he mutters, trying to claim some credit. But he knows his chances of being boss just went up in smoke. He gives me that same look from before. Full-throttle, slow-burning hatred. I may be ahead right now, but I need to remember to watch my back.

"Shut up," I say, but I'm smiling. Actually smiling. And just like that, the whole atmosphere shifts. My head clears. My spine straightens. I can breathe again.

Just then, right on cue, Patrick Lyle walks in.

"Grace," he says, with a pleasant nod. "How are things going?"

I smile like a woman who's just eaten her favourite death row dinner *and* dodged the electric chair.

"Come into the office, Patrick," I say. "You're going to want to sit down for this."

CHAPTER 33
OLIVER

Of course, the simplest thing would be to go to the police.

He could walk into the station and calmly explain how Grace manipulated him – an innocent, a therapist, a helper – into doing something unthinkable. That he has been exploited, groomed, and gaslit into believing he was helping someone in need, when all the while she's been playing him like a fiddle. It's not his fault that he acted out of duty. He was just the weapon. It was she who pulled the trigger.

But the police wouldn't understand the nuances of the dynamic. They'd twist everything. Did you kill him? Yes or no. What they'd miss is the process. The context. The psychological scaffolding that led up to it.

Besides, a prison cell wouldn't help Grace. And that's the point, isn't it? *Helping* her. You don't help a person grow by removing them from a situation. Arrest is avoidance. And Oliver doesn't believe in avoidance. He believes in transformation.

What she needs – what she truly needs – isn't punishment. It's perspective.

And he's the one to give it to her.

Her *actions* are evil, but *she* is not evil. She has forgotten her principles. Perhaps she never had the chance to fully develop them, likely as a result of some childhood trauma or neglect. It could be any number of things. But now, she's spinning in the wrong direction. Her values have become distorted. She is like a twisted rod. She needs to be bent back into shape.

Right now, she's lost. She's become addicted to power. She's developed a dysfunctional relationship with ambition. And if she achieves success in this new job, it will confirm to her that her flawed actions reap positive outcomes. The association will lead her to commit worse and worse deeds. Her brain needs rewiring. She needs to associate her poor choices with poor outcomes. That's why the job itself must be undermined. It must be rendered meaningless. Only then can she rebuild.

He wakes up his laptop and goes to the Lancaster & Lyle website. There she is: Grace Harper, Branch Manager, Scarborough Office. Arms crossed in a white blouse, smiling that friendly-but-professional smile. That smug little bio. *"Passionate about helping clients find the right property solution."* He almost laughs. Helping? She didn't even know what helping looked like until he came along. That's why he took Justin out of the picture. She needed someone to step in and take decisive action. And he did.

But she didn't thank him. She fired him. Because that's what manipulators do. They extract what they need and discard the rest. And now she has her pathetic prize job, what good is it doing her?

He finds himself a new page in his notebook and writes:
Goal: dismantle false self → rebuild authentic identity.

It's not difficult. He doesn't have to destroy everything, just make sure the cracks widen. All she needs is a few small nudges. He recalls her saying how busy she is. "Overwhelmed." That's useful. If he applies pressure at just the right angle, he can trigger a controlled break, like a bone that's healed badly and which needs to be rebroken to set properly.

HE ALREADY HAS her work email and her home address, and uses them to sign her up to everything he can think of. Hearing aid brochures. Quotes for double-glazing and bi-fold doors. Leaflets on laser eye surgery financing. A sample pack of vegan protein powders. Information about a Christian Singles Retreat in Norfolk. Requests for adoption paperwork for a child in Guatemala.

He fills in the forms with abandon. A free starter pack for fertility tracking and ovulation tests. A coffin catalogue. A subscription to *Cat Lovers Quarterly*. Dozens of them. All sent directly to her inbox or posted to her house. He signs her up for trial accounts too: Rightmove Premium, Photobook Pro, Digital Business Cards Monthly, a paid Zoopla account, and a daily motivational quote service that texts you every morning.

Then come the food deliveries. He scrolls through local classifieds and finds three pizza places still operating their own delivery systems. He places an order with a scheduled delivery, three nights in a row. Always late. Always confusing. Always cash on delivery. Next, he opens Uber Eats and schedules orders to her office – three vegan curry pots and a Thai salad.

Taxi bookings. Two for 5:45 a.m. tomorrow. One from her house to the train station, one from her house to the beach. Both pre-paid, non-refundable. Then he calls a cleaning agency and requests an urgent deep-clean of her house, citing a "sanitation emergency." They'll arrive on Thursday.

He books a private yoga taster session to show up at her

home, along with a man claiming to be a 'ukulele virtuoso' offering one free lesson. On Friday, twelve pints of fresh milk from a farm in Whitby will be delivered to her door before dawn.

He feels giddy. Euphoric. There's a tingling at the base of his spine, a coiled energy radiating up through his body and out of his fingertips. He hasn't slept in nearly thirty hours, but it doesn't matter. He's more alert than ever. This is what Maureen calls 'therapeutic synchronicity'. He is locked in. Intuitively aligned with Grace's trajectory.

Maureen. She left a long message yesterday. Something about accountability and structure. She sounded disappointed. That slight catch in her voice when she said, "You're isolating, Oliver. That worries me." It's the same tone he used with Grace when she said she didn't want to continue coaching. When she made the mistake of thinking she could manage without him.

He ignores Maureen's voicemail.

The screen burns his eyes, but he doesn't look away. He opens another tab and books a courier to deliver five back issues of Commercial Property Today to Grace's house, care of "The Commercial Queen of Scarborough." He laughs aloud at that. Then claps his hands together and says, "Good work."

It's nearly 3:30 a.m. when he finally stands and stretches. His body's vibrating with an internal tremor, like his nerves are humming. He knows this is the cortisol and adrenaline cocktail you get when the sympathetic nervous system kicks in. Perfectly natural during breakthroughs. It's what patients sometimes call the clarity before the storm. But in this case, the storm is what will wash it all clean.

He pauses for a second to savour the feeling. It's not euphoria. It's better. It's purpose. And it's calm.

He doesn't feel angry anymore.

Just focused.

CHAPTER 34
GRACE

It has been the most incredible day.

Patrick practically dances for joy in our meeting. He runs his fingers down the profit projections, nodding so hard I think his neck might snap. Then he looks up, grins and says, "I love it when a risk pays off."

He means me. He says it while he's looking straight at me. For the first time in weeks, I feel like I can breathe.

"Great work, Grace. Seriously. I had a feeling in my gut I was right to back you after Justin. Nice to see I wasn't wrong."

I almost tell him I've been hyperventilating in the office toilets for three weeks, but I don't want to ruin the moment. It takes everything I have not to beam like a schoolkid who just got a gold star.

Even Kyle seems marginally less unbearable than usual. When I ask him to pull together the site portfolio for Martijn de Vries, he actually does it. He stays late, helps format all the documents, and colour-codes the whole thing. I don't even have to bribe him with cupcakes. Maybe he's just showing off because Patrick is in the office, but whatever. I almost feel guilty for hating him. Perhaps he's just been trying to survive, like the rest of us, and finally realises we need to pull together.

The funny thing is, it's not even just that I get to keep my job and add to my savings for university. It's more than that. I had an idea, and it worked. I pulled it off. Maybe it's only for one day, but right now I actually feel pretty good about being the manager of a successful estate agency.

Adam notices something different as soon as I get home.

"Wow. You look happy. Have you won the lottery?"

I fill him in on everything. He hugs me and kisses me. He's beaming almost as much as I am. He puts some raucous music on in the kitchen while we wait for the pasta to cook, and we even shuffle around in a bit of a dance until his back can't take any more, and he sits down, rubbing his neck, a bit pained but still happy. It creates a mood that I'd almost forgotten: fun. I'm not anxious, not checking my inbox every twenty seconds like a deranged pigeon with a Microsoft addiction. It's normal. Ordinary – in all the right ways. I didn't realise how much I'd missed this.

We eat, clear up and turn off the music.

"Shall we head up?" asks Adam, with a cheeky twinkle.

"Sure," I say. "I just need to send this email off and I'm done."

I settle with my laptop at the kitchen table to do a final check of the documents before sending. I open Kyle's PDF, expecting it to be fine.

And that's when I see it.

The floor plans are mislabelled. The site access diagram is back to front. The freight summary's completely wrong – he's listed Scarborough as having a deep-water port, which it hasn't. It gets worse the more I look. Key figures have been flipped. Two pages are duplicates. The font size changes three times. There are typos. Whole sentences just… trail off. The profit estimate tables are missing decimal points and look like a monkey's inputted them during a power cut.

I stare at the screen, my stomach falling through the floor. Even Kyle isn't that bad by accident. It's not just shoddy. It's sabotage.

I tell Adam we won't be getting that early night. He's brilliant about it. He gives me a soft smile. "It's okay, luv. Your work is important. You crack on. I'll go and watch something needlessly violent on Netflix."

I work late at the table, laptop in front of me, checking, fixing, checking again.

What must be about two hours later, Adam pokes his head round the door. He's finished his film and he's going to bed. He makes me a cup of tea and kisses the top of my head. I still haven't finished making all the corrections. I insist I'll be ten minutes.

The next thing I know, I'm waking up to the doorbell. I must have fallen asleep at the table. My neck aches. My laptop is gone, and I panic for half a second – then I see Adam in his dressing gown, gently sliding it away from where my head has been slumped.

The doorbell rings again, and I shuffle to the door, rubbing sleep from my eyes.

A cab is idling outside. The driver winds the window down. "You Bob?" he says.

"What?"

"Taxi for Bob?"

I squint. "There's no Bob here."

He checks his phone. "Thirty-two Sycamore Grove?"

"That's us. But there's no Bob here. I didn't order a cab."

He scowls. "Well, someone did."

He just stares at me, like I'm supposed to conjure Bob out of thin air.

"There's no one called Bob here."

He looks at his phone again, then back at me. "This address. Postcode matches."

"Well, it's wrong. We didn't order a cab. Sorry."

He mutters something abusive under his breath and speeds off.

I shut the door, assuming it's just some stupid mistake.

But the next night, it happens again. This time it's two pizza deliveries. Both Hawaiian. Both hours after I'd gone to bed. I hate pineapple. Then there's a call from someone about double-glazing, which apparently I requested. The David Lloyd gym rings to welcome me to their 'Elite Package'. A magazine subscription I've never heard of sends me a letter welcoming me as a 'Platinum Plus Lifetime Member'.

What the hell is going on?

Leaflets start to pile up on the doormat. By the third day, my front hall is a shrine to junk mail. Mail-outs for three-piece suites and window blinds and holiday villas in Cyprus. I haven't signed up for any of it.

The only person I can think of who'd do it is Kyle. As I'm leaving for work, the postman hands me a brochure for an elite boarding school in Kent and another for walk-in bath-tubs. I don't say anything to Kyle when I get to the office. I refuse to give him the pleasure of confronting him. It's exactly the kind of crap Kyle thinks is hilarious. But the truth is, it isn't hilarious. I'm stressed and exhausted from getting woken up in the middle of every night.

The worst part is that I still haven't heard from Martijn. Not a peep. I keep checking my inbox. Nothing. I tell myself he's travelling, busy, time zones, meetings – but it's no use. It's been nearly a week now. I've run out of excuses to tell myself. The silence feels personal now.

I come home Thursday evening after another draining day of faking optimism, to find Adam standing ankle-deep in glossy flyers.

"Oh my God."

"It's good, isn't it?" says Adam. "We weren't sure what wallpaper to use in the spare bedroom. Now we can do it in luxury cruise brochures."

I know he wants to make me feel better by making a joke of it, but it's wearing thin. I'm tired and snappy. I grab a bundle of catalogues and storm outside in the pissing rain to chuck them in the recycling bin. It's windy, and they blow out of my hand, soaked, and stick to my legs. I tear them off me and dump them with a scream of frustration. By the time I get back inside, I'm drenched.

I try to go to sleep, but the storm outside has been building all evening. Sheets of rain hammer the glass of our bedroom window, keeping me awake. In any case, I'm like a coiled spring, waiting for the doorbell to ring with some bull-shit curry delivery I didn't order.

Then I hear it– Bang. Bang. Bang.

It's the bloody kitchen window. The big broken one.

I leap out of bed and march in there. The wind has found the gap and ripped it open. Papers are blown about every-where. Everything on the kitchen table sits in a vast puddle of water, including my bloody laptop.

Adam appears in the kitchen doorway, looking groggy. "What's happening?"

I turn on him. "That fucking window. You said you'd fix it a month ago."

"I haven't had time–"

"Yet you've miraculously had time to watch the entire fifty seasons of *Law and Order*."

He snaps. "You want to talk about time? You've been so deep in this work stuff I never see you. You don't even hear yourself anymore."

"I'm doing this for us!"

"Are you?" he shouts. "Because it's starting to feel like

you'll throw everything away if it gets you five minutes of praise from your boss."

I look at my laptop. It's probably ruined. Adam looks sheepish.

"If I'm up to it, I'll get to it this week."

"That's what you said *last* week."

I storm over and wrench the window shut so the neighbours can't hear us tearing strips off each other. Adam just stares at me. He can tell I'm still hurt.

"Look, I'm sorry, okay? I didn't mean what I said about your work. My neck's been bad today. I know you're stressed. I get it. I really appreciate all the hard work you're doing for both of us."

He rubs his neck.

"You've come so far. I know you can't fuck this up now."

My chest tightens. "Thanks."

"No, I mean... look, that came out wrong. I just meant you've worked so hard. You're doing everything right."

I stare at him. There's something in his tone. The way he's phrased it.

"You sound like Oliver," I say quietly. And as soon as I say it, I hate myself. But it's true. The tone, the pressure, the way I suddenly feel small. I sink onto a chair and press my fingers into my temples.

He sighs. "I'm just trying to help. I'm sorry." He comes over and puts his hand tenderly on my shoulder. "You get to bed. I'll clear this up."

He gets a big wodge of kitchen roll and starts dabbing at the table. I stand and give him a hug.

"I'm sorry too," I say. I go upstairs and get into bed.

I feel bad. Of course Adam's trying to help. But I can feel the knot tightening again. The hopeful version of the week already feels miles away. Martijn dangled hope in front of me, and I clung to it like a lifeline. But now he's vanished.

The stress of work is getting to me, and now it's messing with how Adam and I are getting on as well.

I lie there, staring into the dark, unable to sleep. I thought I'd climbed out of the hole. Now I'm dangling at the edge, hanging on by my fingernails.

CHAPTER 35
OLIVER

He's parked across the road, two doors down, with the engine off, hidden just enough in the long shadow of the silver birch outside number twenty-seven. From here, he has a clean line of sight to Grace's front window and the path up to the door.

He's been here most nights this week, watching. He has drinks, snacks, a blanket and one of those squidgy neck pillows for sleeping on planes. Not that he sleeps. His work is too compelling. Monitoring the fallout, notebook in the passenger seat. Observations, timings, sequences. It's important to document things properly.

Of course, in the old days, he'd be watching this unfold in a consulting room, under safer, more sanitised conditions. But this – this is closer to fieldwork. Raw, unpredictable, more authentic. A chance to observe real human transformation *in situ*.

Oliver watches calmly as another taxi pulls away from the kerb. The driver looks irritated. Good. That particular strand of the experiment is yielding consistent responses. Third unexpected cab in two nights. So far this evening, there has been one cab, two pizzas and a call from a woman offering an at-home hair-cutting service.

He records the time. 21:48.

He's just settling down with a mug of hot coffee from his thermos when he's surprised to see the front door open. Grace exits, holding a large bundle of papers, brochures and some glossy flyers. She's illuminated briefly by a flash of lightning, then she goes to the side of the house.

He can't see her.

Oliver makes a decision and steps out of the car to get a clearer view.

Out of nowhere, she hurls the pile across the garden, papers catching the wind like startled birds. He sees her mouth open in a furious, wordless scream. She looks demented.

He makes himself small against the neighbour's hedge – not because he is ashamed, but because she is making such a scene, others might start to look. He imagines voices murmuring behind glass. He doesn't want to become part of the data set.

She is drenched, hair stuck to her forehead, eyes wild. Screaming at no one, or possibly at the storm. Thunder cracks overhead like a gunshot, and she doesn't even flinch. Just stands there, soaked and raging. It is instructive. Humbling, even. The storm creates the perfect sensory distortion. A natural accelerant.

Grace returns to her house and Oliver to the comfort of his car. He makes some notes. What's unfolding now is a delicate phase in her process, and he knows how fragile these moments can be. She's clearly under strain.

02:12. A delivery of semi-skimmed milk arrives, even though Grace is lactose-intolerant. He remembers her saying that once, at the very beginning, when he offered her tea. She said it lightly, almost as a joke. He didn't forget.

Then, at 03:05, in the height of the storm, she inexplicably throws open the kitchen window and launches into a shouting match with someone. She and the boyfriend, presumably. Oliver winds the car window down, the rain lashing against his face as he cranes to hear. He can't make out their words, which are swallowed by the storm – but their tones carry. Accusation. Defence. Hurt. Fury. Thunder rumbles low and long above them. A flash of lightning bathes the house in silver. And there she is again, silhouetted against the glass, face twisted in something halfway between rage and despair.

Perfect.

This is, in therapeutic terms, the breaking of the false self. She's been clinging to the wrong scaffolding her whole life – bad family, bad men, bad job – and now the supports are coming away. He's clearing the clutter. Burning off the dead wood.

He leans back in the driver's seat, pleased. Her pain is not a symptom of damage – it's a signal. A marker of progress. You have to tear down before you rebuild. You have to let them fall, fully, before they can stand.

This isn't cruelty. This is kindness.

CHAPTER 36
GRACE

It's amazing how quickly things can turn around. For two days, I've been one minor inconvenience away from handing in my notice. A printer jam. A slightly over-toasted crumpet. Something small and stupid that will tip me over the edge. I even draft an email to Patrick. *"Thank you for the opportunity,"* as if I've been in on work experience, not just flushed six years of my life down the toilet. For some reason, I sign off with *"Wishing you all the best."* I don't. I hope the building floods.

And just as I'm about to press 'send', an email appears in my inbox–

–from Martijn de bloody Vries!

He's full of apologies. He's been speaking at some major cycling convention in Belgium and barely had time to scratch his arse, let alone reply to emails. But he's seen the proposal now. Loves the site. Loves the potential. Yes, the infrastructure needs investment. Yes, the buildings are creaking like they were built in 1882 – which, inconveniently, they were – but it would be the perfect UK base for their expansion plans.

His word. *Perfect.*

I could cry. Suddenly, I'm not the idiot who's one sandwich short of a disciplinary anymore. I'm the woman who might just pull off the biggest commercial let in the region.

He wants to do a site visit and bring his full team of lawyers, accountants, global production lead, to do a full assessment. That's how seriously he's taking this. He's even chartered a private jet.

A. Private. Jet.

So here I am, shopping in *Nettle & Silk* for a power suit I can wear to the meeting. I'd never come in here normally. It's one of those places where if you need to ask what something costs, you can't afford it. But this is my big moment, and I need to dress to impress.

The assistant looks down her nose at my shitty coat like I've just walked off the street in *Pretty Woman*. But then I spot the perfect outfit on a mannequin like it's been waiting for me since the shop opened. I try it on and look at myself in the mirror. Ink-black, razor-sharp tailoring, the kind of suit that shouts money and takes no shit. The blazer is all clean lines and structure; the trousers are ankle-grazing and fluid. Pardon me, but I look a-ma-zing.

I walk home with the suit in a bag as I practice a few phrases of Dutch from YouTube. *"Hoi! Goedemiddag! Leuk je te ontmoeten. Welkom in het Verenigd Koninkrijk."* I'm sure people are looking at me like I'm an absolute dick, but I don't care.

On the day of the meeting, I know I look shit-hot.

Kyle's already lurking by the coffee machine when I arrive, faking indifference. He raises an eyebrow as I walk past and stares at my suit. "Oh, I'm sorry, boss," he says. "Did somebody die?"

I smile sweetly. "Yes. Your chances of promotion."

When this deal goes through, and just before I use my big bonus to launch my university fund, I'm going to get him transferred to a satellite branch in rural Wales and tell him they need help cracking the goose farming market.

He must read something in my eyes, because he stops smirking. "Good luck with your big day anyway. I hope you got your beauty sleep," he says.

Something in his tone makes my skin crawl. Because actually, no, I *didn't* sleep well. At 3 a.m., I was woken up by a dead-eyed teenager at my door holding four rice, four naans and eight lamb pasandas.

I don't flinch. I don't give him the satisfaction. I just say, "Like a baby," and grin too widely. The worst part is, I can't prove it's him. Yet. But one day soon I'll catch him blinking in the wrong direction, and I swear to God I will end him.

Patrick and his team arrive. They've been out looking at the warehouse this morning, and now we're all driving to Teesside Airport, where we'll meet Martijn's team. There are three limos; two for us lot and an empty one for the Dutch contingent.

Patrick gives me one of his actual smiles and says I should join him in his car so we can go over last-minute details. The drive to Teesside feels like a movie. The three black limos purr down the A171 like we're in a Bond film. Patrick talks shop a bit, but then starts chatting about his wife, his three kids, and how his daughter's just graduated with a First. He laughs. We talk about travel, art, all sorts. I feel like I've been invited into the inner sanctum.

The drive takes us just under two hours. As we pull up at the airport, he turns to me and claps his hands together. "Right. Let's show them what we can do."

We're early, of course. But that's fine. This is *Martijn de Vries*. He flies private. He's probably drinking a fresh-squeezed orange juice in a leather seat at thirty thousand feet while his legal team discusses Brexit import laws and someone else hands him warm nuts in a bowl.

The waiting area in the airport is less Bond, more bus terminal. The private flight lounge is closed, so we end up squatting by a sad-looking Costa that's out of sandwiches and has one working coffee machine. There's a group of lads in matching "Sexxxy Steve's Stag Do" T-shirts loudly comparing their planned tattoos. One of them, Sexxxy Steve presumably, struts up and down in a full wedding dress and a large inflatable penis hat.

I check my phone. The flight should have landed twenty minutes ago. Maybe there's been a delay. Or maybe private jets don't announce their arrival with the same regularity as Ryanair.

Patrick's team huddles in the corner and mutters. Patrick's expression starts to shift. No relaxed chat now, just staring into space. I offer to get him another coffee. He doesn't want one.

I sneak around the corner and try calling Martijn. No answer.

I try texting. Still nothing.

Half an hour later, we're both standing by the arrivals desk, scanning every single man in a blazer like we're at an aggressive speed-dating event. Nothing. Nobody. No team of Dutch cycling executives in sight.

Patrick starts pacing.

I try calling again. Voicemail.

We wait.

And wait.

Then my phone rings.

Martijn.

I answer on the second ring and practically sing his name.

"Martijn! We're here. Have you just landed?"

"Grace," he says. His tone is strange. I've only heard him like this once, when he was asking about the asbestos surveys. "Is Patrick with you? Can you put me on speaker, please?"

His voice is brisk, a little colder than before. Something about the way he says it makes my stomach drop.

I tap the speaker icon.

"Patrick," I say, keeping my voice bright. "Martijn's on the line."

"Hello," Patrick says. His tone says 'charming', but his face says 'tense'.

"I wanted to call personally. I'm sorry to do this," Martijn says. "I appreciate your efforts, Grace. And it was a compelling idea. But I'm going to withdraw from the site assessment. We won't be pursuing the opportunity further."

Silence.

Patrick folds his arms.

"I thought you were… on your way," I say. It comes out weak and pointless.

"There were several pieces of information we were expecting, but we never received them. Some vital site data and some legal clarifications. It has created too much uncertainty for our team. We've decided to explore other options."

"I sent everything," I say, panicked now. "I sent the documents on Monday. And then again–"

"I'm very sorry about that, Martijn," says Patrick, jumping in. "Is there anything we can do to get you to reconsider?"

"I'm sorry, Patrick," Martijn says. "Your team seemed enthusiastic. But the follow-through wasn't quite there. I wish you the best."

Your team.

He doesn't say my name. He doesn't need to. We all know he means me.

Patrick thanks him flatly, and hangs up.

I lower the phone.

"Can I just–" I start, but Patrick holds up a hand.

"Let's get back," he says.

The journey back is different. Patrick reorganises the seating so that one of his team can ride with him to go over "a few things." I'm demoted to another car like a disgraced child. It's subtle. But it's not.

I spend the next hour and a half staring out of the tinted window, my face burning with silent humiliation. Nobody says anything. Even the driver doesn't attempt small talk. I replay the past week over and over in my head. I *sent* those documents. I checked the attachments. I remember clicking send. I even followed up.

Did I forget something? No. No, I didn't. I was so careful. *Obsessively* careful, because I knew how important it was.

Unless–

Unless something got in the way. Unless someone got in the way.

Just then, my phone buzzes, and for a second I hope it's Martijn, saying he's checked his junk mail, he's got my messages, he's made a terrible mistake. But when I look, it's an email confirmation for a 12-month subscription to *Irish Dancing Monthly*.

I press my forehead against the window and try not to laugh, cry, or scream.

By the time we pull up back outside the office, I've got a migraine brewing behind my right eye. Patrick doesn't look at me as he gets out of the car.

Nobody has to say anything.

I know what they're all thinking.

She blew it.

CHAPTER 37
OLIVER

The phone buzzes again. Oliver watches it flash, listens to the hum of the vibration against the table. Grace's name, bright on the screen.

He doesn't answer. He waits.

Eventually, it stops.

Silence.

Then again. Buzzing, pulsing, that name lighting up like a beacon.

He still doesn't move.

Because it's not his phone. It's *Martijn de Vries's* phone.

Oliver waits for it to stop ringing, then calmly switches it off. The silence that follows feels energised, like a struck bell fading into stillness. He opens the back, removes the SIM card, and cuts it into tiny fragments with scissors from the kitchen drawer, the ones with the blue handles he uses for blister packs and cardboard. He scatters the tinsel shreds of plastic into the bin. Then he opens the clamshell of the phone itself and snaps it in two. He goes to the drawer where his mother stored plastic carrier bags, hundreds of them, and removes one. He places the broken halves of the phone in the bag, takes the rolling pin from a cupboard, and smashes the phone into pieces, hard, twice, three times.

He doesn't know the technical details of how Pay-As-You-Go phones work, or if any of this is necessary. But in any case, it feels satisfyingly final. Necessary things often do.

Anyway, he has others.

He places the shattered fragments in the plastic bag onto the table, next to the other burner phones laid out like surgical tools. Each one is labelled in biro on masking tape: *Pizza Palace; Eastern Spices; Diamond Cabs; Creamways Dairy; Deliveroo.*

Some of the numbers are due for retirement. But there's no time now. He checks the clock, grabs his bag, and hurries to the door. He walks briskly across town and nearly misses his train, but makes it with seconds to spare, panting, sweat prickling through his shirt as he sinks into his seat.

He enjoys the journey. The repetition of motion. There's a single direction, and the sense of being carried forward by something larger. He opens his notebook on his lap and runs his fingers down the list he's copied out at least ten times.

Destabilise. Isolate. Reveal. Rebuild.

Tick one. Destabilisation achieved. The Martijn call was exquisite. That final speakerphone humiliation. Grace trying to stay calm, to salvage something, and Patrick witnessing her crumble. Textbook collapse of false self. Clean rupture.

He hasn't slept in three days, but that's often the way at this stage of the process. There's too much to track. Timing is everything. You have to be responsive. In many senses, he's never felt more awake. It's fascinating how alive he feels.

A uniformed woman appears at the end of the carriage, pushing a refreshments trolley. He orders coffee and a sandwich in the Dutch accent he's been refining. The woman doesn't even blink. Oliver smirks to himself as she clatters off. It's important to find a place for humour in the work.

Maureen's stair-lift creaks up the banister like an old dog coughing.

"You need to get that thing serviced again," he calls down as she rises to meet him.

"We may be rickety and past our best, but that's what gives us character," she shoots back.

She makes them tea and sits. He likes this part – the ritual. Cups, milk, sugar.

"I'm glad you've come to see me at last."

"Yes." Oliver settles into his chair. "I'm sorry it's taken so long. I've been very busy."

"With your clients?"

"Yes. Lots of good work. It feels like clarity."

"You look different," she says, sliding from her wheelchair into the chair opposite him.

"Do I?" he says, smiling. "That's encouraging. I hope."

"You're sitting differently. You look… alert."

"I am."

"But you also look like you haven't slept."

He smiles genuinely. She's sharp. She always has been. He doesn't bother trying to hide from her. He doesn't want to seem evasive. "I haven't, no. Not properly."

She lifts one eyebrow. "Why not?"

"Overactive mind. I'm not distressed."

Maureen sips her tea. "We were discussing one of your new clients in our last session. Grace?"

"Yes." He sits forward. "She's in the transformation zone. It's intense. High-level processing. The pushback's begun – anger, rejection, confusion. But that's all expected. We're breaking down old defences. Clearing the noise. She's started to access the real material now. The truth. You can hear it in her voice."

Maureen nods slowly. "And how does that feel for you – being the one guiding her through that?"

He doesn't tell Maureen that Grace has attempted to end the formal coaching relationship. She wouldn't understand the necessity of his extending the contract. He leans back. "It feels satisfying. Like the work matters again."

"And you feel grounded in that?"

"I feel useful."

There's a pause. She's watching him, but not in a challenging way. "Useful?"

He has to be careful with Maureen. She's good. He's not afraid of her, exactly. But he decides to protect himself from her and shield the more complex data. He suspects where she is going with all this and decides to head her off.

"I thought about what you suggested last time. That my interest in Grace was transference of my guilt about Julia."

Maureen nods gently, waiting for him to continue.

"They're different cases. Julia is gone, but Grace presents with her own issues, her own needs. She's come to me for help, and I'm helping her. *Her*," he says, for emphasis.

"Helping?"

"Yes. Not saving. Not rescuing. Helping. We're doing the work."

"And how is the work progressing? How are things with her 'overbearing' boss?"

He leans back and gets a flash of Justin's lifeless eyes. The deep cleft in his forehead. Oliver focuses on the stone sculpture on the table in front of him, allowing its smooth, flowing, abstract lines to do their job, calming him.

"That situation has resolved itself," he says. "We're working on new goals now."

"Personal goals?"

"Core values. Issues around the locus of self-worth."

Maureen sets down her cup. "There's a crossover between who we are in the workplace and who we are in our wider lives, of course. But remember, Oliver, you are her coach, not her therapist. Are you sure there isn't any shift in that dynamic?"

He lets the silence settle. He curls his lip, as if he is seriously considering what she just suggested. But inside, he knows. Maureen doesn't see the whole picture. She can't. She's watching the process from the outside. He is *in* it. With Grace.

He smiles faintly. "I'm mindful of the boundaries."

"Your terminology is interesting. It's technical. Detached. But your tone says otherwise."

"I'm calm."

"You're sleep-deprived. And maybe a bit... elevated?"

"Elevated's not necessarily bad, is it? Clarity can feel like a kind of euphoria."

"It can," she says carefully. "It can also be a warning sign. Especially in someone who's had difficulties with intensity before."

He doesn't reply.

Maureen's voice softens. "I know that feeling, Oliver. Like you're approaching the centre of the maze. Like everything's converging. It feels clear. Clean. But that's also the moment you need grounding the most."

His face tightens. He imagines himself in her chair, that he sees what she sees. He comprehends the false conclusion she's moving towards.

"You think I'm manic."

"I think you're at risk of losing perspective. Which, by the way, is not a moral failing. It's something we *all* do when we're close to the material. But it's also why we're here. Together. To catch those moments before they run away with us."

He looks away. Her voice is steady. Her presence, infuriatingly constant.

"You're *close to the material* too, Maureen. Is it possible you're getting a bit over-excited in rushing to solve your own puzzle?"

Has he been too confrontational? He attempts to soften it with a smile.

"I'm fine."

"You say that like it's something to prove."

He swallows. There's a burn behind his eyes. Residual exhaustion, maybe.

"I was actually thinking of finishing therapy," he says lightly. "Mine, with you, I mean. Stepping away. You've been an incredible support, as always. But this all feels... manageable now."

She doesn't react at first. Just nods slowly.

"Oliver... I'm going to ask you not to make any decisions just yet. When we've worked this long and this deeply, there's often a temptation to 'graduate' as a way of avoiding something uncomfortable that's coming up. Let's sit with this. Explore it. You've made great progress, yes. But I'd feel irresponsible if I encouraged you to end the work prematurely."

He nods, as if accepting this.

But inside, he knows.

She doesn't understand.

Grace does. Grace understands what he's doing.

Or she will. One day. And when she finally sees it, she'll thank him.

CHAPTER 38
GRACE

I dial again.

It doesn't even ring this time. Just a flat, dead voice. *"The number you have dialled has not been recognised."*

I hang up and stare at the phone. My stomach clenches. I'd get it if Martijn de Vries didn't want to take my calls. But I don't understand this. It's not just that Martijn isn't answering. It's that the number no longer exists.

Maybe there's a fault with his phone. I know I'm clutching at straws, but I Google *Blue Pedal* again. If only I could speak to him, maybe I could change his mind. I scroll through the glossy website full of Euro-bike clones with glowing teeth and find the contacts page. I call the general number, expecting a menu, a robot, a polite Dutch brick wall.

Instead, I get a real person.

"Blue Pedal Group. Good morning."

"Hi," I say, like I'm not dying inside. "Could I speak to Martijn de Vries, please?"

"May I ask who's calling?"

"Grace Harper. Lancaster & Lyle. We've been in talks

about a UK expansion site. He was due to visit earlier this week."

There's a pause. I can hear typing.

"Could you just check with him? Please?"

Another pause.

"I'll see if he's available to return your call."

I give her all my details again, and she hangs up.

I try to zone out the contest Kyle and Mohammed are having to see who can make the biggest ball out of elastic bands. I keep myself occupied sorting through house sale enquiry emails I've neglected while I've been concentrating on the warehouse. But I might as well be doing a cryptic crossword in Chinese for all I take in. I can't concentrate on a word.

Twenty minutes later, my phone buzzes. Dutch number. I nearly drop it.

"Grace Harper speaking."

"Yes, this is Martijn de Vries," says a voice I've never heard before in my life. Calm. Measured. Forty, maybe fifty. Much deeper than the Martijn I've been speaking to.

"I think there's been some confusion," I say. "I spoke to a Martijn de Vries a few weeks ago about a UK site. You asked for floor plans, freight access... everything. We were arranging a site visit where you'd fly to England, to visit Scarborough."

"I'm sorry," he says. "I've never spoken to you before. I've only just returned from holiday. I was in Norway with my family. We export to the UK, but we're not looking to set up any kind of base there. But thank you for your enquiry."

He hangs up. I sit very still.

Then I laugh. Just once. It comes out strangled and wet. Somewhere between a sob and a bark.

Kyle and Mohammed are staring at me. But I don't care. Because of course I didn't just lose the deal – I lost it to someone who never existed. Someone used a real man's name, borrowed a real company, spun it into a pantomime, and fed me every line. And I ate it up like a starving idiot.

Whoever did this didn't just trick me. They studied me and reeled me in. They sabotaged me.

BY THE TIME Patrick arrives at the office and asks to speak to me, I've already rehearsed the entire conversation five times in my head. We meet in the side room, which I've now started to think of as my personal torture chamber. Patrick doesn't sit. He stands by the table like he's addressing an underperforming sixth-former.

"I want to understand what went wrong," he says. His tone is clipped. Not angry. Disappointed. Which is even worse.

I nearly say: *"Kyle impersonated a CEO. He pretended to be Martijn de Vries. He's been undermining me for weeks. He sabotaged this on purpose and I don't know why, but I swear it wasn't me."* But I don't. Because I know how it sounds. It's just the sort of smug, elaborate prank Kyle would find hilarious – but I can't prove it. And even if I could, what sort of a useless manager does it make me look like?

So instead I tell Patrick, "I gave Martijn everything he asked for. Site plans, freight data, everything." I sound like a woman explaining how she wired ten grand to a man in a cowboy hat who promised her diamonds and a puppy.

"So why did he pull out like that? Did you do your due diligence?"

I didn't. I was so pleased to have his personal email and number, I never once called the actual offices.

Patrick sighs. Not theatrical. Just tired.

"I've spoken to HR," he says. "This needs to be formally recorded."

He slides a letter across the table like it's something distasteful he doesn't want to hold any longer.

"It's a written warning."

I take it. I don't look at it. I just nod, because really, what else can I do? I should argue. Explain. Scream. But I don't have the energy. I just say, "Thank you," like he's handed me a consolation biscuit, and walk back to my desk.

Kyle's already there. Leaning on my desk like he owns it.

"Patrick looked thrilled," he says. "You must have nailed it."

I realise he's looking at the written warning letter I've put on my desk. I cover it with some paperwork.

"Just back off."

He smiles. "You're tense. Can I make you a milky drink?"

I shouldn't say it. Not here. Not now. But it boils up anyway.

"You've been sending shit to my house, haven't you?" It's out before I know it.

He blinks. That exaggerated, innocent blink he does when he's lying.

"I beg your pardon?"

"The taxis. The food. The gym memberships. The time-share villas in Crete. All of it."

Kyle's eyes flash with mock surprise. "What are you on about?" He's a bloody good actor, I'll say that for him.

"I'm serious."

He puts up his hands defensively. "Wasn't me. I've been too busy organising the funeral for your sales figures."

Then his laugh subsides. He looks directly at me.

"Grace, whoever's pranking you, it's not me. But if someone else is, maybe it's because you're such an easy bloody target."

I stand so violently that my chair rolls backwards and

bumps into Mohammed, who's been silently loitering behind me like a ghost.

"What about you?" I snap at him. "You get off on this too?"

Mohammed looks away. He doesn't answer. Which of course is an answer.

I try to remember... were there ever moments when I took a Martijn call with Kyle nearby? And if not Kyle, then what about Mohammed? He's quieter, less obvious. But I've seen them together. Whispering. Laughing. Watching me.

I take a step forward.

"Was it you on the phone? With the accent?"

Kyle snorts. "What are you even *talking* about?"

"You pretended to be Martijn. Or maybe he did." I jab a finger in Mohammed's direction. "Or maybe you took turns."

Kyle raises both eyebrows. "Are you hearing yourself? This is *insane*. If you think we've got time to prank you with fake Dutch CEOs, you really do need a holiday."

"You had *plenty* of time," I say. "You've been sulking about, doing as little as possible on my warehouse project, trying to fuck it up."

"Oh, *your* project," he says. "The one that tanked the month's commission? Brilliant work, by the way. You should put that on your LinkedIn."

My hands are shaking.

"I'm reporting this."

"To who? Patrick? He's already given you a written warning, and you want to walk in and tell him about mystery men and prank calls?"

He smirks.

I turn to Mohammed again. "You think this is funny too?"

He shakes his head. "No. I don't."

And that's worse somehow. The pity in his voice cuts worse than Kyle's sarcasm. Like I'm already written off.

That's when I see Patrick, standing in the doorway of the side office, having witnessed the whole pathetic scene.

CHAPTER 39
OLIVER

The weather has turned again. Rain, thin and sharp as needles – not quite sleet, but near enough. It beads on his coat and soaks through the cuffs, but he doesn't care. The sensation keeps him alert.

He cuts through the town centre, the shops lit up defiantly against the grey of the afternoon. Through the thinning crowds, past the closed cafés and chain stores and bins overflowing with rubbish. He doesn't rush. He has purpose. He is calm.

He isn't going to talk to her. Not today. He's just going to observe.

Stage 1 is a success. She's fractured. Now he needs to see if Stage 2 is taking hold, whether she's starting to lose her external supports.

He crosses the car park and makes his way over the bridge. He turns onto the Esplanade and slows by the lamp-post where he last encountered Justin. A bunch of flowers tied to it is already browned and wilting. He gives a small, knowing smile. Forgotten already. It hasn't even been a month. That's how fast people disappear. The world doesn't grieve for long.

He doesn't linger. He crosses the street and keeps walking until he reaches the agency building. He doesn't go in. Of course not. He's not a fool.

He finds his usual position, concealed just behind a hedge by the bank. He removes the small binoculars from his coat pocket and lifts them. A therapist sometimes has to monitor behaviour in real-world settings. It's perfectly ethical when done for the client's benefit.

Through the rain-smeared glass, he sees her.

Grace.

Sitting at her desk. Not working – not really. Her posture's too tight. Shoulders high. Neck hunched. Her hands keep moving: mouse, keyboard, mouse again. But there's no flow. Classic indicators of anxiety and stress.

She's fraying.

In contrast, Kyle's body language is all theatrical confidence and crocodile charm. He approaches her desk, leans over, says something which Oliver assumes to be smug. He sees Grace freeze. Then she stands up. Her mouth moves sharply. A confrontation. Good. Mohammed's hovering too; the quiet accomplice.

Eventually, the men wander off, and Grace is left alone at her desk. She doesn't move for a long time. Just sits there. Completely still.

That's the Grace he is hoping for. Not the performative mask she usually wears at work, all fake smiles and bravado. This is the Grace who cried in his sessions. Who talked about her parents and the fear of being fundamentally unlovable. Who apologises too quickly and always tries to manage everyone's expectations.

This is the real Grace.

He feels a vibration on his phone – his *actual* phone, the one still connected to his everyday life, such as it is. A message has come through from Pete, one of his clients.

Hey, Oliver. Can we talk? Rough week. Need a session if you've got space.

Oliver stares at the message for a moment, then types.

Pete, I'm afraid something's come up. I think you'll be best served by another coach. I wish you all the very best.

Send. Done.

He doesn't have space for other clients now, not while Grace is in this state. This is what the work looks like when it matters, when it's real. It demands focus. Total presence. Nothing less.

When he looks up again, Grace is leaving the office. It's early. Just after 4:30. She just puts her coat on and walks. He lifts the binoculars and sees it, just as she closes the door and steps into the street. Her face. She's crying.

He imagines her walking home, damp coat clinging, her face blotched with tears. Tears are good. They mean she's letting go.

He doesn't follow. Not today. She needs to be truly alone.

He turns and walks away. Not home, not yet. He is too full of energy to confine himself to that small, quiet house. His feet carry him instinctively to the harbour. The low road, the one that hugs the edge of the town like it's trying to keep it from slipping into the sea.

There's no one around, just the gulls and the rain. He stands at the railings, hands in his pockets, and watches the water batter the seawall. The waves are relentless. No poetry. Just raw, mechanical violence. The sea throws itself forward again and again, like a dull beast trying to escape its cage.

In the distance, the spire of the church cuts through the mist, lit from beneath by the sodium glow of the streetlamps. He thinks of Anne Brontë again. Her grave, that crooked bench beside it. Thirty-nine, that's how old she was when she died of consumption. A disease that hollows you from the inside, slow and invisible. Like guilt.

He wonders if Julia felt like that, eaten alive from the inside. Whether her death was a slow surrender or a snap of panic. Did she plan it? Or was it a moment she couldn't step back from, the compulsion to jump once your toes touch the edge of the drop?

He presses his palms to the cold railing.

He tried so hard to help Julia. But with Grace, it will be different. Because this time, he's doing it properly. This time, he's winning.

When he makes the final turn towards home, the street is washed in orange. The tree at the top is darker than the others, the bark still visibly gouged where he struck it. He pauses and touches it gently, fingers over the torn edge of wood. Something once whole. He remembers the sound Justin made when he hit the windscreen. The dull thud. The glass cracking like ice. The way the body tumbled, loose and awkward, like it didn't belong to itself anymore. Eyes open. Staring.

At home, he leaves the lights off. He doesn't need them. The shadows are enough. He's exhausted. He can't remember the last time he slept. Three days? Four? It doesn't matter. There's clarity in the sleeplessness. A kind of focus. The brain stops lying when you strip it of comfort. He's closer to the truth now than he's ever been.

He lies in bed, still dressed, the room dark. He remembers the mirror. The way it steamed up. The shape of her face disappearing behind it.

He won't let it happen again.

Grace is alone now. Stage 2: Isolate.

Except she's not *truly* alone.

She has him.

And he won't let her fall.

CHAPTER 40
GRACE

I'm sitting at my desk, trying to remember how many formal warnings you get before they kick you out. One? Two? Is it like football – yellow card, red card, then you're off?

Because if so, I'm one clumsy tackle away from being ejected. And Kyle and Mohammed know it. Of course they do. I could feel it the second I walked in. Kyle gave me the kind of smile that says "Don't worry, your secret's safe with me," while radiating the smug energy of someone who's already written my goodbye card.

And today, because the universe has a sick sense of humour, I'm doing Mohammed's performance review. His annual one. The one where I'm meant to look like a manager, speak like a leader, and offer career development suggestions – like I haven't just spent the last week flushing my own career down the toilet.

I've never done one before. I Google *'performance development review structure'* and skim through an article that's chock-full of jargon and buzzwords. I scribble a few notes.

Talk strengths
Celebrate achievements

Set goals
Challenges
Performance indicators
(Don't cry, swear or punch anything)
That last one's for me.

The review is in my diary for ten, and it's already five past. It's bad form to start late, so I wander over to Mohammed's desk.

"Shall we?" I say.

The two of us walk to the side office.

"Remember you two, one foot on the ground at all times," says Kyle, with a schoolboy grin.

I ignore him like you ignore a misbehaving toddler showing off, and we go into the office. Mohammed sits and folds his hands defensively. Before I can even open my mouth, he says, "What happened yesterday – that wasn't okay."

It lands with a thud.

"Sorry?"

"The way you spoke to me. Accusing me. It was inappropriate."

My face is still, but inside, my brain starts pulling fire alarms.

"I get that Kyle can be a dick sometimes," he goes on. "I don't contradict him because I don't want the aggro. But I don't agree with him half the time. I'm just trying to keep my head down, do my job, and build a career."

His tone doesn't waver. He's calm and steady.

"I'm not like him. But this... all of this lately? You've made it impossible. You're accusing me of things I haven't done, treating me like I'm part of some conspiracy. It's not on."

It's the most I've heard him say in three years. And every word hits like a slap I probably deserve.

Maybe I got him wrong. Maybe he's not the enemy. I just threw him into the same mental bucket as Kyle because it was easier than admitting I don't know who's behind any of what's been happening to me.

I nod slowly. "You're right," I say, voice low. "You're right. I lost it yesterday. And I shouldn't have taken it out on you."

"I don't want to stir more shit up," he adds, "but I've had enough of it. I've thought about making a formal complaint."

"About Kyle?"

He looks surprised. "No. About you."

I nod once, playing for time. Shit. Not just embarrassment now – real trouble. I didn't just lose my temper. I gave him ammunition.

"Look," I say, "I know yesterday was a mess. I was out of line."

"*Waaaaay* out of line."

"I'm under a lot of pressure," I offer, then immediately regret it. "Not that that's any excuse."

He just stares at me.

"Listen," I say, "I know I screwed up. But please, don't go to HR. I'm on a formal warning already. If there's another complaint against me, I'm finished. I'm properly finished. Please don't put one in. Let me fix it."

Now he looks uncertain. Suspicious.

"How?" he asks.

I scramble again.

"I'll... support you more. You said you want to do well here – I'll help. We'll work out a proper development plan, training, whatever you need."

He watches me. Still cautious. But maybe a little less guarded.

"Okay," he says eventually. "But I want a real plan. Something useful. And soon."

"You'll have it," I say. "Monday."

He nods, stands, and leaves.

I exhale slowly. I've been in this branch too long. In this pressure cooker, trying to fix everything, solve every problem. And with this promotion, trying to save money for uni, prove I deserve to be here. And all it's done is prove I'm on the verge of cracking.

I'm not incompetent. I know that. I've done real work here. Closed deals. Held it together when it mattered. But lately I've been all reaction and no strategy.

I'm out of steam. Out of tricks. And very nearly out of a job. If I'm going to claw this back, I can't do it on my own.

I need help.

And I need it fast.

CHAPTER 41
OLIVER

The stair-lift creaks its way up the banister with arthritic defiance.

Oliver no longer finds it charming. Before, he imagined it a physical manifestation of Maureen's humility, her self-deprecating warmth. Now, it's just an annoying waste of time.

He resists the urge to sigh. Instead, he stands and waits, hands loosely clasped in front of him like a mourner. He doesn't want to be here. But Maureen insisted, and his professional reinstatement depends on her. She's the last box to tick.

Maureen finally arrives at the top of the stairs. Floral blouse, cardigan, the studied casualness. Her uniform. They exchange greetings, the usual conversational warm-up. Weather. Rail disruptions. Her sympathetic shake of the head at the news that his refreshment trolley was out of hot water. There's something rehearsed in her kindness. He can feel it now, how tightly it's managed.

They've barely sat down before his phone vibrates. Loud in the stillness. He's already reaching for it as he apologises.

"I thought I'd turned it off," he says. "Forgive me."

Maureen tilts her head – calm, neutral, a slight half-smile that says more than words. Phones, of course, are a boundary violation. The therapeutic chamber must remain sealed.

But then Oliver sees the name on the screen.

Grace Harper.

He hesitates for only a second. "I think I need to take this. It's patient-related."

"Of course, if you must." Maureen's permission is pregnant with disapproval.

"I won't be long. Sorry. This is important."

He steps into the hallway and answers.

"Grace."

"Hi. Sorry to call out of the blue. I wasn't sure if you'd still… be available." Her voice is small and flat, he thinks, like something that's been pressed between two panes of glass. "But I need someone. A coach. You were the first person I thought of."

He closes his eyes. The moment blooms in his chest. Not triumph, but a deeper, cleaner satisfaction.

"I'm glad you called," he says gently. "What's happening?"

"Work." She exhales. "It's a mess. I've hit a wall. I thought I could manage it all, but I can't. I just feel like I'm failing, like I'm losing control."

"Yes," he says, soft and supportive, "that's a painful place to be. But it's also where real work begins."

They agree to meet later that day at her office. Familiar ground. That's good.

She thanks him. She actually *thanks* him.

Oliver returns to the therapy room, his brain tingling with thoughts of what's to come. But first there's this to be dealt with. He centres his breathing, regains his composure. Maureen is waiting in her chair, notebook on the table at her side, toying with the pen in her hand. She smiles thinly as he settles into the chair opposite.

"Everything alright?"

"Yes. In fact, better than alright. Grace has reached out. We're resuming our work together."

Her name bubbles out before he knows it, such is the excitement that fizzes inside him. He can't help himself.

Maureen purses her lips. "Resuming?"

"She'd paused the therapy. A while ago. I'm sure I mentioned it." He knows he didn't. "But she's realised, I think, that she was premature. That the process wasn't complete."

"And so she asked to resume it?"

"She did."

Maureen sets her pen down. "Oliver, you referred to her just now as a patient."

"Did I?" He smiles mildly. "Slip of the tongue. I meant client."

"You also said 'therapy', not coaching."

"I misspoke. The work overlaps. Coaching, of course."

"I understand," she says evenly. "But definitions matter. Especially in your case."

He doesn't respond.

"Tell me, how do you see your role with Grace?"

"I'm her stabiliser. Her disruptor, if needed. She's caught in poor relational boundaries, workplace trauma, and impostor distortions. She needs someone to help deconstruct the false self so the authentic self can emerge."

"Oliver..." she says slowly. "You're describing a clinical framework. Not coaching."

"I'm describing what *she needs*."

"And you believe you're the best person to give it to her?"

"I *know* I am."

There's a pause.

Maureen speaks carefully now. "I need to be honest. I don't think you're ready."

"You said I was improving."

"I said I was hopeful. But you're sleep-deprived. Manic. Obsessed with a client you're no longer ethically permitted to work with."

"She *wants* to work with me."

"That doesn't make it safe."

He stares at the stone sculpture on the table between them. It isn't calming. It's just a formless mess of bumps and dimples and bulges. It doesn't make any sense.

"You've never understood the work Grace and I are doing."

"You're right. I don't. Because you've withheld. Because you're performing in our sessions rather than truly pursuing therapy."

He smiles. "I appreciate your concern."

"I think we need to review the framework we're working in," she says. "I think you need to step away from all client-facing activity for now."

"No," he says. "You don't get to sabotage this."

She doesn't flinch. "This isn't sabotage. It's responsibility. You're not well, Oliver."

"I have patients I need to protect."

"I am protecting them, Oliver. And I'm protecting you."

He stands. "I've never been clearer."

"Oliver–"

He thanks her. Smiles. Leaves.

She listens to the angry stamp of his feet on the stairs and the heavy slam of the front door. She breathes in. Presses one hand to her diaphragm. Old grounding techniques. They work, mostly. Then she leans behind her chair and steers her wheelchair round, moves herself into it slowly.

She crosses to the window, watching the dusk bleed into

the sky. She has known Oliver for the best part of twenty years. She remembered the first time he sat in her office as a student. So articulate. So desperate to do good. And now she feels incredible sympathy for him, for everything he has experienced. But she doesn't know how to help him in this moment if he doesn't want to be helped. A wave of sadness runs through her.

She flicks through her notebook, then picks up her phone. Googles until she finds the number.

"Is Grace there, please?"

She waits while someone goes to fetch her. She notices herself fiddling nervously with the pen in her hand and puts it down.

Eventually, a woman comes to the phone. "Hello? Grace Harper."

"Hello, Grace." Maureen jots down the surname. "My name is Maureen Crouch. You don't know me, but I'm an associate of Oliver Smallwood. I believe he was your executive coach until recently?"

The young woman confirms. Her voice is light, and Maureen can hear a note of nervousness in it, which could be anxiety or confusion.

"I was wondering if we could talk briefly? In person, ideally."

"What about?"

"I'd prefer to talk to you in person, if that's possible. I could meet you somewhere in Scarborough, later today even, perhaps after you've finished work. I won't take up much of your time, I promise," she says, lightening things with a laugh, doing her best not to spook Grace. It's important she agrees to meet her. Maureen needs to explain where Oliver is in his therapeutic journey, that he's at a point of crisis, that he's not ready to see clients, and that Grace has to terminate coaching with him immediately.

A pause. Then agreement. They settle on 6.00 p.m.

"I'll come to you," Maureen says. She ends the call.

She closes her eyes. She knows this has to be done. But even so, it feels like a breach. A rupture in the sacred contract. But there are times when confidentiality isn't protection. It's danger. And Oliver is a danger now, particularly to Grace, whom Maureen suspects has become the unwitting object of some kind of unhealthy obsession, all of Oliver's unresolved trauma transferred from Julia to this new subject.

She cannot let this go.

She turns to pick up her phone again, to check the train times from York to Scarborough–

And stops.

Oliver is in the doorway.

She stares. "What are you doing?"

"I thought you might do something reckless," he says. "So I stayed. Just in case."

Her expression shifts, just slightly. "You need to leave, Oliver."

"You just phoned Grace."

"She has a right to be safe."

"I *am* keeping her safe," he says, and his voice is calm, clinical even. "She needs someone who won't look away. Someone who won't abandon her. You're the one disrupting the process."

"Oliver–"

"I hoped it wouldn't come to this," he says.

"Then don't let it."

"I have a duty of care," he whispers. "I won't let you get in the way."

Maureen's hand rises, a word half-formed on her lips. But he strikes before she can speak. The calming stone sculpture is heavier than he anticipated, and it takes some effort to lift high enough to bring down on her head with real force, even with her seated as low as she is in the wheelchair.

The first blow cracks the sound from her. The second sends her toppling to the floor. The third is insurance.

He stands there for more than a minute, staring at her, watching for any signs of life. But she's still, and her body doesn't rise and fall with breathing. The only thing moving is the expanding puddle of blood that pools around her head.

He goes to the kitchen and pours himself a large glass of water from the tap. He drinks it, then wets a cloth and returns to the consulting room. He wipes the statue clean and places it gently back on the table.

He removes his jacket, then drags Maureen back to her wheelchair. He lifts her upright as best he can and places her on the seat. He wheels her carefully to the head of the stairs, then lets go.

The sound is heavier than he expected as her limp body tumbles down the stairs and the wheelchair clatters after her against the wooden treads and the metal pipe of the stair lift. There's a distinctive thud as she reaches the bottom, like splintering open a coconut with a hammer.

He looks at her sprawled body and the upturned wheelchair beside her. The pose looks plausible. An accident. A misstep. Age. Gravity. A tragedy. He is gratified to see that her head is resting on the tiled floor of the hallway, and that blood begins to pool out again.

He checks the time. He's due to meet Grace at her office in two hours.

He takes his notebook from his bag, sits back in his chair and begins to make notes.

There's still a session to prepare for.

And Grace is waiting.

PART FOUR

CHAPTER 42
OLIVER

He cleans up the consulting room, the landing, the top of the stairs, then puts all the soiled kitchen roll and tea towels into a black bin liner he tears from a roll under the sink. He squeezes it into his bag. He'll put that in someone's wheelie bin in a side street on the walk back to the station.

Oliver pauses at the top of the stairs. The scene is quiet now. He allows himself a moment of stillness. Not regret. Just professional reflection. Maureen's death is... unfortunate.

But regret is not a clinically useful concept. Maureen had become a contaminant in the process. She had threatened the sanctity of his work with Grace. Her actions constituted a clear breach of trust. In such circumstances, one must be guided not by emotion, but by principle.

He has a duty of care. To Grace.

The therapeutic relationship, if it is to be effective, must be unpolluted by sentimentality, social convention, or even the law. He knows how crucial it is to act in the best interests of the client, even when those actions are misunderstood.

Oliver presses the button on the stair lift and lowers it a couple of steps before he stops it. He has seen it in its unreliable operation so often, seen the engineers visit – and fail – to fix it. It's perfectly credible that it might get jammed before it reaches the top, that Maureen might stretch too far to reach it, that her wheelchair shifts across the top step and tumbles down the stairs. An elderly woman. Faulty equipment. Unlucky timing. What other logical explanation is there?

He returns to the consulting room. It's still warm, the radiator humming, the two teacups cooling on the table. He picks up his and drains the last of it, then washes both in the kitchen sink, as he imagines Maureen would have done after their session. He scans the surfaces. Checks the carpet. Nothing visible. No cast-off. No blood spatter.

He walks carefully down the stairs, stepping over the body and past the wheelchair, with professional detachment. He's learned from the mistakes of Justin – the mess, the panic, the improvisation. That was an emotional response. This is strategic.

Then he lets himself out. No rush. No fuss. A professional leaving at the agreed time.

OLIVER ARRIVES at Grace's office ten minutes early. He stands under the awning and straightens his coat. There's a serenity to this moment – the quiet street, the crackle of tyres on wet tarmac, the sodium glow of the streetlights reflected in the puddles. Everything slick and clean.

When he goes in, it's Kyle who greets him. Oliver finds Kyle difficult to look at. Something in the man's face, all bravado and adolescent menace, makes his skin crawl. He wonders how Grace survives in this environment at all.

He waits, composed.

And then she appears.

Grace.

She smiles, a little too brightly, masking her tension. She leads him through to a side office and closes the door.

"Thanks for coming," she says. "I know it's a bit out of nowhere."

He nods. "It's good to see you."

They sit. She smiles again, nervously. "I wasn't sure you were coming, actually…"

She must mean after Maureen's phone call. He feigns ignorance. "No?"

She changes tack. "I thought it might be awkward, considering... how things ended."

"They didn't end," he says gently. "They paused."

"That's good," she says, sounding relieved. "Because I wanted to ask if you could do some coaching for me again."

"Of course."

She's come back to him, as he knew she would.

"When would you like to start?"

"Oh, sorry," she says, "it's not with me. It's with Mohammed."

He pauses. "Mohammed?"

"Yes. He's one of my team. Junior, but he's ambitious. I've promised him a bit of development support, and I remembered how helpful you were when we worked together. I thought maybe coaching sessions with you might be good for him."

There's a long moment. Oliver nods slowly. "So you're referring him to me. For coaching."

She launches into a little speech: how much she appreciated Oliver's work; how insightful he was; how he helped her see things differently. But it's all too polished. The gratitude sounds thin and scripted, like she's telling the story she thinks he wants to hear.

He lets her talk. And as she does, something in him recalibrates.

She is, once again, resisting the truth. Still avoiding her reckoning. Still refusing to submit. This, too, is part of the process. A regression before breakthrough. He blames himself, of course. Challenge can be a hard tool to wield correctly, and he can see she has built up a tough shell across the years. He hasn't pushed her hard enough.

Not yet.

But he will.

"I'd be happy to take Mohammed on," he says.

Her shoulders relax a little. "Great. Thank you. Honestly, it means a lot."

"Of course," he says, standing. "Whatever you need."

CHAPTER 43
GRACE

"Look. There. See? It's juddery again."

Adam's pointing anxiously at the television like it's had a stroke.

"You can really see it in the panning shot – the ball blurs for a second. It's the refresh rate. That's what does it."

I squint at the screen.

"It looks fine to me," I tell him. "I mean, you couldn't hang it in the Tate Modern, but the picture's sharp, the sound's on, and there's a man kicking a ball. What more do you need?"

But Adam's still watching with a frown.

"Is this one of those man things?" I ask. "I mean, I can see from your face that something is offending your sense of masculine order."

"Ag, well, you can mock, but it's because it's LCD," he says, flipping open a leaflet I didn't even see him pick up. "There's this OLED at Richer Sounds, fifty-five inch." He shows me the picture with the reverence of a man who's seen God in a display catalogue. "Was four grand, now it's down to £2,499. Absolute bargain."

"Two and a half grand?" I say, too loud. "For a television?"

"It's a *bargain*," he says, like I've just insulted his nan. And that's when I realise there's a bit of him that isn't joking.

"A bargain is a tenner off a toaster, not the entire GDP of a small country for a massive screen to watch *Line of Duty*."

"Okay, okay... I'm relieved now I didn't show you the sixty-five-inch one."

And that's when I feel it – the shift. Something hot and fast boiling up under my skin.

"I'm on a *formal warning*, Adam," I snap. "We might not be able to afford a tin of beans next week. There's a letter on my record, and Mohammed's about to go to HR. Kyle's circling like a baby vulture... And you're flipping through TV porn like we've just won the lottery."

"Okay, let's leave it. It's just a telly. It's not like I was suggesting we buy a bloody yacht."

I clear up a few dirty teacups in silence. I should really leave it there, but I don't.

"Fine. I mean, I'm sorry I'm not a cash machine," I mumble, "but you're not exactly raking it in either."

His face drops. I see the hurt register. He shifts awkwardly, rubbing his neck under the neck brace.

Shit.

Instantly, I regret it. But it's too late. I know I'm stressed. I can make all the excuses under the sun, but it's really not fair to unload on him.

"I didn't mean to upset you," he says quietly. "I was just trying to take your mind off things."

"I know you were. I'm sorry to bite your head off."

I sit in the chair. He comes over and starts to massage the back of my neck. It feels sooo good.

"Blimey, Grace, what are you keeping in this neck of

yours? Golf balls? You've got more knots than a set of Christmas lights."

"You know what'd take my mind off things?" I say. "Not being five minutes away from total career collapse. You know I need money if I'm going to make this university plan happen."

He keeps massaging. "You'll get there, Grace. You're a superstar. And I'd help, you know. If I could."

"I know," I say, voice flat. "But you can't. I get that you can't. But it does leave us kind of stuck, even though I know it's not your fault."

There's another long pause while he keeps massaging.

Then, in a careful tone I assume he's using so as not to piss me off again, he says, "If you're really that worried about money... maybe it's time to have the conversation."

"What conversation?"

"You *know* what conversation."

"Oh right," I say. "*That* conversation."

He means Bridget. The house. The thing I've been dancing around for months. He says it anyway.

"I just think you need to talk to her about money and the house. About sorting things properly. Officially."

I pull away from his massaging, spin round and cross my arms. "Right. And how do you think that'll go?"

He shrugs. "She's your sister."

"Exactly."

He pushes on. "Look, your parents died without a will. You've lived here ever since. You gave up years to look after them. That matters. I like Bridget, but let's be honest, what did she do? Sweet F.A. And let's not pretend Bridget and Dave are struggling in their little mansion."

I let out a bitter laugh.

"I'm just saying, if she's decent, she'll understand."

"That's the problem," I mutter. "She might not be."

It's not that he's wrong. He isn't. But no amount of massaging can get rid of the stress I feel about this. I gave up everything to be here – university, any kind of career I could have been building. I bathed them and cut their toenails and wiped their bums. Poured morphine into little cups at four in the morning. I held their hands. All Bridget did was turn up for an hour at Christmas and act like she was doing me a favour.

And now, legally, this house is in both our names. If I could remortgage, I could free up all the cash I need to quit my lousy job and go back to my university course. But I don't even know if I *can* remortgage without her. I hate the idea of crawling to her.

But unless I fancy selling a kidney on eBay, I don't really have a choice.

I grab my phone and write a quick message.

Can we meet this week? We need to talk about the house.

I hit send before I can change my mind.

Adam comes over and leans down to give me a hug. "Well done, luv. It's the right thing to do."

But it doesn't feel right. It feels terrible. I'm not ready for this. I get that sick feeling you get when you're going into an exam you haven't revised for.

To my surprise, her reply comes through seconds later.

Okay. When?

No fuss. No delay. Just that.

I look up at Adam. "She's coming."

Adam nods. "That's good, right?"

I don't answer.

Because although it is good, it terrifies me.

CHAPTER 44
OLIVER

Oliver sits at his kitchen table, sleeves rolled up. Dinner has been eaten, a ready-meal pasta, and the plate put to one side.

He considers his meeting with Grace earlier. Asking him to coach Mohammed instead of her is a classic avoidance strategy. Clearly, she still doesn't understand. She hasn't fallen far enough. She isn't ready. But it is his job to break her down, to peel away the defensive layers, to get her to a state of readiness.

Now comes the real work.

He lays down newspaper on the kitchen table, sheet after sheet, shielding the surface beneath like a surgeon preparing for an operation.

He thuds the heavy black bin bag onto the table with an organic squelch. One of the corners leaks something thick and brown. He'll have to check if the same sticky substance has seeped into the boot of his car. He didn't notice anything when he was loading up – but he was in a hurry in case any of her neighbours might be out and about. He puts on his yellow washing-up gloves and slices the bag open with a kitchen knife, splitting it like a carcass.

The smell hits him immediately. Sour milk, damp bread, rotting fruit. But this work has no place for squeamishness. He reaches into the bag with gloved hands and begins.

The first layer is pure domestic squalor. Banana skins, crusted takeaway cartons, loose clumps of soggy cereal. Junk mail bleeds into greasy chip wrappers. He works through it all with quiet focus, peeling away layers like a crime scene technician. People think their secrets are kept in locked drawers or whispered confessions. But this is where the truth lives: in what they throw away.

He pulls out a wine bottle – cheap pinot. A sports supplement vitamins leaflet stained brown by tea bags. A receipt for a coffee and a sandwich. A crushed envelope with an electricity supplier's logo smeared across the front like blood in water.

Then he strikes gold. A letter from her credit card provider about a missed minimum payment. A utilities bill, final warning. An overdraft extension. He extracts them delicately, smoothing each one out like a love note, placing them in a neat pile at the far end of the table. He uses an old tea towel to blot one envelope dry.

He can see Grace is behind on at least two payments. She is struggling. She's kept the mask on, still walking around with her sad little to-do lists, still pretending she's in control.

But she's not.

And soon, no one will be able to pretend otherwise.

His own financial implosion comes back to him in bright, unpleasant flashes. A council tax letter shoved through the door. The smell of his ex-wife's perfume disappearing from the house, just as the electricity was cut off. The sheer, grinding shame of it.

He fishes out one of her bank statements, then peels off his gloves. He makes a quick search online and dials the number.

The fraud line rings twice before a young man with a chipper voice answers.

"Good evening. You're through to Lloyds. How can I help?"

"Yes," Oliver says, allowing a nervousness to creep into his voice. "I found a Lloyds bank card on the pavement. The name on it is Grace Harper. I thought I should report it before someone else uses it."

The man thanks him. Routine questions follow. He supplies the account and sort code details from her jam-smeared bank statement.

"I hope I've done the right thing calling. I was worried it might have been taken by pickpockets."

The man assures him he has. He promises to freeze the card immediately and contact the customer.

"Thank you so much. That does put my mind at rest."

Oliver hangs up and stares at the wall. That should throw her into a bit of a tailspin. She'll try to pay for something small, petrol or coffee, and the machine will spit her out. She'll feel the eyes of the queue behind her. She'll go home and start making phone calls. The creeping doubt will begin. *Did I spend too much? Did I miss something? Am I losing my grip?*

Good.

Let her lose it.

The caterpillar doesn't become a butterfly through tenderness. It dissolves inside its own skin.

CHAPTER 45
GRACE

When I get to the pub at the time we arranged, Bridget's not there.

Of course she isn't. That would require basic respect and a functioning moral compass.

Instead, Dave's waiting, sitting at a corner table, pint in hand. He spots me and stands up, trying to look warm and cheery, like this is a lovely surprise for both of us.

"Grace," he says. "Glad you made it."

I glance behind him, just to make sure she isn't crouching behind the fruit machine. "Where's Bridget?"

He gestures to the opposite seat. "Sit down, pet. I'll explain."

I sit, knowing exactly what's coming, that awful feeling in my stomach that I'm about to be humiliated. I've been here too many times.

"Bridget couldn't make it," he says. "She's sorry."

"No, she isn't."

He frowns. "Well, she–"

"She knew I wanted to speak to her. Not you. No offence, Dave, but she's my *sister*."

"She thought it might be easier if we just had a quick chat. You and me."

"For me or for her?"

He just sort of shrugs at that. How can he defend her?

"Money," he says apologetically. "It's a tricky subject. She didn't want it to turn into... you know."

"A scene?"

"Well, not my words..."

"Not yours, no." I glance around. Of course she sent him. Neutral pub, public setting, maximum embarrassment if I cry or lose my temper. Coward.

"Can I get you a drink?"

No, I don't want a drink. I just want to get on with it.

"Maybe you could take her a message. I want to discuss the house," I say, already tired. "I'm not doing great at work. I just needed to talk through a few things."

"Sorry to hear things have been rough."

"Thanks."

Dave nods, very slowly, frowning like he's reading the subtitles to a difficult film. "Thing is, Bridget's been patient for a long time."

"Patient?"

"She never pushed for her half," he goes on. "Not when your mum and dad died. Not when you were finding your feet. But it's been what, three years?"

"Four," I say. "But who's counting?"

"It's just... she doesn't want to feel she isn't getting what she's entitled to."

I stare at him. "And what *does* she feel she's entitled to? She doesn't live there. She moved out at nineteen and disappeared with you. I came back. I looked after them. I gave up my twenties, university, the lot."

"That was your choice," he says.

I've known Dave since I was fifteen. Back then, he used to

take us to Filey in his mum's Fiat Punto and buy us WKDs from the off-licence. But since then, Bridget's become practically a stranger.

"She didn't want to say this to your face," he goes on, "but she thinks she's been more than generous letting you live there all this time."

"Oh, does she?"

"She said she's been patient long enough. That you've coasted. Her word. Not mine."

The floor seems to tilt beneath me.

"She said she'd be happy to split things properly. Fairly."

"Fairly," I echo. "Right."

"She wants to put the house on the market," Dave says. "She wants her half. That's the way it is, I'm afraid."

I stare at him. The pub hums with the chatter of people having a much better day than me.

"I nursed our dying parents in that house," I say quietly, "while Bridget was off living her best life. She let me drown so she didn't have to get her hands dirty."

"She didn't mean it cruelly," he mumbles.

"She sent *you*." My voice breaks. "She knew exactly what she was doing."

He just shrugs again and takes a long gulp of his pint. "I'm just the messenger, Grace."

I push my chair back. "Tell her she got what she wanted."

I THUNDER out of the pub, too angry to think. I've been walking for a minute before I stop and take stock of where I am. I'm supposed to be meeting Adam, but I don't even know if I'm heading in the right direction. I get my bearings and turn down a side street.

I'm glad he's meeting me after his physio. I need to tell him what just happened. I'm fuming and I'm upset. I check my phone to see if we're still meeting at The Ship & Anchor and notice my hand is shaking with fury.

"Alright, luv? Did it go okay?"

"I'll tell you in a minute," I say, and I can hear the wobble in my voice. "I need a drink."

"Okay," he says, "let's get one."

He takes my hand and walks me along the road. We only go a few doors down before I find myself outside a window with a huge display of televisions.

"Oh look," says Adam, as he stops walking. "We're just next to Richer Sounds. Come on, we might as well take a quick look."

Without waiting for my answer, he heads into the shop. Now I understand why he chose The Ship, a pub we never go to. So he could bring me here.

The showroom's brighter than Las Vegas. Rows of televisions blare out different parts of the same sports commentary in surround-sound torture. Adam's drifted over towards the home cinema section.

"I thought we were going to talk," I say angrily.

"I *want* to talk," he says earnestly, turning to me. I'm taken aback at just how serious he sounds. He looks small under the light. Tired and pale.

"Adam? What's up?"

"I know it's not a great time," he says, rubbing his neck, "but... physio's not working. Not really. My mobility hasn't improved. The pain's not much better. And I have to keep this bloody thing on for another month." He points angrily at his neck brace. "I can't drive. Can't work. I'm in the house all day. It's like–" He gestures helplessly at the wall of screens. "This is it. This is the world."

I want to be angry – with Bridget, with work, and with Adam too. But here he is, looking desperately sad and lost, telling me his only friends in the world are me and a television.

I don't want to be like Bridget. I don't want to be petty and cruel and miserly. I want to be generous and caring, even if it makes no financial sense.

"Let's get it," I say. "The TV."

He blinks. "Really? No, you're right, we can't afford it. Let's get that drink. Two halves and a very small packet of peanuts."

"No, I mean it," I say. "Let's get it."

I smile, but it doesn't quite reach. My stomach's a ball of lead.

"But what if they fire you? How the hell are we going to live on the streets with a 55-inch television?"

"They're not going to fire me," I tell him, hoping it's true. "And if they do, we can always live in the box."

His whole face lights up. He grabs hold of me and kisses my cheek. "You're amazing."

The sales assistant goes off to get someone else, and then there's a grand performance – the giant box wheeled out on a trolley like a sacred object, one person to push, two to steady it, another in front to move the other customers back. People look as it's paraded through the shop like a carnival float. It's a production.

At the till, I hand over my card. PIN in. Waiting…

DECLINED.

I blink.

The assistant frowns. "Want to try again?"

"Sure," I say, heart hammering. "Weird."

I try again.

DECLINED.

Try another card.

DECLINED.

I want the floor to open up. The manager comes over.

There's a conference. The TV gets wheeled back into the storage zone like a failed experiment. We skulk out of the shop like criminals.

Outside, the sky's gone grey and mean and the air smells like rain.

"Well, that wasn't at all embarrassing," I try to joke.

But Adam doesn't say anything. He's not looking at me. Just staring straight ahead like I kicked a puppy in front of him.

"I didn't know," I say. "I didn't think it was that bad."

"It's not your fault," he mutters. "Come on, let's go and get that drink."

But I can tell he's angry with me. He wanders off towards the pub, and I glance back at my distorted reflection in the shop window, like a ghost laid over the colourful screens full of lush green football pitches and summer holiday beaches. I want to scream. Or cry. Or curl into a ball and vanish. First work. Then the house. Now this.

Five minutes later, Adam comes over to our table with a couple of pints of beer.

"We'll be okay," he says. "At least you've sorted things with Bridget and the house."

I don't tell him about the excruciating conversation I just had with Dave, and that we might need to sell the house and move out to God-knows-where we could afford with half the money. Some crappy bedsit with a mouldy fridge and a shared bathroom.

I'd like to talk to him and tell him about everything, but I feel it choked up in my throat, like someone's closing their hands around my neck.

CHAPTER 46
OLIVER

The following morning, Oliver arrives early at The Driftwood Café. He chooses a quiet table in the far corner with a clear view of the door. He likes to watch clients arrive. There's something about that first unguarded moment that reveals a lot. He orders a flat white and a croissant, wanting to make it appear he's in command of the space.

Mohammed is perfectly on time. Oliver recognises him from his frequent observation sessions outside the agency. He stands and offers a warm handshake. He gestures to the seat opposite.

"So, Mohammed. I'm sure you've researched coaching and know what it's all about."

They skip the usual small talk. Oliver can barely be bothered with the coaching niceties. He gallops through the contracting phase like a formality.

"Let's not waste time," he says. "You're here for a reason. You want change."

Mohammed shrugs. "I guess."

Oliver leans forward. "Then let's start. Tell me a bit about how you've arrived here."

Mohammed talks. He gives a potted personal history and gets to when he joined Lancaster & Lyle. He talks about his ambitions.

"And how are those shaping up?" Oliver asks, leading Mohammed to what he wants to talk about. "You know, under the new management?"

Mohammed talks about Grace. About the pressure she seems to be under. About how she's unpredictable, snappy and distracted. But he pulls back before he gets too critical. "I don't know. Maybe she's just under a lot of stress."

Oliver smiles. He positions himself as kind and encouraging. "Yes, perhaps. But we're here for you today, not her."

"Fair enough."

Oliver shifts forward slightly, and lowers his voice.

"I wonder what would happen if you didn't edit yourself quite so much."

Mohammed blinks. "What do you mean?"

"I mean… let's put your concern for other people to one side for a moment. Let's focus on what *you* want and need."

Mohammed nods, and Oliver sees him sit up a bit more confidently. It's amazing how empowering it is when someone gives you permission to be selfish.

"You're ambitious," says Oliver. "You wouldn't be here if you weren't. But let's ask ourselves for a moment, what's the good of that ambition if you don't put it into action?"

Mohammed blinks. "I don't know…"

"I think of it as stifled potential."

He lets the thought hang there between them for a moment. The room is silent but for the strangled hissing of milk being frothed.

"Let me show you something."

Oliver takes a pen and pad from his bag. He draws a dot on the paper.

"This is you, getting your qualifications, landing your dream job at Lancaster & Lyle."

As he speaks, he draws a line from the dot upwards and right at a steep angle.

"You're climbing, climbing, climbing."

He begins to make the line less steep.

"And this is you recently, evening out, no new things coming in. The successes are fewer and fewer."

He lets the line resolve to horizontal.

"And here you are now. You're flat," he says softly, tapping the flat line. "You've stalled. And once you stop rising, that's how people disappear."

Oliver drops the pad onto the table between them. He watches Mohammed take it in as he stares at the disappointing curve of his stalled career.

Finally, Mohammed nods. Just a small tilt of the head.

"I'm not here to coddle you, Mohammed. If you want to be a leader, start acting like one. If you want that line to start climbing again, we have to remove whatever or whoever is in your way."

He doesn't say her name, but they're both thinking it. Grace.

"Well," says Mohammed tentatively, "I was toying with the idea of writing a letter of complaint..."

Oliver leans back.

"I notice you use the word 'toying', Mohammed. It's interesting, because who plays with toys?"

"Children."

"Yes, and I wonder if you're not allowing yourself permission to grow beyond your junior role, to push for what you want. Do you want to toy with ideas, or do you want to put those ideas into action?"

The words land. Oliver watches them sink in.

"For the sake of argument," says Oliver, " let's assume

you were going to write that letter of complaint. What would it say?"

He picks up the pad and pen again and effectively begins to take dictation. Oliver writes down all Mohammed's moans and gripes. Together, they write a list of allegations: erratic leadership, failure to communicate, emotional outbursts, negligence. Oliver tightens the language into something dangerous. He leads Mohammed by the nose down exactly the path he wanted. He has weaponised coaching, and Mohammed is the hand grenade he intends to throw into the middle of Grace's life.

When he comes to an end, Oliver reads it back to him. He exhales like he's just conducted a symphony.

"How does that sound?"

Mohammed slumps back in his chair, looking pale. "Jesus."

"You've done something brave," says Oliver. "Most people never do."

He claps Mohammed on the shoulder and tells him the session has been a triumph. But really, he's congratulating himself.

Mohammed looks uncertain, like he's only come for a paddle and the tide is in danger of sweeping him away.

"I mean," Mohammed says, faltering, "I don't want to get anyone fired."

"No," Oliver agrees gently. "But you do want to be heard. I'll type that up for you, so you can see just how far you've come."

"Do you think I should send it?" Mohammed looks terrified.

"Only you know that," says Oliver. "But from where I'm sitting, I just watched a man come out of the shadows and step into the light."

CHAPTER 47
GRACE

I've been staring at the same Excel sheet for half an hour.

The numbers are wrong. Again.

I'm meant to be compiling a month-end financial summary, but nothing makes sense. The spreadsheet is a Frankenstein's monster of tabs and colour-coded chaos. The figures bounce around like popcorn in a microwave. Truth is, I'm so distracted by the idea that I might be out of a job at any moment, I can't concentrate.

Get a grip, Grace.

I start again, slower this time. Then I freeze.

Three thousand pounds. I check again. And again. I check the formula. Double-check the totals. It's still short. My skin prickles. The back of my neck sweats. Where the hell has three thousand pounds of company money gone? My stomach lurches like I've just driven over the crest of a hill too fast. That faint, woozy feeling of something about to go very, very wrong.

Something pops into my head – the flicker of a memory. Kyle grinning, sugar on his fingers, waving the company credit card like he'd won a prize. That Friday morning, I sent him out for coffee and cakes. I should have known it was a bad idea. I remember when he handed me the receipt, his joke about getting champagne next time. I laughed, but it stuck in my throat.

No. He wouldn't. That'd be madness. Wouldn't it? Anyway, he couldn't take out three thousand pounds. It's ridiculous.

I should speak to Patrick.

But what if I do and I've got this wrong? Then I look like a bloody useless manager in a different way. I need more information first.

I sneak a look across the office. Kyle's at his desk, headphones on, chewing a pen like he's in school detention. I watch him for a moment, trying to work out what I'm even looking for. Guilt? Fear? Glee? I walk over slowly, as casually as I'm able.

"Hey," I say. "Quick one. Do you remember those coffees and pastries you picked up a while back? Did you get a receipt for that?"

"I did," he says. "And I gave it to you."

"Oh, did you?" I say, as innocently as I can make it sound. "Only I'm doing the monthly financial report."

He shrugs. "What's money in this economy anyway? It's all just numbers on a screen until the lights go out."

"Kyle. Head office look at all that *very* carefully."

I make it sound serious, like Interpol might be on to him. I'm hoping he'll point his wrists my way so we can put the cuffs on. But all he does is raise an eyebrow.

"Jesus, you auditing me now? The Great Espresso Heist of 2025? If Lancaster & Lyle's gonna sink over ten quid's worth of croissants, I'm heading for the lifeboats."

I laugh. "No. I'm just reconciling the card statements.

Trying to get the paperwork straight. There's some odd totals showing up. Thought maybe you'd gone wild in Pret."

"Must've been the hazelnut syrup in those cappuccinos." He leans back, stretching. "Or maybe I bought a Rolex and a round of lap dances."

I keep smiling.

He gives me a long, slow look. "Are you actually accusing me of something? Because I can't decide if this is offensive or just tragic."

I laugh too quickly. "No, no. Just some weird discrepancies, that's all. Probably nothing."

He tilts his head. "Are you okay, Gracie? You look like you're about to faint."

"Don't worry," I say lightly. "I'm fine."

"You sure? Only I've seen pensioners on mobility scooters with more sparkle."

"Thanks."

"No worries. Tell you what, if I ever *do* decide to rob the place, I'll cut you in. We could run away to Portugal. Set up a rogue estate agency. You do the spreadsheets. I'll distract the clients with charm and baked goods."

He watches me go, expression unreadable.

Back at my desk, the sweat is prickling at the back of my neck. I can't prove anything. And I can't just do nothing. I pick up my phone and check the train times to Leeds.

WHEN HIS ASSISTANT shows me into his office, Patrick's mouth is doing that thin, disapproving expression people have when their dog's just done a shit on the carpet. It doesn't do much for my nerves.

I don't muck about. I explain everything – the three grand shortfall, the repeated checking, the fact that it *can't* be a simple error. My voice stays steady, but inside I feel like I'm standing on a cliff edge.

He listens, nodding, his fingers meshed together like the villain in a crappy low-budget drama.

"I think we'll need to have some kind of investigation," I say to finish.

He leans back. "Well," he says, after a pause. "Thank you, Grace. You were right to bring this to me."

Relief punches through me, fast and hot. "Good. Thank you."

"But," he adds, "in order to protect the process, you'll need to step back."

I blink. "What do you mean? I've done nothing wrong."

"I didn't say you had."

"But you're treating me like I have."

My mouth opens. Then closes. My brain has stalled. Patrick continues talking gently, like a vet euthanising a rabbit.

"A temporary suspension. It's completely standard, purely procedural. It's important no one feels the process is being influenced."

"You're suspending *me*?"

"It's not punitive," he says, too quickly. "Just a formality."

"Because I reported something?"

Patrick folds his hands. "This is in your own interest. Trust me, Grace, the optics matter. Especially given the letter."

I stare at him. "What letter?"

He stops and his mouth hangs open a bit. He looks like a man who's just said something he very much wasn't supposed to. He straightens a paperclip, then sets it down. "It's nothing. A minor complaint. HR have the details. I'm sure you'll be contacted formally."

He sent it then.

Sod you, Mohammed.

A chill washes through me. Patrick must read it on my face.

"Honestly, Grace, this isn't about blame. It's about clarity. You'll be on full pay. Take the time to rest. Let the investigation run its course."

I feel like I've stepped out of my body. Watching this scene from above. I nod like I'm fine, like I'm not dying inside.

"When?" I ask.

Patrick looks at his watch. "You'll probably make it back before closing," he says gently. "Go now. Take half an hour to gather your things."

OUTSIDE, the wind catches my coat like a sail. I walk fast back to the station. I feel like I'm being watched. Paranoid, like everyone knows what just happened.

Except things *keep* happening. Taxies and takeaways all hours of the night. This money at work and some weird transactions in my personal account. The junk mail and phone calls. Bloody Martijn de Vries. Three grand doesn't just *vanish.*

By the time I reach the office, it's just before 5.00 p.m. I'm hoping Kyle and Mohammed will have gone early, but they're still there.

Mohammed doesn't look up. Kyle glances over, then says something to Mohammed I can't hear.

I pack up my desk, assuming they know exactly why, like I've been caught with my actual hands in the actual till. No one says anything, of course – they just pretend to type a bit harder.

For a second, I consider standing on the desk and screaming *This is not my fault.* But I don't. Instead, I slide my laptop into my bag. Pull the charger from the wall. I turn to make as swift an exit as I can, but my bag catches the tin of pens on my desk and they go flying everywhere. I fall to my knees and gather them up as quickly as I can. I don't think I've ever felt more humiliated.

And just when I think it can't get any worse, that's when I see him.

Oliver.

CHAPTER 48
OLIVER

Oliver arrives at the estate agency five minutes early, not because he's eager, but because Mohammed needs watching. The boy is soft. Soft people need firm guidance. He's here to ensure the complaint letter about Grace has been sent. If not, he'll run another impromptu coaching session – some exercise about values, a discussion about assertiveness or something. That'll give a nudge that tips him over the edge.

Oliver pushes the glass door open and steps inside.

The sight that greets him is unexpected.

Grace. On her knees, as if in prayer. A manic expression on her face, and a fistful of pens in each hand. She looks up at the noise of the door. When she sees him, her body jolts, and she rises with unnatural speed, seizes him by the elbow and pulls him into the side office.

Her face is flushed. Her hands are shaking.

"What the hell are you doing here?"

He raises both hands in placid surrender, barely containing his glee at seeing her so distraught. "Grace, I'm here for a coaching session with Mohammed."

"Cut the crap," she hisses. "I know what you've done. That complaint letter to HR. I know you're behind it."

Wonderful. The rug has already been pulled out from under her.

Oliver arranges his expression with care: a mixture of hurt and just enough confusion to seem plausible. "I can't comment on the contents of any client's session," he says gently. "Confidentiality, I'm afraid."

She just stares at him like she might be on the verge of committing some act of violence.

"I understand you're distressed," he continues in his studied, calming tone. "I'd be the same in your position. All I can say is that Mohammed has been under pressure. He's... impulsive."

He figures this will be a strong enough hint for Grace to grasp that Mohammed has sent the complaint letter without his approval – even though, of course, it was entirely Oliver's doing. He watches her mentally rearrange the pieces. She looks confused and drained and running on empty. He sees his opportunity.

"I can see you're hurt. I know how hard you've been working for this, Grace. It must be very upsetting for you."

Tears start to form in her eyes and she wipes at them furiously. She hates herself for it, he can tell. That only deepens the pleasure.

"You're under enormous pressure. And this – this rage you're directing at me? I don't think it's really about me, is it?"

She blinks, emotionally punch-drunk and on the ropes. That's the moment to move in.

"Grace... I want to help." He takes a tentative step closer, like she's a horse he doesn't want to spook. "I have time now, if you want to talk. We don't have to call it coaching. Just... a conversation. About what's going on. About everything."

She hesitates, torn. Then, slowly, she sits. She nods, almost imperceptibly.

And like that, he's in.

He allows himself a small smile. Takes a seat opposite her, just far enough to seem respectful, just close enough to create intimacy.

"Let's start with something simple," he says, reaching into his bag. "A self-audit. You feel you're in a bit of a hole. Let's see if we can dig you out of it."

He shows her the small packet he's holding. "These are strength cards." He slips them out of their box and lays them out on the desk like tarot, watching her read each one as he does so.

Resilience. Confidence. Leadership. Composure. Relationship-building. Reliability under pressure. Optimism…

Her eyes dart nervously across the cards with increasing anxiety. Eventually, they are all on the table.

"Now split them into three piles," he says, "As you feel they apply to you: *Strong, Developing,* and *Needs Attention.* There's no judgment," he says, gently. "It's just data. And the more honest you are, the more we can fix."

He chooses his words with the precision of a sniper. *Fix.* As though she's broken.

Grace sighs and starts picking, slow and mechanical, dragging the cards into piles. *Decisiveness.* Pause. *Assertiveness. Self-Belief.* Her hands hesitate more than they move.

"Good," Oliver says, when she's done. He points to the smallest pile. "These are the *Strong* ones?"

She nods, vaguely embarrassed.

"Tell you what, let's jump right in and start with the *Needs Attention* pile."

He picks up the largest stack of cards with both hands and makes a comic face at her, while he pretends the pile is heavy.

He does it as if he's trying to lighten the mood, but he's pleased she doesn't smile back.

He flicks through the pile with a frown, slowly, saying nothing. He pauses on one card.

"If you had to pick… would you say you're stronger in *Leadership* or *Following Instructions*?"

She snorts faintly. "Is there a third option? Hiding in the toilet?"

He chuckles indulgently as he lays the cards face up on the table.

"This actually explains a lot. Your lack of confidence at work, your struggle with emotional regulation, the difficulty managing challenge… You know something's wrong, but you can't quite put your finger on it. Am I close?"

She stiffens. "Are you reading my fortune?"

He laughs softly. "No. I'm listening. You're saying it all without words."

She stares at him. "I thought you were meant to make people feel better, not worse."

"I'm not a cheerleader, Grace. Imagine you're a car. We're doing the MOT. Better to find the faults now, in a safe space, than have a catastrophic breakdown on the motorway."

She laughs once, sharply. It's half-amused, half-horrified. "Are you calling me a Skoda?"

He presses on. "You've been struggling. I know it. You know it. The great thing is, we can work on this. Together. We can rebuild."

She nods slowly. He can almost taste her surrender. He could lead her anywhere.

He lets the silence stretch.

She speaks eventually.

"What are you doing here?"

She lifts her head. And the look in her eyes – he recognises it too late. Steel.

"I don't need rebuilding," she says. "This isn't coaching. You're acting like it's concern, but it's actually cruelty."

His mouth opens, but she's already standing. Something's shifted. He sees it in her posture. The way she looks at him now.

"Grace, let me help you."

"Of course. Because what I really need is a man to explain how broken I am."

Her voice is full of rage. He's hit her too hard. He can see he's made a tactical error.

"You're worse than Justin. At least he didn't pretend to care." Her face is flushed now. "You're a crap coach," she says. "And honestly, a bit of a creep."

"Grace–"

"No. Fuck off."

She storms to the door, throws it open.

Oliver leaves the meeting room without another word. They must have heard the argument in the main office. He races past Mohammed, hunched down, trying to make himself invisible behind his screen. He barely registers Kyle, leaning back in his chair and grinning like it's Christmas.

Outside, he walks fast, blind with fury. She was supposed to cry. To *need* him. How dare she? After everything he's done for her. The hours, the patience, every sacrifice he's made, and this is how she repays him? With contempt?

He stops beneath a lamppost, pressing his palms against it, gasping for air. He feels dizzy, as if the ground beneath him is shifting. He recognises the symptoms of a panic attack, closes his eyes and concentrates on his breathing. One, two, three, four, five. One, two, three, four, five.

When he opens his eyes, his vision clears slowly. This is the lamppost where he ran into Justin. He recognises it even though the flowers have gone. Just a miserable-looking bit of string remains, tied round the post like a snare.

Justin. Another one who refused his help. Oliver stares at the ground, his anger giving way briefly to an absurd thought, almost comic in its bleakness: perhaps getting rid of Justin was a mistake. Perhaps Grace deserved him after all. Maybe they deserved each other. A pair of arrogant fools determined to wreck themselves, despite all of Oliver's attempts to intervene.

He straightens slowly, feeling suddenly emptied out, exhausted by the ingratitude. He's done. Enough. Finished. If Grace Harper wants to destroy herself, fine. Let her. You cannot help someone who refuses to be saved.

He steps away from the lamppost and walks slowly into the darkening street, no longer certain of anything at all.

CHAPTER 49
GRACE

I watch as Oliver skulks away with his tail between his legs.

I can't believe it. A coach is supposed to be on your side, not rip you to shreds. That was a horror show. A psychological mugging with strength cards.

Once he's gone, I look around the room. Kyle's smirking, but once I make eye contact with him, he sinks behind his computer like a startled rabbit. Mohammed's keeping his head down too. Good. He knows I've clocked he sent that complaint letter about me, and he's waiting for me to tear him a new arsehole.

I sit at my desk and catch my breath. My heart is thumping. It must be the adrenaline rush of telling Oliver to fuck off.

Actually, I feel amazing. Oliver's done me a favour, because in a weird, twisted way, it worked. Yelling at him felt... good. Not okay-good, not spa-day-good. *Righteous.* Like something clicked back into place and I remembered who I was before all this – before Justin, before Kyle and the spreadsheet from hell and midnight pizza deliveries and double-glazing deals and bank cards that cancel themselves.

That's who I am under all this. Someone who doesn't put up with bullshit.

Which makes me think about Bridget. All the cancelled meetings, vague texts, casual brush-offs. Always some excuse, like she's too busy or tired or overwhelmed to deal with me. And always Dave, fobbing me off like a nightclub bouncer. Well, *I'm* tired of all *her* bullshit too.

I get up, grab my coat and my box of things and head for the door. As I pass Laurel and Hardy, I pause.

"That's right, boys. I've been suspended. Enjoy it while it lasts – because when I come back, I won't be taking prisoners."

BRIDGET ANSWERS the door in slippers and a dressing gown that's seen better decades. She freezes when she sees me.

"Are you letting me in or what?"

She hesitates. "I didn't know you were coming."

"Of course you didn't. I didn't give you time for Dave to make excuses for you."

I step past her into the hallway

"Grace–"

"No. Not this time." I spin to face her. "I need to talk, properly, to the organ grinder, not the monkey. I need the money from the house and I've completely had it with being fobbed off while you hide behind your boyfriend."

She bites her lip. The cogs are creaking. Something flickers in her eyes, a flash of something real.

"Grace," she says, "this isn't a good time. Dave won't like–"

"Who gives a crap about what *he* likes? This is between you and me."

I walk towards her and she flinches. She actually *flinches*. Like she thinks I'm going to hit her.

"Oh, don't be so dramatic," I say. "I'm not here to mug you."

She breathes out. Half-smiles. "Sorry. You startled me."

She says nothing else. Just stands there, small and pale. Tense. And then, like someone's yanked back a curtain, I see it. Not just tiredness. Not just reluctance.

Fear.

"Bridget," I say slowly, "are you okay?"

She blinks, confused. "What do you mean?"

Footsteps. A shadow on the glass in the front door. A key touching the lock.

Shit.

Bridget freezes. We stare at each other. We don't need to speak.

I grab her hand and pull her upstairs, into the spare room. We close the door softly and crouch behind the bed.

"Babe?" Dave's voice, casual. "You home?"

We don't breathe.

He's moving through the house. I try to make out where he is. The squeak of a plank in the hallway. Keys going into a bowl in the kitchen. The sound of the fridge opening.

His footsteps creak up the stairs.

I can hear my heartbeat in my ears.

Then he stops outside the door.

Silence.

Then the bathroom door opening. A breath. The toilet flushing. A pause. He walks away. Back down the stairs. The front door groans open. Closes.

We wait. Count to ten. Twenty.

Still nothing.

I look at Bridget's face. She's terrified.

"Bridget," I whisper. "Is he hurting you?"

Her eyes go wide. Her lip trembles. "No," she says brightly. But she says it *too* brightly.

That's the moment I know. She hasn't been managing me. *He's been managing her.*

"We're leaving," I say.

"What?"

"You're coming with me. Right now. You're going to stay at mine."

"I can't just go."

"Why not?"

"Dave–"

"Exactly."

Am I right to drag Bridget into this? Am I overstepping?

"Pack a bag," I say.

She hesitates. She looks at the door as if going through it would be like climbing Mount Everest.

"Now," I say urgently. "Before he comes back."

I see a shift in her eyes. That's enough. I charge around and throw things in a holdall. A jumper, toothbrush, charger, whatever I can grab. I spot her passport in the drawer and shove it in too. Just in case.

We bolt. Out the door. Into the car. She gets in the passenger seat, clutching her bag tightly. Her face is white.

I turn the key and pull away.

As we drive up the road, a car turns at the corner and drives towards us.

"Oh, shit," I whisper. "Get down."

"What?" Bridget turns to me.

It's a silver Peugeot, the car Dave drives. He must have forgotten something. I flash my panicked eyes at her. She hesitates, then sinks down into her seat.

Sure enough, as the car gets close to us, I can see it's Dave. I look straight ahead, but I can see he's spotted me.

I keep driving, flicking my eyes to the rear-view mirror. I see him pull over by their house. Then he pulls out again and does a U-turn.

He's following.

"Jesus."

I drive out onto the main road, concentrating on the traffic and trying to ignore Bridget muttering and whimpering in the footwell. Dave's car joins the road about five cars back. I speed up, my heart hammering so hard I think it might leave a bruise on my ribs.

I get to the lights at the junction just as they're turning red, but I floor it. I take the corner fast, tyres whining.

I look in the mirror.

He's there.

My hands are shaking, but I speed up again.

"What is he doing?" Bridget whispers.

"He's not going to catch us."

We head across town as fast as I dare. But whenever I check the mirror, he's a few cars back. He's not just following. He's chasing. This goes on for what seems like an eternity. Eventually, I zigzag down a side street, loop through a short-cut, and screech into my own road. I slam on the brakes, cut the engine, and half-drag her up the path.

Dave pulls up behind us just as we get to the door. He winds down his window and yells.

"Bridget! What the fuck is this?"

I fumble with the key. Shove the door open.

Then we're inside. I lock it, top and bottom. Slide the chain across. Bridget leans against the wall, shaking.

I peer into the kitchen, then the living room. No Adam. His neck brace is lying on the sofa. He must have gone out.

"Upstairs," I say and drag her with me.

As we hit the landing, there's a loud thump at the door. Then shouting.

"Open the door, Grace. I knew you'd do something like this. Knew it. You can't *stand* to see anyone else happy, can you? Always got to make it about you."

I steer Bridget into the bedroom. She crumples onto the bed, clutching her knees, while Dave keeps yelling.

"It'll be okay," I say, hoping I'm not lying.

It goes quiet. I go over to the window and sneak a look. He's outside, pacing on the path, his face red, staring up at the house and considering his options.

"Bridget! Babe. Let me in."

She stares at the floor, pale and shaking.

"Come on, babe. Just come outside and have a proper chat, yeah?"

Old Mr Sefton from number 26 comes out onto the pavement, craning his neck to get a look at what all the fuss is about. Dave turns on him instantly.

"Can I help you, Baldy?"

Mr Sefton blanches.

"Yeah, that's right, you, you old twat. Mind your own fucking business!"

That's enough to send him scuttling back into his house.

Dave starts walking back up the path. I stand on tiptoes to see him until he disappears out of view.

Then the door handle is rattling. Then he's pushing. Testing it.

I go rock-still and look at Bridget on the bed. She's frozen too, her eyes wide.

He pushes the letterbox open.

"Come on, babe. Talk to me."

I glance at Bridget. She looks like she might be sick. She looks up at me.

"Maybe I should just go out and talk to him."

"No fucking way." I move between her and the door. I can see how scared she is. I don't trust her to hold out after years of this sort of crap.

Then, as if he senses she's hesitating, he says it.

"You don't want to make me angry."

She looks at me, eyes wide.

"If you don't come out now," he says, "I'll come in."

That's it. I pick up my phone. My hand is shaking so badly I can barely tap the screen.

The letterbox slams shut. Silence. Then a single, sharp thud against the door.

I hit 999 and pray the police answer before the locks give way.

CHAPTER 50
OLIVER

His temper has subsided. He can see now he pushed too hard and damaged their valuable rapport. He was angry with her, but he mustn't let emotion get the better of him. He crouches behind the hedge opposite Grace's house, wet soil seeping into the knees of his trousers. He doesn't feel it. He is perfectly still, utterly focused, his breath low and measured.

He needs to formulate a plan.

He thinks he might knock. Apologise, perhaps. Invite her to talk. Not to beg forgiveness, of course, but to explain what she doesn't yet understand: that her resistance in the coaching session was simply confirmation of how much she *needs* his help. It is a classic reaction to therapeutic challenge. He feels sure he can lure her back.

But just as Oliver is considering all this, Ash arrives. Or Dave, as he now calls himself, as if changing your name erases who you are.

Oliver hears his voice before he sees his face, loud and obnoxious. Pacing, shouting, kneeling at the letterbox, then rising to boot the door with the flat of his foot, over and over, until the paint is scuffed black and the frame judders.

Oliver can't hear every word, but the shape of the situation is obvious. Grace and her sister are inside. Ash is outside, like a bad actor, arms thrown wide in theatrical outrage. His whole performance is grotesque. A tantrum in a grown man's body.

Men like this disgust him. Predators, prowling outside the homes of women who no longer want them. Bullying. Lurking. Convinced they're entitled to be let back in. Men like this have no self-awareness. They don't realise how they look.

Suddenly, there are flashing lights, and a police car pulls up at speed. Two officers emerge. Ash tries to confront them. There's a scuffle, and Ash is down on the pavement. One officer has a knee in his back, while the other restrains him.

The police lights strobe against Oliver's skin, illuminating his face in stark pulses. He feels suddenly aligned with their purpose, an ally in pursuit of the greater good. Clearly, the entire family are as bad as each other. A pack of feral, sociopathic dogs. Animals in clothes. Apes who think they've evolved because they hold a mobile phone.

Oliver watches Ash's stunned expression as the cuffs lock tight. Ash isn't fighting, just bewildered. And for a moment Oliver sees Grace's face there instead. A flicker of satisfaction surprises him, then hardens. He feels the clean pulse of justice.

Like a bolt of lightning striking him, it suddenly makes sense: the wrong person is in custody. Grace. *Grace* should be the one in cuffs, head bowed in shame. He thought he could coach her, that redemption was hers to choose. But Grace rejected every offer. Every opportunity. She didn't want help; she wanted escape. And the law exists precisely to stop people escaping accountability.

How could he have not seen it? He once thought she was damaged. Lost. Something to be fixed. But she isn't damaged. She's guilty.

Oliver considers the way she stood by while Justin was killed. How she set the kindling around Maureen's feet and handed Oliver the match. What she *made* him do. She let Kyle needle her, let Patrick discipline her, let Ash terrorise her – and still, she has the audacity to act like the victim. The poor, overwhelmed woman, trying her best.

But she is not overwhelmed. She is guilty. It's a moral failing, not a clinical one. A rot at the root of her character. And watching Ash, Oliver realises saving Grace means bringing her to justice. Real justice, legal and public. It isn't cruelty, he reasons; it's salvation.

Oliver stands slowly, brushing the leaves from his coat. A curtain moves in an upstairs window. A shadow flickers. It doesn't matter. He walks away without looking back.

Grace is guilty.

And Oliver now knows exactly what role he's destined to play in her story.

Not coach.

Judge.

PART FIVE

CHAPTER 51
OLIVER

A week has passed. Oliver has been wrestling with the knotty problem of Grace's retribution, but he finds he can't properly concentrate, in spite of thinking about nothing else. He's taken to walking, leaving the house early, while it is still dark, and marching across town to the castle. Then onwards along the ragged edge of the coast. He turns it all over in his mind as he stomps along, the sea at his shoulder, often forgetting to stop for lunch, usually not returning home again until after dark.

Today, he's almost home when the idea arrives, fully formed. A sudden clarity that cuts through the drizzle and the dark. He almost laughs aloud in the street. The thought is too perfect. How had he not seen it before?

Rain patters, cold against his hair, seeping down his neck. The streetlights smear amber across the wet pavement. He doesn't bother to pull up his collar. Oliver's thoughts are elsewhere.

He sees Justin's face in his mind's eye. The slack mouth. The glazed eyes. He remembers how his hands shook on the steering wheel afterwards. He'd been surprised at the damage – the caved-in bonnet, the shattered windscreen. You think of a car as solid and a human body as soft, but that night he learned the truth: the human body is not weak. It's a mass of bone and tendon, dense and heavy. It broke the car as much as the car broke it.

He turns the key in the door and steps inside, leaving his waterlogged shoes on the mat. He crosses the hall and goes to the cupboard under the stairs. Water drips from his coat in quiet plinks and pools onto the lino around his stockinged feet. He flicks on the little bulb and squats down, rummaging in the gloom. He moves the mop and bucket and the ancient hoover and looks on the shelves, scrabbling among old tins of paint and cleaning supplies until he finds what he's looking for: his father's battered red toolbox. His fingers close around cold metal. He lifts it out and sets it down on the hallway floor. The rusty clasps pop open with a satisfying snap.

The smell hits him immediately – old oil, metal, and wood shavings. He rummages through chisels, screwdrivers, assorted nails in an old tobacco tin. At the bottom, he finds what he's looking for – the claw hammer, heavy, balanced, old enough to have belonged to his grandfather. The wooden mallet, broad-headed and scarred with years of use. He tests their weight in his hands.

You think of a head as hard, a skull as strong. But bone cracks under force. Bone gives way to iron. His chest tightens with something almost like anticipation.

He doesn't take off his coat. He tucks a tool in each pocket. As he goes to turn the light off, he spots an old dust sheet, paint-stained and stiff, folded behind the hoover. Might be useful. He pulls it out and slings it over his shoulder.

Outside, the drizzle has thickened into a steady, pene-trating rain. The wind gusts harder now, rattling bins along the street. Thunder growls low in the distance, promising worse to come. He walks quickly, leaning into the storm, his pockets heavy.

By the time he reaches her street, her house is dark. Good. He takes up his familiar position in the hedges opposite her drive, hidden in shadow. He's seen her car, parked a few houses up, shadowed and half-concealed by trees.

Justin's face flashes across his mind again. Flesh isn't soft, not really. The human body is dense with secrets. Hard things do terrible damage to soft things. But bodies damage hard things too.

He checks his watch. Too early. People are still coming home from pubs, the odd dog-walker still dragging their mutt around the block. He forces himself to be patient. Patience is half the work.

He watches her windows. Dark. The neighbouring houses too. He waits, motionless, as the hours bleed away. He pulls the dust sheet from inside his coat and tears it in two along a frayed edge. He takes the hammer and mallet from his pockets and wraps each tightly in a section of the sheet. He weighs the tools, heavy in each hand. The sheet will muffle the impact and deaden the blows which might alert a witness.

He remembers striking Justin, the sound of it. Metal against flesh. The wet, final impact of something meeting its immovable end. His mind is clear, crystalline with purpose.

After midnight, thunder begins, low and distant at first, then building into deep, rolling detonations. Lightning flickers over the rooftops, splitting the sky in bright, jagged streaks. Perfect. Nature itself has come to assist him.

When the street is silent and lightning cracks directly overhead, he moves.

He crosses quickly to her car, hunkers down low beside it. He waits, counting the seconds between flash and thunder.

Flash. One. Two. Three. Four. Five–

He swings the hammer in a tight, vicious arc. The glass of the headlight implodes with a soft, muted crunch.

Flash. One. Two. Three. Four–

The mallet slams into the front wing, crumpling the metal with a solid thump.

Flash. One. Two. Three–

He times each blow to the masking thunder. Another headlight. The bonnet. The windscreen. Wing mirror. He works systematically, shifting his position, alternating hammer and mallet, moving along the car like a surgeon along an incision, recalling the damage Justin made to his own car. The dust sheet spreads the force, avoiding obvious impact dents. It's all in the details.

By the time he's finished, the car is fractured and broken, its metallic skin ruptured and split, leaking oil like dark arterial blood. His shoulders ache and his fingers are numb from the cold, but inside, he is alight.

By 2.00 a.m. he is home, soaked through and trembling. He shrugs off his coat and lets it fall to the floor. He goes upstairs and peels off his wet things, then towels himself dry. He slips on his dressing gown, ties it snug around his waist, and sits for a moment on the edge of the bed, breathing steadily until he calms his pulse to normal.

He picks up one of the unused burner phones, taps in the Crimestoppers number, and waits for the click and shuffle of the connection. His voice, when it comes, is mild and almost apologetic.

"Ah, yes, hello. I'd like to give someone some information."

He explains that he's just got back from holiday and only now seen the news about that poor man killed in a hit-and-run. He can't be sure, of course, but that night he saw a car driving erratically in the area. He remembers the date because it was the day before his flight. Yes, he says, he remembers the make. He even remembers the partial plate, because it's the same as one of his lottery numbers. He gives them a chunk of Grace's number plate, digit by digit, describing her car and its colour. He's calm and helpful. No, he'd rather not give his name. He's just a citizen doing the right thing.

When he hangs up, he lies back on his pillows, staring at the black square of the window. He slides beneath the covers, listening to the rain lash against the glass.

He imagines them tracing the number plate, heading for her address, closing in. To all intents and purposes, she killed Justin. It's only right she pays the price. This is what happens to people who persist in their illusions. It's only fair that consequences are felt equally. Let the punishment fit the crime.

For the first time in months, he sleeps soundly. The peaceful sleep of the just.

CHAPTER 52
GRACE

Luckily, my insurance has given me a posh new hire car. Mine's out of action because it was set upon by vandals. Smashed wing mirror, headlights obliterated like someone took a sledgehammer to them. Adam said it'll be idiots turning out of the pub, pissed. But I can't help wondering if it might have been Kyle, furious I reported that missing three grand. Petty little arsehole. I've told the police, of course, but they didn't seem wildly interested. Just gave me a crime number for the insurance and told me not to hold my breath.

But today is about Bridget. We've had a busy week, setting her up in a new place, and today is the day we ferry Bridget's life in black bin bags from her old place with Dave to her new rented flat. She's nervous, but I can tell she's also excited. It's a new start for her. A new start for both of us, getting our relationship back on track.

Adam can't lift the heavier stuff, but he carries some of her bags down and loads them into the boot.

"Careful with this one," he says, lifting a bag dramatically. "Feels like you've packed half of Dave in here."

Bridget laughs and rolls her eyes. It helps relieve a bit of the tension.

"Glad we sorted this limo for you, Bridget," he says. "You'll be arriving in style anyway.

He's been so lovely to her while she's been staying this week, knowing when to joke about and lighten the mood, or when to sit back and listen and let her have a good cry. He puts a bag in the boot and hugs her.

"Good luck," he says with real meaning as he gives her a squeeze.

He releases her and she gets in the car. I take my turn to give him a cuddle. "Thanks, Adam. I'll stay and get her settled. I don't want to leave her on her own. I'll be gone all day."

I load the final bag in the boot and get in. Bridget leans across and takes my hand. She squeezes it.

"Thanks, Grace. I couldn't have... Thanks."

She doesn't have to say any more than that. We know.

We set off. Bridget's quiet in the passenger seat, staring out at the passing streets, clutching a half-dead spider plant like it's a kitten rescued from a drain. I know she's still reeling from everything, Dave's arrest and the police interviews. Her hair is tied back in a scrappy ponytail, and she's wearing her favourite fleece with the cartoon owls on it. She looks fragile, like she might blow away in the breeze. But every now and then I can see sparks of the old Bridget surfacing – the twitch of a smirk, the tiny eye-roll at my driving – and I hang onto those moments like lifelines. She's still in there. Just needs coaxing out.

We arrive at her new flat. I unlock the door and push it open with a flourish worthy of my finest viewings.

"Welcome," I announce, gesturing theatrically, "to your exclusive top-floor studio apartment. Original features include authentic nicotine-stained woodwork, a beautiful heritage damp patch in the corner, and state-of-the-art single glazing for optimal winter character."

Bridget snorts. It's an actual snort, and it makes me so happy I want to cry.

"Very upmarket," she says, hauling a bag inside. She sniffs. "Do you think I should get scented candles or tell everyone I've changed my perfume to Eau de Mildew?"

"Start with the candles," I say. "And maybe a tetanus booster while you're at it."

For a few precious minutes, I forget about work. About Kyle, Mohammed and Patrick. Oliver. The fact I've been suspended for a missing three grand I didn't take. But I push it away. Today isn't about that. I almost let myself imagine I could just be here, forever, helping the sister I've finally got back settle into her new life.

She notices my silence as we're wrestling the vacuum cleaner out of the boot.

"What about you?" she asks quietly. "How's everything going?"

"It's fine," I lie breezily. "Work's just sorting out some admin stuff. You know how it is."

She nods, but her brow creases. "Well, tell them to get their heads out of their arses. You're brilliant."

I smile and hug her quickly before she can see the tears pricking at my eyes. God, I've missed her.

She heads upstairs, and just as I'm unloading another bag from the boot, my phone buzzes. Withheld number. I answer distractedly, thinking it might be the hire company wanting their car back early.

"Grace Harper?"

"Yes, speaking."

"This is DC Patel from North Yorkshire Police. We'd like you to come into the station for a chat. Today, if possible."

My stomach drops. "Is this about Dave?"

He resisted arrest on the way in and punched one of the coppers. He's also got a previous conviction for something violent. The policeman who interviewed us said he wouldn't be getting out on bail. But I'm scared now that something has changed.

A pause. "We can discuss that when you come in."

I hang up and head back into the flat. Bridget's kneeling in the hallway, sorting through a bag of tangled coat hangers. She looks up and sees my face.

"What is it?"

"Police. I think it's about Dave. They want me to go in."

She nods, looking worried. "Should I come too?"

"No," I say, forcing a smile. "You stay and clean up. But don't touch anything without a hazmat suit."

THE POLICE STATION is a rundown sixties prefab that feels like a clapped-out old school. DC Patel leads me into an interview room with no windows. Another policeman is in there who introduces himself as DC Taylor. The fluorescent light buzzes faintly overhead, like one of those things they have in chip shops for zapping flies.

"Before we begin, I want to make it clear that you're not under arrest, but I will be interviewing you under caution."

What?

DC Patel reads me my rights like they do on TV. The words swim in and out of focus. She says I can have a lawyer, but as this is about Dave, I figure they just want background info, so I don't need one. They fiddle with knobs on a box and start recording. They say all our names again. I keep waiting for her to mention Dave, but she doesn't.

"This is about Justin Trott," she says.

My mouth goes dry. I blink at her. "Justin? What about him?"

"We're investigating his death as a suspicious incident. Hit-and-run. We've had some information suggesting your car was seen driving erratically in the area that night."

"I... what?" My voice comes out absurdly high. "No. That's not possible. My car was parked outside my house, I think."

She looks at her notes, unbothered. "Can you remember what you were wearing that evening? The evening of Mr Trott's death?"

"I... what? I don't know. I changed from work, a work suit, then I went out to dinner with my sister. I answered all this in the office the day after Justin died."

"Would you have washed those clothes since then?"

I stare at him. "Yes. I wash my clothes all the time. Is that supposed to be suspicious now? Doing laundry?"

I can feel the panic rising in my chest. I try to push it down and sound less defensive.

"Like I told the other officers, I was at work with Justin that afternoon, yes, but I didn't leave with him. He left first. If the clothes stuff is to do with DNA or stuff like that, it's possible my DNA might be on him, but only because I was there, in the office, talking to him. That's normal, isn't it? That's not proof of anything."

But the more I speak, the more suspicious I sound. My voice is trembling, and I'm talking faster and faster. Then I remember something else.

"Oh yes, and I hit him, accidentally, with a key, the keys to a flat we were selling. It was an accident. I can't remember if I told your colleagues this before. But there was a bit of blood, so I guess that might turn up in tests or something. Though come to think of it, that was on a different day, earlier."

I'm spiralling out of control. I can feel my face flushing red.

"I didn't kill him."

She flips through her notes again.

"We've also spoken to your employers, Lancaster & Lyle. We understand you're currently suspended, under investigation for fraud?"

"What? No. That's... that's nothing to do with this."

"That's incorrect?"

"No. I mean... yes, I'm suspended, but on full pay, so they can do a proper investigation. But I'm pretty sure it's someone else in the office who's taken the money."

DC Patel pauses and looks at me. "Is it possible," she says, with a kind of half smile, "that Justin found out you were stealing, and he confronted you?"

"No," I say forcefully. "No, that's not what happened."

"He confronted you, and you knocked him down with your car to stop him from reporting you."

"No. No. Not at all."

"We've recovered your car, Grace. It has damage on it consistent with striking a body."

"No," I say, "that was vandals. That was just last night. I reported it. I reported it to you."

"It's with our forensics team now, so they'll be able to tell us if it struck someone. So it would be better for you if you told us now anything we should know."

"But that's ridiculous. That was ages ago. My car only got damaged last night. My neighbours will have seen my car parked out front, looking normal, between when Justin died and now. Ask them. Loads of people will be able to testify they've seen me parking the undamaged car outside my house for the last couple of weeks. I'm sure they will."

I *hope* they will. My mind races. Would anyone even notice or care?

"I didn't kill Justin."

DC Patel just looks at me. She closes her notebook. "Well, let's see what forensics say. We won't keep you longer today.

You're free to go, for now. But we will need to speak to you again."

For now.

For now.

The words echo in my skull, louder and louder, all the way home. By the time I get back to the house, they're deafening.

CHAPTER 53
OLIVER

He watches from across the road as she emerges from the station. No cuffs, no escort. Just Grace, walking free. Oliver's breath stalls in his chest.

He allowed himself a brief moment of hope to flicker inside him as he waited. Hope that the system would do its job and justice would be served. That the police, in their drab polyester uniforms and righteous certainty, would prove useful. That they would drag her out in handcuffs, push her into the back of a van, and lock her away from the world she pollutes.

But the system has failed. Justice has let her slip through its fingers. There she is, before him on the pavement, free.

He grips the steering wheel, feeling the leather creak beneath his hands, knuckles whitening with pressure. The police had their chance. They had her in their grasp, under the fluorescent light. They had her, and they let her go. Blind fools fumbling in darkness, unable to see the rot staring them in the face.

He exhales slowly, the air hissing between his teeth.

Of course they did. They don't know her like he does.

They haven't done the work, lifted the lid, peered into the dark, toxic mass that festers inside her, like a nest of baby rats. The fact is, she killed Justin. Maybe not with her own two hands, but with her poisonous selfishness that corrupts everything it touches. And let's not forget poor Maureen. She didn't deserve her terrible fate. Grace has the blood of two people on her hands now. Even Oliver himself is a victim, he realises, caught in her corruption. She drove him to it.

And still the police let her walk free, back out into the world to continue her monstrous enterprise. All they see is a tired woman with smudged mascara and anxious eyes. But Oliver knows better. He sees what she really is. The diseased animal. And there is only one thing you do with a diseased animal. It has to be removed before it infects the rest of the herd. It's not cruelty. It's necessity.

Oliver watches her, smug and triumphant. His jaw tightens. She thinks she has slipped through the net. She thinks she'll walk away from this. That if she tells enough lies, cries enough tears, the world will forgive her trespasses. She won't go to court, won't face a judge.

He feels an incredible sense of calm, realising the truth of the matter. Grace will never see the inside of a courtroom. But justice is bigger than courts, bigger than laws and uniforms. Justice demands balance. An eye for an eye. A life for a life. If justice won't act, he must. And if Grace Harper is to be stopped, he'll have to do it himself.

He closes his eyes, remembering the feel of the steering wheel vibrating under his palms as he drove it into Justin. The sudden resistance, then the lurch as metal met flesh, the dull final thud as the body crumpled.

The road outside the police station is busy, traffic streaming past in both directions, headlights sweeping across his dashboard, illuminating the calm, serene expression on his face. Too many people. But he feels no impatience. No need to rush.

He starts the car, calm now, resolved. No more games. No more waiting for others. This time, he will deliver justice himself.

He knows where she's going.

And when she gets there, he will be waiting.

CHAPTER 54
GRACE

I can't go back to Bridget's new place.

I want to. I want to be there, unpacking her mugs, making jokes about her dead spider plant, pretending for just one afternoon that I'm not under police investigation for a murder I didn't commit. But I can't. I feel like I've been scooped out and left hollow. My hands are trembling so badly I can barely type as I text her.

Something came up with work. I'll call later. xxx

I start walking, past a blur of houses and shops. I just want to go home. Shut the curtains. Crawl under the duvet and vanish.

As I turn onto my street, I see a white delivery van parked outside the house. At first, it doesn't register. Then I see Adam, standing by the open back doors, talking to the delivery guy.

I stop and watch from a distance, confused. He isn't wearing his neck brace. He's moving easily, lifting something from the van. It's a box. Not a box. A crate. Massive. Nearly as tall as he is and half as wide. The driver helps him shuffle it onto the pavement. Adam slips his arms around it and heaves it up against his chest. No wince. No twisted expression of pain. He starts carrying it up the path, inching sideways to get it through the front door.

I walk slowly up to the house. My stomach lurches. The front door is still open. I push it and follow the scraping sounds up the stairs. I climb slowly, one step at a time.

He's in the living room, wrestling the huge box into the centre of the floor, panting slightly, his hair damp with sweat. The cardboard is half open, revealing gleaming black plastic and foam inserts.

A TV. A massive flat screen TV.

"What the hell is this?" I hear myself say.

He jumps, spinning round. His face is all guilt and fear.

"Bloody hell, Grace," he laughs. "Don't sneak up on me. You nearly gave me a heart attack."

"What is it?" I ask again. My voice is low and I'm shaking.

He recovers and shrugs, cutting tape with a kitchen knife and pulling the cardboard away. "I told you, they were doing a deal."

He makes it sound like it's the most obvious thing in the world. Like I'm making a fuss over nothing. Something starts to unravel inside me. He looks relaxed. No grimaces of pain. No protective hand pressed to his neck. No wincing when he lifts or twists. Just normal, healthy movement.

"How did you carry it, Adam? Up the stairs. Into the house. How are you standing there unpacking it when last week you couldn't even lift the kettle?"

He turns, looking confused. "I don't get what the problem is, Grace. You're seriously cross because I've got us both a nice television? Okay, next time I'll stick to flowers. Lesson learned."

There's something slippery behind his eyes. He's trying to gaslight me, making out I'm somehow the person in the wrong.

Then it hits me.

"How did you pay for it?"

He doesn't look at me. "I sorted it. Don't worry."

"But how?"

"Like I said, it was a deal, on offer."

"A deal," I repeat. "With what money, Adam? We don't have any money."

"Don't worry about it." He keeps fiddling with the box.

But I do worry about it. I stare at him, really stare, watching him peel back the cardboard.

It all comes into focus with sickening clarity. The missing money from work, and those payments I didn't understand from my account. The security questions he always teased me for making about him, his best friend at school, the make of his first car, the name of his first pet. And all those times I left the work laptop at home.

I picture him, sitting there all day with nothing to do but google and guess and find ways in. It wasn't Kyle. It was never Kyle. It was Adam.

"You stole the money," I whisper.

He freezes. Just for a second. Then he lets out a bark of laughter. "Don't be ridiculous."

But his face looks wrong. The muscles behind the smile aren't moving.

"You lying sack of shit," I say, my voice rising. "You fake an injury, rob me blind, and still manage to act like the injured party? You're unbelievable."

His head snaps up. "What are you talking about?"

"You've been lying to me for months. Jesus, I felt so sorry for you. Guilty you got hurt helping me. I thought you were so brave about it. But you're not. You're…"

"What?" he spits. "Say it."

"Pathetic," I say. "You're pathetic."

He laughs easily, as though I've caught him stealing

biscuits, not thousands of pounds. I turn to go. I need to get away. I head into the kitchen to where he keeps his keys and grab them. But as I move, he's there, blocking the doorway. His shoulders fill the space. His breathing sounds loud in the silent room.

"Oh Grace, come on, don't be like that. Does it really matter who got it? Let's not fall out over a telly. "

He's smiling at me, making out there's nothing wrong. His voice sounds just like Dave's did, talking sweetly to Bridget through the letter box, just before he tried to smash the door down.

"I want you gone by the time I get back," I say.

I go to push past him and leave. But as I do, his hand reaches out and grabs hold of the keys I'm holding. We struggle and eventually he rips the keys out of my hand. They fall clattering to the floor. The shock jolts me back. He still stands between me and the doorway, his eyes narrowed, his breathing heavy.

"Sorry," he says, "but you're twisting everything. I didn't mean for it to get this far."

"Move, Adam."

"No, not until we talk."

I look at my hand, where the key has made a small nick. A bead of blood begins to form. Adam notices. His face flashes with panic.

"Jesus, Grace, sorry. But look, you can't just storm out like this. We have to talk."

"Move," I say again.

"No," he says softly, casually placing a hand on the door-frame. "Not until we've sorted this out." Then he steps forward, his face inches from mine. I get a sudden horrible flashback to Justin, charging towards me in that flat. My heart is hammering and I feel dizzy. "You're not going anywhere."

I shove him, hard, to get him out of the way, just enough

space to slip past. But I must push harder than I intended. He takes a step backwards to steady himself, but his foot lands on the keys. They scrape like ice on the tiles and his leg flies upwards as he loses his balance. Time stops. He falls backwards, and I see his arms windmill, grasping at nothing. He can't right himself in the small kitchen before he collides with the wall opposite. There's a splitting sound as he smashes into the window he never got round to fixing, with its rotten frame and cracked putty. The wood gives way as the window flies open.

He disappears through it, out into the cold evening air. The window is just a white frame of empty blank nothing. He's gone.

There's a dull, heavy thud and a muffled crack that makes my stomach heave.

Silence.

I stand there, frozen, staring at the jagged gap where the window used to be.

I hear myself breathing. Shallow, ragged breaths that don't seem to reach my lungs.

I can't hear anything else.

Just silence.

CHAPTER 55
OLIVER

He parks two doors down from her house and sits for a moment, breathing evenly, feeling his pulse slow down. Rain ticks gently against the windscreen. The wipers squeak across glass, clearing a brief oval of clarity before blurring again. He closes his eyes. Breathes in. Breathes out. This feels like a good moment to evaluate the coaching programme, now that his work with her is coming to an end.

Oliver has done everything by the book. Every technique, every model. Empathetic listening, positive reframing, strengths-based interventions, cognitive challenge. All tools of the therapeutic trade, some gentle, some robust. Each designed to pry open the rusted-shut compartments of a human mind. Most clients eventually soften. Reshape themselves around the insights he offers. That is the process. That is the work.

But not Grace.

Grace resisted at every stage. Mocked him, defied him, closed herself off. She is a festering abscess that refuses to drain. And he is absolutely certain, beyond a shadow of a doubt, that the failure here is not of the process. The failure is hers alone.

She is beyond therapy.

His work is not quite finished though, and he still has one or two more things he can try. More direct, blunter, but effective nonetheless. He reaches across to the passenger seat and feels the cold steel of the hammer. Sometimes a practitioner encounters a subject so damaged, so resistant, that only one tool is appropriate – especially when seeking a final, irreversible breakthrough.

Oliver slips the hammer into his coat pocket and steps out through the car door into the drizzle, the weight of the metal reassuringly heavy as he walks. He imagines it cradled in his palm, the perfect extension of intention into action. He has at last found his way back to the life he should have, his practice re-established, his skills honed to their sharpest edge.

He is on a mission now. An ethical intervention. She has been a most uncooperative patient.

But now the precise moment has arrived to finish this once and for all.

Time to terminate her treatment.

He approaches her house with professional detachment. His pulse is steady, his breathing even. He scans the windows, assessing. Is she alone? Are the curtains drawn? Is she ready for him? But just as he reaches the edge of the road, something erupts above him.

The upstairs window bursts open with a suddenness that stops him in his tracks. Oliver's breath catches in his throat. For a moment, all he sees is flailing limbs. A man topples out, twisting in the air like a dropped marionette. There is a strangled scream, then a dull, wet crack as he hits the pavement below. The silence that follows feels enormous.

Then he sees her.

Grace appears at the broken window, framed by splintered wood. Her hair is wild around her face, eyes wide with horror. She stares down at the body sprawled across the path. Even from here, Oliver can see the unnatural angle of the man's neck.

Three, he thinks. Three deaths now, circling her like vultures. Justin. Maureen. Now this man. She is a plague carrier. A walking infection. Everywhere she goes, death blooms like mould.

She vanishes from the window. Moments later, the front door bursts open, and she emerges onto the step. She stands there, frozen, staring at the dead man. Then her scream tears the quiet street in half. She turns and flees, running up the road, her coat flapping behind her like wings.

She looks smaller somehow. Deflated. Her head is down, her hair pulled forward around her face like a veil. Just for a second, he almost feels pity. But pity is a weak man's luxury. He has moved beyond pity. Beyond mercy.

Oliver slips his hand into his pocket and curls his fingers around the hammer's grip.

This ends today.

He steps out from the shadows and follows.

CHAPTER 56
GRACE

I walk along the beach in a daze.

One second, Adam was there. The next, he just… wasn't, falling backwards through the window in awful, silent slow motion.

I don't remember leaving the house. My legs just carried me, zig-zagging down streets to the beach. Now I'm here. The tide is out and the air is salty and cold. My trousers are damp at the hems, dark and gritty with sand.

I feel nothing. Just empty. Hollowed out, like when Mum died and I came down here instead of going to the hospital to say goodbye. I sat on the beach for hours, staring at the horizon, not able to cry, unable to feel anything but blank terror at how final it all seemed.

It's so surreal that for a second I wonder if I imagined it. Maybe it didn't really happen. Like some kind of awful magic trick gone wrong, Adam was there, and then he disappeared.

But it did happen. Adam is dead.

I killed him.

I keep walking. The grey waves keep rolling in and sucking back out, utterly indifferent to anything. Gulls wheel and scream overhead. It was an accident, but that doesn't matter, does it? You can't just push someone out of a window and run away. I have to come clean. Even if they don't believe me. Even if they lock me away forever.

My phone rings in my pocket, making me jump. The screen says DC Patel. My heart hammers so hard it hurts.

"Grace?" she says. Her voice is clipped and anxious.

"Yes," I say. "It's me."

"I need to see you. It's urgent."

I let out a sound halfway between a sob and a laugh. Thank God. They already know. At least now I won't have to ring up and say, 'Hello, Officer. I seem to have accidentally murdered my boyfriend.'

"Where are you right now?"

I look around at the dull sky and the wind coming in off the sea.

"I'm on the beach," I say. "Down by the south steps."

"Wait right there," she says. "Officers are on their way. Don't move, Grace. Do you understand?"

"Yeah," I whisper. "I understand."

She hangs up. The waves hush and sigh. I stare down at my hands. They're shaking so hard I can barely clench them into fists. I think about Adam's body sprawled across the pavement. About the blood, and the awful crack his head made as it hit the kerb. Will they believe me, I wonder? That he stole the money? That his neck wasn't really injured? That it was an accident, just a push to get him out of my way?

Of course they won't. They think I killed Justin. One body's bad enough. Now two makes it an open-and-shut case.

I stand there, staring at the sea, my breath catching in my chest. A dog runs past me, chasing a ball into the shallows, with its owner laughing in the distance. Then sirens start wailing somewhere far off, drifting on the wind. I close my eyes and feel tears start to come, hot and prickly under my lids. There's no way out.

"Grace."

I spin round.

He's standing ten feet away on the sand. His hair is slicked dark and flat with drizzle, and his black coat is flapping in the wind. His eyes are fixed on me with a focused intensity that makes my insides curdle.

Oliver.

For a moment, I think it's something else I'm hallucinating. How weird to see him now, as if today wasn't awful enough already. But he's real.

"You look… unwell," he says softly. "Do you want to tell me what you've done?"

My mouth opens, but no words come out.

"It's okay," he says gently. "You can tell me."

Something about how he asks makes it okay to speak. "I've done something terrible," I say. It's a relief to hear it out loud. "I didn't mean to do it. I didn't mean for any of this."

He nods, as if this confirms something he's always known.

"Yes," he says. "I know. But you see, Grace, it's too late to be sorry now."

He takes a step closer. There's something in his expression that makes my blood turn cold. I see his hand come out of his pocket. He's holding something. It glints in the drizzle. A hammer. I don't understand.

"I'm sorry, Grace," he says calmly. "But I'm afraid I'm going to have to end our sessions together."

My heart seizes. I stumble backwards onto the sand.

I twist away just as the hammer swings through the air where my head was. Then I run, as hard as I can, shoes slipping on the wet sand, breath tearing out of me in ragged gasps. Behind me, I can hear his footsteps pounding closer and closer.

That's when I see blue lights flare against the dark sky. Police cars are up on the promenade. Uniformed officers spill out, shouting orders I can't hear over the roar of blood in my ears, and then there's DC Patel, moving forward, ready to arrest me. I give myself up to my fate.

But the officers don't stop for me. They stream past, charging down the sand straight at Oliver. I turn, stumbling to a halt, just in time to see them tackle him to the ground. For a bizarre moment I want to call out, 'No, you've got it wrong. It's me.' But they're wrestling him down in a chaotic tangle of limbs and shouts, wrenching the hammer from his hand. He thrashes and yells as his eyes are fixed on mine, wild and staring.

"I was helping you!" he howls. "You needed me. You *needed* me!"

I stand there, chest heaving, as the officers drag him to his feet and march him away across the beach.

The sirens wail. The wind howls.

I crumple down onto the sand. And behind it all, the sea keeps sighing in and out, like it's all just nothing.

CHAPTER 57
GRACE

I sit in the police station waiting room, staring at the scuffed linoleum floor. My hands are clasped so tightly in my lap my fingers ache. Bridget is next to me, sipping vending machine tea out of a paper cup. Every now and then she reaches across and rubs my back in gentle circles, like Mum used to when I was little and poorly.

"I'm fine," I say.

But I'm not. I'm anything but fine. My eyes dart anxiously between her and the door. Every footstep outside makes my stomach drop. I don't understand why Oliver nearly attacked me on the beach. But one thing I do understand is that they know it's my fault Adam fell from that window. And any minute now, they'll come for me.

Bridget leans in close and puts her arm round my shoulder.

"You're shaking," she whispers.

"Yeah." My voice comes out wobbly. "Yeah, I am."

"Whatever it is, Grace… it'll be okay."

I close my eyes and feel tiny and safe. I have my big sister back. I want her to hold me like this forever. Like, if she lets go, I'll fall and I'll never stop falling. But she only believes it'll be okay because she doesn't know about Adam. She has no idea what I've done and what I'm about to be arrested for.

"Grace, I'm here. We'll deal with it together."

I almost laugh at that. *We'll deal with it.* Like it's a fine for dog fowling or a parking ticket. My chest tightens painfully. I try to find the words to tell her, but they stick in my throat. *I'm about to be arrested for murder! For pushing Adam out of a window!* She'll understand, won't she? After everything that's happened with her and Dave?

"Bridget," I say, my voice cracking. "I need to tell you something–"

The door swings open, cutting me off. DC Patel appears, her dark hair scraped back severely. Her expression is sombre and my stomach flips over. This is it.

"Grace," she says. "Could you follow me, please?"

Bridget starts to rise but I touch her arm. "No," I say. "Please. Wait here."

I follow DC Patel down the corridor to a room that looks identical to the one they interviewed me in – the same scratched table, the same blue chairs bolted to the floor. I feel like I'm getting sucked back into a nightmare. I sit down heavily. Patel sits opposite me, flipping open a thin file. For a long moment she just looks at me, assessing. Then she sighs. I brace myself for the words I know are coming.

"Grace," she says gently. "I'm sorry to have to tell you this, but Adam Powell is dead."

I blink at her, confused. "Sorry. What?"

She pauses. "He's dead."

I stare at her, trying to make the words mean something. Why is she telling me something I already know? That's why I'm here. So they can arrest me for it!

"A neighbour called it in."

She just looks at me. My heart bangs against my ribs. Is

this some kind of sick tactic? Throwing me off guard with what I already know? I wait for the next question. *Why did you push him? Why did you run?*

But instead, she glances down at her notes. "Grace, do you know an Oliver Smallwood?"

"Yes. He was my... he was coaching me."

"The man on the beach?"

"Yes."

Patel nods grimly. "We've been looking into him. I'm afraid we have some serious news. His therapist, Maureen Ridley, was found dead some days ago. At the time, we believed her death was an accident, a result of her stair-lift malfunctioning. But when engineers said the fault didn't match how the stair-lift was found, we became suspicious."

A sick chill creeps through my veins.

"Oliver was her last appointment of the day and most likely the last person to see her alive. We read her session notes, and realised she had grave concerns about Oliver's mental state. She was planning to refer him for an urgent psychiatric assessment. We suspect he discovered this and pushed her down the stairs, hoping it would look like the lift failed."

I swallow hard.

"She knew," I say quietly. "She tried to warn me. We were meant to meet. But she never showed."

I think about those sessions, alone with Oliver in that tiny room. His calm voice, his dark eyes watching every flicker of emotion. I sat inches from a murderer who killed a woman with his bare hands.

"When we went to arrest Oliver," Patel continues, her tone flat and heavy, "we linked him to Justin's death too."

I flinch. "What?"

"Traces of Justin's blood were found in Oliver's house. It had been cleaned, but not well enough. In his hallway, his kitchen, everywhere. And we traced a garage where he had his car repaired from damage consistent with the hit-and-run."

The floor seems to tilt under my feet.

"So you don't think I killed Justin?"

"No," says DC Patel. "Oliver killed him."

She sits back and looks at me for a long time. "I know we questioned you pretty hard. About Justin."

My mouth goes dry.

"We were looking in the wrong place," she says. "I'm really sorry."

Her face has a grave, haunted look. I figure now's the moment she's going to ask me about why I killed Adam.

"There's more, Grace," she says. "While we were searching Oliver's house, we found multiple phones and phone accounts. They all have numbers linked to firms that have your details. Taxi firms, takeaway companies... dozens of them. Florists, double-glazing firms, timeshare companies, a donkey sanctuary... The scale of it... it's... overwhelming."

I blink, taking it all in. "I thought it was Kyle. A guy I work with, who doesn't like me. I thought he was making all the calls."

Patel shakes her head. "We found notebooks too, twenty or so. Coaching notes. Every page is about you. Observations. Theories. Plans."

"Plans? Like what?" I ask. I can see the hesitation in Patel's eyes. "Tell me."

DC Patel pauses and looks at the closed door. I get the sense she's not supposed to do this, but she opens the file in front of her. She pulls out a wodge of typed sheets stapled together. Her eyes scan it as she reads to herself. She looks pained.

"Show me."

She passes me the document reluctantly. I pick somewhere random and start reading.

...She is beyond redemption...

...She must be stripped to her foundations to expose the rot...

...Grace is moral gangrene. There is no therapy for wilful corruption...

I skip through, page after page, phrases leaping out at me.

...amputation from the world before she infects everything...

...Cleansing her is not cruelty. It is hygiene....

...I see now my calling is not to save her, but to remove her from existence.

DC Patel leans across the table and takes the document from me. She puts it face down in front of her. She looks tired.

"It's all like that." She lowers her voice. "I'll be honest, Grace... I've never come across anyone remotely like him. We think he's an extremely dangerous individual."

"He was going to kill me," I say softly.

Patel nods. "Yes. We believe he was. You've had a very lucky escape."

I can't wrap my head around it. A complete stranger, obsessed with me. Why me? After everything – Mum, Dad, Dave, Justin. Now Oliver. It's like the world's been slowly cracking and I've only just noticed I'm standing right over the fault line. And the worst part is, it's not over yet. They're going to arrest me for killing Adam. I can feel it coming. And no one's going to care what led up to it.

"Just so you're aware," says Patel, "we've let your employer know what's happened."

I tense. "Right."

"They arranged for you to see Oliver; is that correct?"

I nod.

"We spoke to a Mr Patrick Lyle. He seemed genuinely concerned for you. He mentioned you'd been under internal review for financial irregularities, but that's all been cleared up."

She flips a page in the file.

"Turns out when the firm onboarded Oliver for the coaching programme, their IT department gave him limited access to internal systems – calendar bookings, team directories, that kind of thing. We assume he somehow managed to use that to get into the company payroll details."

But that's not true. That's not what happened.

"We're still piecing it together," she adds.

I shake my head. They think it was Oliver who took the money. They still haven't worked out it was Adam. How am I going to explain? And she still hasn't said a word about... what I did. The silence around it is unbearable. Like waiting for a sentence you already know is coming. I can't take it anymore.

"But what about Adam?" I blurt. Louder than I mean to.

"Yes, Adam." She sighs. "Well, your neighbours heard a scream and saw Oliver outside your house just after Adam fell. We believe Oliver entered the property and killed him. Possibly from jealousy. He was clearly obsessed with you. Anyway, I wanted to let you know Oliver's been arrested for murder. For Justin, Maureen Ridley, and now Adam."

I can't speak.

I don't know if I *should* speak.

Patel reaches across and lays a hand on mine. "You're safe now, Grace."

Safe. The word sounds meaningless. Like saying "calm down" to someone in a burning building.

She closes the file. Breathes out slowly. She looks at me.

I look away. My palms are damp. She still doesn't know the truth yet about Adam's death. Is this the moment? Do I say it? There's a pause. A long one.

Maybe she can see something in my eyes, something unresolved. Maybe she senses there's something more.

"Grace, is there anything else you want to tell me right now?"

I look up at her, wiping my eyes with the heel of my hand. My throat feels raw, my chest tight.

"Yeah," I croak, my voice barely above a whisper. "Next time someone offers me free coaching, I'm gonna tell them to fuck off."

CHAPTER 58
OLIVER

Oliver sits in the interview room, back straight, palms pressed reverently against the scuffed tabletop. The fluorescent light hums overhead, buzzing faintly like an insect trapped against glass. He finds the grey room calming in a way, minimalist and uncluttered. The ideal therapeutic setting, if only the two police detectives across from him weren't disturbing it, leafing through a file that is thicker than it needs to be. Overblown and dramatized, like everything else about this circus. But once he makes them see the truth of the situation, they will thank him.

His solicitor sits beside him, a flabby man in a cheap suit, staring at the floor with bored, dead eyes. But he won't understand. He is used to dealing with criminals. *No comment* was his only suggestion. Useless. It's better that Oliver explains.

The man who introduced himself as Detective Harris looks up.

"Mr Smallwood," Harris begins with theatrical weariness, "do you understand why you're here today?"

Oliver tilts his head graciously. "I understand why *you think* I'm here."

"Do you understand the charges against you?"

Oliver smiles patiently, like a teacher addressing a dim pupil. "I know what crimes you *think* I've committed."

Harris exchanges a glance with the other one, Detective Patel, who suppresses a small eye-roll. Like the solicitor, Oliver concludes they have no practical grasp of what they are dealing with.

"Let's start with Justin Trott," says Harris. "There are traces of his blood in your hallway, kitchen and bathroom. And we have a time-stamped garage invoice for repair work to your car just days after the hit-and-run. Can you explain that?"

He folds his hands serenely. "Yes. I can explain everything. Grace is responsible."

Detective Patel frowns slightly. "Grace... Harper?"

"Yes," he says calmly. "Technically, I was holding the wheel, but Grace is the engine that drove the car. She orchestrated the entire sequence of events. She wanted him gone. She made me understand what had to be done. She manipulated me."

The detectives look at each other. Oliver can see they weren't expecting his answer. How could they? It seems almost unbelievable. But they don't know Grace like he does. Oliver leans forward, earnest and reasonable.

"You're trying to treat the sneeze when you should be treating the virus. I was merely the mechanism. If I was the gun, as it were, then she was the one who pulled the trigger."

Detective Harris scribbles something in his notebook.

"Let's talk about Maureen Ridley instead. You visited her, and shortly afterwards, she fell down the stairs and died of blunt force trauma."

Detective Patel slides a photograph across the table and

looks at him intently, watching for a reaction. The image shows poor, dead Maureen's broken body at the foot of her stairs. Oliver understands the tactic. Maureen was his friend and mentor. They are trying to provoke him with emotion. But they don't need to. He *wants* to tell them the story.

He sighs softly. "She didn't fall. She was pushed. She was struck first, and then pushed. Again, this was Grace. Yes, I pushed Maureen, but it was Grace who forced my hand. She orchestrated everything."

Harris leans back, folding his arms.

"So you're saying that you and Grace Harper conspired to murder Justin Trott and Maureen Ridley?"

Oliver suppresses a sigh. He is already beginning to lose patience with their obtuseness. He leans forward and speaks slowly.

"No. Not a conspiracy. I didn't conspire to do anything. I'm another of her victims. It was Grace. All Grace. She infected everything."

He pauses, frustrated at their blank stares.

"I understand why you might not grasp the subtle ways in which someone with Grace's personality disorder can manipulate an ordinary, trusting person like myself, even an experienced clinician. But she is a runaway narcissist with antisocial features and zero empathy. It's her you should be interviewing."

Harris shuffles his papers.

"And Adam Powell? Neighbours saw you outside the house, running away, immediately after he fell to his death."

Oliver snorts softly, a condescending smile playing at his lips. "That was Grace. She pushed him. She's dangerous. She provokes these situations, these breakdowns in others. She drives people to do things they would never otherwise do."

"Right." Harris closes the file with a snap. "So let me get this straight. Grace really drove the car into Justin, Grace really smashed Maureen's head in and threw her down the stairs, and Grace really pushed Adam out of the window?"

Oliver feels his pulse spike. His composure flickers. "Yes!" he snaps. "She *did*. You're not listening. You're too blinkered to see what she is. I tried to save her, but she's a plague. She destroys everything she touches. She manipulates good, honest people into–"

"Into what?" Harris interrupts, pen tapping against his file with deliberate irritation. "Murder?"

Oliver snarls. "Don't you understand what she is? She's already in your heads. She's manipulated you, too!"

Even his solicitor shifts uncomfortably now. Patel gives a tiny shake of her head to Harris. The detective checks his watch and reaches forward, pressing the stop button on the recording device.

"We're terminating the interview at this stage."

Oliver stares at them, incredulous. "No, you can't. You don't understand what you're doing. She destroys everything she touches."

The detectives stand to leave. Oliver surges forward in his chair, hands flat against the table, voice rising.

"She did all of it! You don't know what you're dealing with. You have no idea what sort of dangerous person you've got right under your noses!"

But they're already gathering their papers.

"Thank you for your insight, Mr Smallwood."

Two uniformed officers come in and begin to manhandle Oliver towards the door. He struggles to get away, to get back to the detectives, to let them know that she's fooled them too, that she's toxic.

"She's poisonous!" he shouts, voice cracking now, rage flooding through him. "She'll kill you all! She'll kill every one of you!"

As they drag him backwards down the corridor, his shoes

squealing against the lino, Oliver realises that his protestations are useless, that they are falling on deaf ears. Just as it was with Grace, so with those detectives – you cannot make someone face up to the truth if they do not want to hear.

Oliver shakes his head and stops resisting. He makes a mental clinical detachment. He washes his hands of her. She is someone else's problem now. He washes his hands of the police as well.

He did as much as he could.

The sad truth is, there's just no helping some people.

CHAPTER 59
GRACE

It's been two months.

I'm back at work now. Properly back, not creeping in on probation or doing forced coaching sessions. Patrick Lyle called me over to his office in Leeds a couple of weeks after they arrested Oliver, and for a split second, I thought he was going to fire me anyway. But instead, he smiled his thin, awkward smile and said, "Grace, I think it's time we made your role permanent. And there's a raise. You've earned it."

I almost cried right there on his ridiculous geometric carpet tiles. It was like all the feelings came together in that one moment. Adam and Bridget and Oliver and everything. But I managed to keep a lid on it instead, and just said, "Thank you," in a calm, composed voice. Then went home and screamed into a tea towel.

Today I'm giving the agency a bit of a makeover. The grim grey vertical blinds have come down, replaced with… nothing at all. It immediately feels modern and open, and less like some 2000s dental surgery. I've rearranged the display boards and the desks so people can see each other without craning their necks like pigeons. I ordered some fantastic scandi chairs online that were such a bargain I was terrified they'd be doll-house-sized ones. But they're great. There's little potted plants now. I've got a plant on my desk too. Bridget gave it to me. It's a peace lily. She says it's a symbol of new beginnings.

Kyle is gone. I thought about firing him, but I was really grown up about it. I took him for a coffee and gently suggested that he might be happier working elsewhere. He rolled his eyes, marched back to the office, threw his stapler in a box, and muttered on his way out, "I'd say it's been a pleasure, but we both know that's bullshit."

What I wanted to say was, "Don't let the door hit your overinflated arse on the way out," but I bit my tongue and just smiled. I figure I'm the boss now. I don't need to have the last word. And the tranquillity he's left behind is absolutely blissful.

I promoted Mohammed to Deputy Sales Manager. It turns out he's quite a nice guy, once he's out of the shadow of Kyle's toxic sarcasm. He bought me a novelty desk plaque when I got the permanent role, bright gold plastic with black engraved lettering:

WORLD'S OKAYEST BOSS.

Cheeky little shit. I laughed so hard I snorted coffee through my nose. He got me a Terry's Chocolate Orange too. That all feels like another new beginning.

I'm meeting Bridget for lunch later. She's brighter these days. Dave's been recalled to prison for violating his bail. I guess threatening voicemails and mysterious drive-bys will do that. Her victim liaison officer says he's got previous convictions, and he's going to be going away for a long time. Good riddance. So she's safe again.

Last week we had a laugh on that spa weekend I booked her. We spent half the massage giggling because the therapist kept calling our shoulders 'traumatised tissue.' Bridget cried in the steam room. But good tears, she said.

We're thinking about selling Mum and Dad's house, maybe renting somewhere together for a bit. We've wasted too many years letting men make decisions for us. Now it's just us.

I've joined the local gym too. Swimming on Tuesdays, spin classes on Fridays. My shoulders ache in a good way now, not from hunching over spreadsheets 'til three in the morning.

Last weekend, I packed up the last of Mum and Dad's things. The boxes have sat in the hallway so long they'd become furniture in their own right. And Adam's stuff, too. All gone. I thought of phoning his brother, but then I decided it would feel more satisfying to put all his beloved video games and DVDs in a skip at the dump. And it did! The house feels emptier but lighter. Like there's finally space to breathe.

And – cue fanfare – I've finally arranged going back to university again. Back on the course I left when Mum got sick. Different faculty now, different entry requirements, but I'm going to go back and finish what I started. I've worked out my savings and though it'll be tight, I can do it. I haven't told Patrick I'm leaving yet, but I'm already signed up for next September.

So, everything's good.

Or it should be.

I almost let myself believe it. That I'm free. That I'm getting back to normal. But maybe normal isn't possible anymore. Because the truth is, despite all the fresh paint, the brighter office, the gym classes and peaceful nights, there's still something dark and heavy pressing at the edges.

I killed him.

I tell myself it was an accident, that he slipped, that I

never meant it. But it doesn't matter what I meant. Adam's dead. And I ran. Left him lying on the street like a sack of rubbish.

I didn't tell the police anything. I didn't tell Bridget either. And the guilt of it sits in my chest like lead. They all think Oliver did it. The crazy, murderous psychopath with two bodies to his name. And I let them.

I catch myself thinking about Oliver a lot. The horror of him. The damage he did. But weirdly, I also think about the truth he forced me to see. Coaching unlocks things. It helps you realise what matters. Of course, Oliver's methods were utterly insane, but in the end, he nudged me forward. Without him, Bridget would still be with Dave. I'd still be working for Justin. And I'd still be with Adam. It's insane to think it, but meeting him ultimately made my life better.

And there's another thing I learnt from him. You can't hide the truth. You can pretend you've buried it under work, under redecorating and pot plants and spin classes. But it never really stays buried. It's still there, ticking like a time bomb, waiting to upend everything. It rots you from the inside. That's something Oliver taught me.

The guilt about Adam comes in waves. I'm brushing my teeth and think of his body. I take the bins out, and I see the blood pooling. Sometimes I forget, for hours. And then I remember. Pushing Adam. Adam falling. The terrible sound of a crack I can't unhear. Adam smashed on the pavement. A ripple of nausea, a shortness of breath. It swells, towering over me like a black wave, threatening to crash down and drag me under.

Is any happiness I have now just me pretending, ignoring what's really happened? Can I ever move on, carrying this secret? Will I ever truly be free if I don't tell someone what I did? I still have DC Patel's number in my phone. I scroll past it every couple of days. I've thought about ringing her at 2 a.m., just blurting it all out. But I don't even know what I'd say. *'Hi. Remember me? The one who almost died? Turns out I'm a murderer too."*

So I haven't called her – yet.

I look out of my office window at the street outside, the low sun flaring off car roofs like shattered glass.

Maybe if I ever want to truly be free, I have to tell someone what I did.

Because if I don't... it will drown me.

Won't it?

I guess we'll see.

CHAPTER 60
ONE YEAR LATER

Oliver smooths the lapels of his white coat. He adjusts his posture to appear open, receptive, and authoritative. Exactly as a good clinician should.

"Let's pick up where we left off last week, shall we?" he says, voice soft and even.

"Okay, Doctor."

George looks at him with wary eyes. A large man, mid-forties, thick hands scarred with old burns and self-inflicted cuts. His past trauma is extensive. Childhood neglect, sexual abuse from multiple perpetrators, persistent violent conduct disorder escalating to adult antisocial personality disorder with sadistic features. Long forensic history: robbery, aggravated assault, grievous bodily harm, sexual assault, attempted murder. Multiple imprisonments. Court-mandated treatment here after attempting to gouge out a cellmate's eye with a toothbrush.

A uniformed orderly stands discreetly over by the barred window in the day room. Oliver appreciates that a patient like George can never be completely trusted not to react in some unpredictable or violent manner. But Oliver pushes such thoughts to the back of his mind. It's vital he has unqualified compassion so he can do his work effectively.

Oliver gauges George's mood. His hands tremble slightly as he pulls repetitively at a small thread on the cuff of his grey sweatshirt with HMP PROPERTY stamped across the back. His hair is cropped harshly close to the scalp, and he can see bare, red patches where George must have been scratching obsessively.

"It's okay," Oliver says gently. "You're safe here. You can talk about it."

George shifts in his seat. Sweat beads on his upper lip and settles in the deep worry lines etched around his mouth.

"I just... I keep seeing it, Doctor," George mutters. "That night. When I broke his nose and he couldn't breathe. The noise he made..."

George shifts. His trainers squeak against the linoleum. Somewhere down the corridor, a man begins to shout in guttural, wordless terror before staff voices intervene, soothing or commanding.

"Close your eyes for me," Oliver says. "Feel your feet on the floor. Your back against the chair. Notice your breathing."

Oliver works systematically to remove George from the hostility of his environment, the chipped chairs bolted to the floor, the empty TV bracket, the fire exit alarm covered with a protective cage. The institutional despair. He watches George's shoulders rise and fall. Calm. Focus. Authority. This is what he was trained for. Real work. Work that matters. Guiding the unreachable towards feeling... something. Dignity. Recognition of their humanity, however fragmented.

"Good," he says softly. "You're re-experiencing the event. That's natural. The trauma loop traps you there. But today, we're going to walk back through it together. Safely. Like rewinding a film and seeing each frame clearly."

Oliver leans forward, steepling his fingers. "Now tell me

about the moment before you kicked him. Where were you standing?"

George swallows. "Near the sink."

"Good. And what did you see?"

He guides him, question by question, step by step, through the memory: the metal glint of the tap, the sour smell of unwashed plates, the feel of blood underfoot. Oliver notes every tic, every hesitation, grounding him with clinical skill, with the steady rhythm of his voice, filing away clinical observations to write up later. Progress is minimal with men like George, but that's not the point. This work isn't about cure or discharge. Nobody here will ever leave. It's about containment, management, harm reduction. Giving even the most damaged mind a measure of calm within its darkness.

Inside, Oliver feels a quiet bloom of satisfaction. After everything, the lies, the trials, the humiliations, he is finally doing what he was born to do. Helping people.

Across the room, the medication trolley rattles closer, pushed by Nurse Hammond. She is brisk and broad-hipped, with bleached hair scraped into a bun. The heavy keys at her waist clink softly as she walks.

"That's time for today, George," Oliver says warmly. "Thank you for your honesty."

George exhales like a deflating tyre. "Thanks, Doctor."

Oliver exchanges a courteous, professional nod with Nurse Hammond, who then dispenses George's meds into a small paper cup. Oliver notes the tablets. Quetiapine, olanzapine, sodium valproate. Antipsychotic, mood stabiliser, anticonvulsant. A standard cocktail here. George swallows them obediently and shuffles away under her watchful gaze.

"A good session with George this morning," Oliver tells Nurse Hammond. "He's managing to work through traumatic incidents in a structured way. Cathartic even."

"That's good."

"I'll share my notes with you later," he says. "It's important we work as a team."

"Thank you," says Nurse Hammond. She turns to Oliver, rattling the little plastic cup in her hand. Her expression is kind but firm.

"And now you, Oliver."

He smiles at her. "Of course."

He takes the cup and looks down at the white, pink, and yellow tablets. Clozapine for treatment-resistant psychosis. Sodium valproate to stabilise mood. Lorazepam for anxiety.

He places them on his tongue and swallows with the offered water.

"Good lad," Nurse Hammond says, her voice tired but gentle. "Back to your room now."

Oliver rises obediently, smoothing his white coat once more. The uniformed orderly escorts him as he walks back along the corridor, under flickering fluorescent lights, through the faint chemical smell of antiseptic. He nods at the patients staring blankly from their doorways through their small, reinforced windows. He wonders if they'd trust him with the meds trolley if he asked. He could be so helpful here.

Oliver reaches his room and steps inside. The door closes behind him with a magnetic snick. He stands there for a moment in the quiet, looking down at his trembling hands.

Helping people. That's what matters.

And he smiles, serene, as the lock slides shut.

END

THANK YOU FOR READING

Did you enjoy reading *Trust No One*? Please consider leaving a review on Amazon. Your review will help other readers to discover the novel.

ABOUT THE AUTHOR

Caleb Crowe is a British writer of psychological thrillers, and is fascinated by stories where extraordinary things happen to ordinary people, and the mundane is transformed into the menacing.

He's afraid of the sea, fearful in the countryside, panicky in large open spaces and terrified of small, confined spaces. He finds eerily quiet villages and bustling impersonal cities equally unsettling. There's nowhere, and no one, that doesn't possess some kind of dark, brooding anxiety just waiting to have the lid prised open and turned into a twisty, suspenseful, nerve-shredding story.

He lives in Manchester with his partner, two children and two cats, who probably have their own mysterious agendas. Whether he's navigating the urban jungle or wrestling with the daily challenges of family life, Caleb draws inspiration from the unpredictability of everyday existence.

Find Caleb on his website: www.calebcrowe.com

ALSO BY CALEB CROWE

Printed in Dunstable, United Kingdom

71089842R00194